"I'm sorry if I misinterpreted your motives,"

Laura said grudgingly. "And I appreciate the use of your tent."

"Well, you didn't have to sneak into it. I would have let you in ... maybe."

"I would have asked your permission, but you were sawing wood, Slater. Do you always snore so heavily?"

"I never had complaints about it before. And I've never had a woman sleep with me without an invitation before, either."

"I slept beside you, not with you," she corrected him. "There's a big difference."

"Well ... I think you should give me credit for not taking advantage of the situation."

"Hah! How could you? You were dead to the world."

"Yeah, but I'm up now, Laura." A smile eased across his wide mouth as he slowly, ever so slowly, began unzipping his sleeping bag. "And you know what? I sleep in the nude."

Dear Reader,

Welcome to Silhouette **Special Edition** . . . welcome to romance. Each month, Silhouette **Special Edition** publishes six novels with you in mind—stories of love and life, tales that you can identify with—romance with that little "something special" added in.

November brings plenty to be joyful and thankful for—at least for Andy and Meg in *Baby, It's You* by Celeste Hamilton. For with the birth of their child, they discover the rebirth of their love . . . for all time. Don't miss this compelling tale!

Rounding out November are more dynamite stories by some of your favorite authors: Bevlyn Marshall (fun follows when an abominable snowman is on the loose!), Andrea Edwards, Kayla Daniels, Marie Ferrarella and Lorraine Carroll (with her second book!). A good time will be had by all this holiday month!

In each Silhouette **Special Edition** novel, we're dedicated to bringing you the romances that you dream about—the type of stories that delight as well as bring a tear to the eye. And that's what Silhouette **Special Edition** is all about—special books by special authors for special readers!

I hope you enjoy this book and all of the stories to come.

Sincerely,

Tara Gavin
Senior Editor

BEVLYN MARSHALL
Above the Clouds

Silhouette Special Edition

Published by Silhouette Books New York

America's Publisher of Contemporary Romance

SILHOUETTE BOOKS
300 East 42nd St., New York, N.Y. 10017

ABOVE THE CLOUDS

ISBN: 0-373-09704-2

First Silhouette Books printing November 1991

Books by Bevlyn Marshall

Silhouette Special Edition

Lonely at the Top #407
The Pride of His Life #441
Grady's Lady #506
Radio Daze #544
Goddess of Joy #562
Treasure Deep #598
Thunderbolt #665
Above the Clouds #704

BEVLYN MARSHALL

has had a varied career in fashion, public relations and marketing, but finds writing the most challenging and satisfying occupation. When she's not at her typewriter, she enjoys tennis, needlepoint, long walks with her husband and toy spaniel, and reading. She believes that people who read are rarely bored or lonely because "the private pleasure of a good book is one of life's most rewarding pastimes."

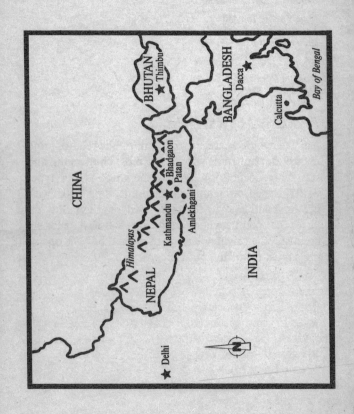

Chapter One

Steve Slater's mood was as foul as the weather when he entered the Kathmandu Hotel, soaked to the skin. He couldn't be bothered with such encumbrances as an umbrella, even during the monsoon season in Nepal. As he shrugged off his dripping-wet canvas jacket, the bell captain came forward, smiling obsequiously.

"More better luck today, sahib?" he asked.

Steve glowered at him and then reminded himself not to take out his bad humor on someone who had done nothing to cause it. He forced a tight smile.

"Seems Lady Luck has deserted me, pal," he replied. During his week's stay at the hotel, he and the bell captain had become fairly chummy.

"She will return when the rains relent," the Nepalese assured him in his lilting accent.

"But I need her now." Steve ran his hand through his wet black hair, his fingers making furrows in the thick mass.

"I'm having a devil of a time trying to find a guide willing to take me to Jewel Mountain."

"It is not the time to travel up treacherous mountain paths. Mud slides and such." The bell captain shuddered at the very thought, smoothing down the front of his pristine white Nehru jacket. "You must have patience."

Steve laughed at that. Patience was the one thing he didn't have too much of, especially when he was after a hot story. "Surely there's one guide in a city the size of Kathmandu willing to brave a little mud and rain for the right price. I'm willing to pay double the going rate."

During his years as a globe-trotting journalist, Steve had learned that almost everyone had a price. This had disappointed and depressed him when he was in his twenties. Now, at thirty-three, he accepted universal greed with weary detachment. He dug into his pocket, took out a handful of rupees and gave them to the bell captain.

"Ask around for me, will you, pal? I can't wait for the monsoon to pass. I want to get to Jewel Mountain as quickly as possible."

"Surely." The man accepted the money with a formal bow. "But why such a hurry, if I may ask? Nothing there but wild sheep and a few poor mountain villages."

"Yeah, but I hear the view is terrific."

Steve wasn't about to reveal his real reason for wanting to go there. He didn't want the rumors he'd heard to spread until he had investigated them for himself. Perhaps it would turn out to be a wild-goose chase—a wild-yeti chase, that was. Or maybe, just maybe it would be the story of the century. He could just about see the headline: *Abominable Snowman Proven To Exist!*

Feeling a rush of adrenaline as he imagined the story with his byline below it, Steve turned away from the bell captain and glanced toward the hotel entrance. His eyes narrowed with interest as he watched a young blond woman in an ankle-length raincoat hop out of a ricksha and run into the lobby, her movements graceful and lithe.

The bell captain noticed her, too, and sprang to attention, ringing the little silver bell attached to a red sash around his waist. She was immediately surrounded by three eager porters, which irritated Steve because they blocked his view of her. He heard her speak to them in Nepali, and this piqued his interest in her even more. Because of her appearance and long athletic stride, he'd assumed she was an American, but not many Americans spoke Nepali. A porter ran out to the ricksha to get her one piece of luggage, a canvas duffel bag. This added to Steve's favorable first impression. He liked a woman who traveled light.

His mood brightened considerably. He'd been bored biding his time at the hotel, but now that this fascinating young woman had arrived, she might offer a delightful outlet for all his restless energy.

She breezed right past him and headed for the registration desk, however. Steve wasn't used to women ignoring him as if he were invisible, but he shrugged it off. There was always a first time for everything. That's what made life so interesting. And *she* certainly was interesting. Because it was such a small hotel, he figured that she would have to acknowledge his presence sooner or later. Most women did....

In one quick glance, right before the porters surrounded her, Laura Prescott had taken him in—a tall, lean man, hair as dark as night, and features rugged enough to be carved into Mount Rushmore. Although she didn't know his first name or his last, she guessed his middle name was Trouble. There was something about him that made her wary. He exuded a disquieting intensity, and his hooded eyes were sharp and watchful.

But Trouble would be easy enough to avoid, Laura assured herself. If all went well, she would be spending only one or two nights at the Kathmandu Hotel, and she had no intention of making this stranger's acquaintance during her brief stay.

As she filled out the registration card, she sensed he was still watching her, and it took a great deal of self-control to stop herself from looking back at him. Eye contact would be a big mistake. Her mission was to reach Jewel Mountain as soon as possible, and she had no time for romantic detours, no matter how short, along the way.

Not that Laura was inclined toward short romantic interludes with tall, dark strangers in the first place. She was far too prudent. Besides, she was still in a state of shock over having a long, serious relationship end on no uncertain terms just hours before she had taken off for Nepal. Surely the apathy she was feeling over this break-up was due to shock. Or else she was far too concerned about her father to allow room for other emotions right now. Later, when she'd taken care of more-urgent matters, she would have a good cry over Jerome, she decided. Yet when she looked down at her left hand resting on the desktop and no longer saw the engagement ring on her finger, all she felt was...relief.

From the corner of her eye she glimpsed Trouble walking toward her, and she stiffened. Riveting her attention on the registration card, she ignored his approach. As he stood beside her, not too close but close enough, she could feel the heat of him and smell the rain on his clothes and skin. She kept her head bent, her face averted.

"My room key, please," he requested from the clerk.

His voice, husky but soft, cut right through Laura. In the next instant he was gone. And now, when relief would have been a suitable reaction, Laura surprised herself by feeling disappointed instead. She swallowed down the temptation to ask the clerk who he was. What did she care?

Begging her forgiveness, the clerk informed her that her room wouldn't be ready for a little while. Laura's heart dropped. She had spent enough time in Nepal to know that "a little while" could mean endless hours of waiting. She also knew that protest would be futile. Waving away more effusive apologies, she headed for a lobby sofa and sank into it, exhausted. The flight from New York to Delhi had been over sixteen hours long, then the plane to Kathmandu had been delayed for five. In all, she'd been traveling a full day and night and longed for some uninterrupted sleep. Since she had an aversion to sleeping in public places, she closed her eyes for only a moment.

When she opened them, Trouble was sitting on a chair right across from her, observing her with a little smile on his wide mouth.

"You were really zonked out," he informed her unnecessarily.

"It's rude to watch people sleep," she told him. She adjusted her raincoat around her, feeling totally exposed under his gaze. "Besides, I wasn't really sleeping. I was just resting my eyes."

"Then I wasn't being rude," he countered. He checked his watch. "You've been resting those big gray eyes of yours for a good half hour."

"And you've been sitting here all that time? Don't you have anything better to do than stare at defenseless women?"

"It's exactly because you looked so defenseless that I stuck around when I spotted you sleeping here. I didn't want anybody bothering you."

She wasn't going to let him pass himself off as some knight in shining armor. "Well, *you're* bothering me," she said.

Her remark didn't seem to disturb him in the least. "Better me than somebody else. A woman alone in a place like this should be more careful. If you can't afford a room, I'll be happy to share mine with you."

"How kind," she said dryly. That was exactly the sort of offer she had expected from Trouble. "But no, thanks."

"Then let me lend you some money for your own room."

Laura hadn't expected *that* offer. She gave him a closer look, but his deep-set eyes revealed nothing. Their amber color fascinated her, but she couldn't pin down the child-

hood memory they conjured up. Something wonderful...
yet dangerous.

"I mean it," he said. "I'll give you some money, no
strings attached." He pulled out his wallet. "I know how
tough it can be to be short on cash when you're so far from
home. I once got my pocket picked in—"

"No, really, I don't need any money," she interrupted.
He seemed genuinely concerned about her, and she smiled
at him for the first time. "They're getting a room ready for
me. Or at least that's what the clerk claimed. But I have a
sneaking suspicion my reservation was lost, and I'll have to
wait for another room to free up."

"Hell, that's not right. Let me go see what I can do about
it." Trouble got up, looking determined to cause some.

"Please don't bother." Laura stood and stretched her
stiff limbs. "It won't do any good. When you're in Nepal,
you have to go with the flow."

"You've been here before, I take it? I heard you speak to
the porters in Nepali."

"Just a few words I remembered from childhood. I
haven't been back for years." She didn't want him to ask
any more questions and quickly changed the subject.
"Lord, I would appreciate a nice hot shower right now."

"Here." He tossed her his key. "Take one in my room.
Don't worry. I'll stay down here and leave you alone."

She hesitated for only a moment and decided to trust him
just a little bit. He had shown her nothing but kindness and
concern, after all, and it was an offer she didn't want to refuse. "Thanks," she said, clutching his key. "I appreciate
it. My name is Laura, by the way."

He smiled slowly. "I was hoping you'd get around to
mentioning it. And I'm Steve."

They didn't shake hands. They just stared at each other
a long moment.

"Maybe we could get on a last-name basis over dinner
this evening," Steve finally said. "Will you join me?"

Laura felt that it would be uncivil to refuse a man her company during dinner after accepting the key to his room. Besides, she could see no harm in sharing a meal with him if they kept things impersonal and light.

"I'll meet you in the dining room," she said. "In twenty minutes or so."

"Take your time. I would never rush a beautiful woman."

Laura ignored the compliment and slung her duffel bag over her shoulder. She hurried to the elevator before one of the porters had a chance to help her. She didn't feel like explaining, in her halting Nepali, why she was going to a strange man's room.

The whirling ceiling fans in the hotel dining room did little to dispel the heavy humidity. Steve requested a table for two on the terrace instead, where it was cooler and fresher. He sat there alone, waiting for Laura.

The rain had let up for the time being, and through a thin veil of clouds he could make out the ghostly outline of the Himalayan mountains in the distance. By the time the waiter brought him his gin and tonic, darkness had cloaked his view of them entirely. Still, Steve raised his glass to the tallest mountain range in the world and offered a silent toast. He admired greatness in any form because he came across it so seldom.

He didn't often come across women who captivated him, either. Not only did Laura's good looks attract him, but she also had a certain mystery about her despite her big, guileless eyes. What was she keeping back from him beside her last name, he wondered. Steve was good at finding out what people didn't want to tell him, but he was inclined to let Laura remain a mystery. Usually he was disappointed in the secrets people revealed to him. He didn't want Laura to be a disappointment. Their time together would be too short to get to know each other well, but he intended to enjoy it to the fullest. A little conversation, a little flirtation—that's all he expected from their evening.

Of course, if things developed further, so much the better, he thought as he watched her walk toward the table. She was wearing a simple black knit dress that showed off her legs, slender arms and long neck. It was the kind of dress that raised a man's expectations considerably. Not that it was deliberately sexy. Actually it was rather demure. But oh, how good she looked in it! He stood up when she reached the table.

"Is this all right?" he asked her. "Or would you prefer eating inside?"

She handed him back his room key and took a seat. "No, this is perfect."

So are you, he thought, sitting down across from her. The paper lanterns strung along the terrace trellises cast a soft glow on her face. Her shoulder-length hair looked darker in this light, then Steve realized that it was still wet from her shower. She smelled of his soap, and he imagined her drying off her shapely body with his towel.

"Why are you smiling like that?" she asked him.

"Like what?"

"The cat who just swallowed the canary."

"I'm just pleased to be here with you, Laura. What brings you to Nepal?" It was a casual enough question, but he noticed her tense. "You don't have to tell me if you don't want to."

"Then I won't," she replied simply. She plucked up her elaborately folded napkin and shook it out with a quick snap of her wrist. "And of course you don't have to tell me why you're here, either."

"I came to climb Mount Everest. I thought it would be an interesting way to spend my vacation," he replied truthfully. Why he'd decided to stay was another matter. It was on Everest that he'd heard about Dr. Adam Prescott's yeti research in the Jewel region from a Sherpa whose brother worked for the zoologist. He had no desire to share this information with Laura. He'd learned long ago to keep his mouth shut when he was chasing down a lead.

"Climbing Everest is hardly a relaxing way to spend a vacation," she said.

"I'm not too big on relaxing. I prefer a good challenge."

"Do you?" She met his eyes but seemed uncomfortable with what she saw in them. She looked away. "And did Everest meet your expectations?"

"No, it proved to be a disappointment."

She looked back at him, a trace of defiance in her expression. "Don't tell me the climb was too easy for you."

"No, but it wasn't too hard, either. That's not what disappointed me, though. The area has become too commercial. The trash the summer tourists left in their wake was a real eyesore."

Laura nodded. "Tourism brings desperately needed revenue to Nepal. At the same time it upsets the natural balance of things. And the people are drifting away from their traditional ways."

Steve wondered if she was connected with the government in some capacity. "You seem knowledgeable about this country's economy."

"Oh, no," she protested. "I only know what I've heard from my... from others who have been here recently."

He didn't press her. If she wanted to keep up the mystery-lady act, he would let her. "Would you care for a drink before dinner?"

"I really shouldn't. Jet lag, high altitude and alcohol are a heady mixture."

"Have a soft drink, then." He motioned to the waiter and was surprised when Laura ordered a glass of raksi, the local wine. She was brought a small decanter of it. "I like a woman who knows she really shouldn't, but does it anyway," he teased.

"I assure you, it's a rare occurrence with me," she replied a bit stiffly.

"Well, here's to rare occurrences." He raised his glass to her. "And to the unknown and unexpected," he added.

"Spoken like a true adventurer." There was a note of reproof in her voice, but she clicked glasses with him anyway.

When she tilted back her head to take a sip, Steve admired the curve of her neck, thinking how pleasant it would be to trail kisses down it. "You must have a taste for adventure yourself, Laura. Not many women would travel alone to a place like Kathmandu in the middle of the monsoon season."

"I have my reasons for coming here, but a desire for adventure isn't one of them. Actually I'm very set in my ways. What other people might consider a rut, I consider a comfort."

Her reply disappointed Steve. It didn't jibe with his first impression of her. The moment he had seen her alight from the ricksha, he had felt an immediate connection with her, as if they were fellow travelers headed down life's bumpy road, full-speed ahead. And to do that you had to avoid ruts at all cost. His hunches about people were usually right on target, so he disregarded her claim about being set in her ways. He rarely believed what people told him, anyway, preferring to go by what he saw for himself. And what he saw was a young woman on her own in an exotic country for reasons she would not reveal.

"I think you're a spy," he said, partly in jest, but also curious to see her reaction.

She only shrugged. "It takes one to know one," she shot back coolly.

This time her reply delighted Steve. If she wanted to play games with him, he would happily play along. "We could be working on the same side, Laura."

"Or for opposing forces."

"If we are, I might be willing to trade secrets with you if we could go some place private later." He reached across the table and ran his hand down her bare arm. At first her skin felt smooth to his touch, like polished marble, but then he felt the goose bumps.

She moved her arm away from his hand. "What makes you think I'm interested in exchanging anything with you in private, Steve?"

Her reaction to his touch had. Goose bumps were usually a good sign. The evening ahead had enormous potential, he decided. "Let me pour you a little more wine," he said.

She laughed. "No, you don't, you devil." She covered her glass with her palm. "I need some food in my stomach, not more raksi."

"Whatever you say." He beckoned to the hovering waiter again. "Why don't you order for both of us, Laura? You're the Nepalese expert."

"Not really," she said, but she requested a variety of special dishes she remembered liking as a child, hoping that Steve would like them, too.

She wasn't disappointed. He ate with a keen appetite, enjoying each serving that was placed in front of him with the same gusto as the one before it. Laura found herself wondering if he enjoyed women in much the same manner, relishing one as much as another and then moving on when he was satisfied.

"You look as if you've just eaten something that doesn't agree with you," Steve remarked.

"No, I think it's delicious." She took another bite of curried lamb cooked in mustard oil to prove she did.

"Then it must have been a thought that didn't agree with you. You have a very expressive face, Laura. All your emotions flit across it."

"I hope I'm not that transparent!"

"Better than being opaque. Some people tend to block their emotions before they can rise to the surface."

"Is that what you do, Steve?" She hadn't meant to get so personal, but the question had popped out.

He answered without hesitation. "Absolutely."

"Then I guess that makes you a better spy than I am," she joked to keep the conversation light.

"Oh, I don't know. With a lovely face like yours, you could probably get most men to pour out their deepest secrets to you if you really wanted them to," he told her.

"Most men . . . but not you?"

He smiled. "Try me. I'm not above being seduced."

"But I am," she said quickly, and then felt stupid about this prim declaration of her virtue. She took a deep sip from the wineglass he had managed to refill without her noticing. He made her nervous, but she found his company stimulating. Perhaps a little too stimulating. She pretended a yawn as the waiter cleared the table. "It's time I called it a night."

"But it's early," Steve objected. At that moment he was exactly where he wanted to be with exactly the person he wanted to be with. That was a rare experience for him. He was usually so restless. But now he leaned back and relaxed.

How his amber eyes glittered in the lantern light, Laura thought. And then it occurred to her that snow leopards had amber eyes, too. She had glimpsed this elusive Himalayan mountain cat as a child, and that was the memory Steve had stirred up in her. Snow leopards were predators, she reminded herself.

And what sort of animal was this man seated across from her? His room had given her no clues. Not that she had snooped around it. That would have been a betrayal of his hospitality. But she couldn't help noticing how impersonal it had been, even for a hotel room. A travel kit on the dresser, a well-used suitcase and some hiking equipment in one corner, a pair of boots at the side of the bed—those were the only visible signs that he occupied it. Well, she had learned one thing about him. He was very neat.

It occurred to her that perhaps he really was a spy, some sort of secret agent. But then why would he be wasting his time with her? Her only secret had to do with her father, and no government would have much interest in that. Her father had nothing to do with politics, and he was a zoologist, not a rocket scientist. He studied rare and nearly extinct animals in the wild, observing their feeding and mating habits, and he published any new discovery he made about them.

Until now, that was. He had kept his latest discovery to himself for months, thank goodness. No one else knew about it but Laura. And he had just revealed it to her by letter a few days ago. That's why she had come to Nepal. She hoped to convince him to give up his delusions and return home with her. If possible, she also hoped to save his fine reputation and protect him from being ridiculed by the scientific community.

"I've lost you, Laura," she heard Steve say. "You're a million miles away."

"I was just trying to figure out if you were really a spy," she told him. "You don't give away much about yourself."

"But you're the one who's so closemouthed," he reminded her. "I'm just going along with it because it amuses me."

"Oh, does it?" she said sharply. She didn't care to be considered his evening amusement. "You enjoy playing games, don't you, Steve?" Like cat-and-mouse, she thought.

"I would enjoy doing anything at all with you," he replied.

That was definitely her cue to say good-night, she decided. But a band began playing in the dining room, a Nepalese rendition of a Western pop tune, and Laura lingered to listen to them for a moment or two. The off-key melody conjured up the image of her parents dancing together at this very hotel years ago. They would stay here occasionally and consider it the lap of luxury after months of living in the wild.

Although they did it rarely, her parents danced well together. They had done everything well together, working side by side at research sites in the wilderness. Their complete happiness together had made Laura's childhood happy. It didn't matter that they'd never had a "real" home. Home truly was where the heart was, Laura had learned, be it a trailer, a hut, even a tent. She had traveled with her parents all over the world—Africa, South America, India and Nepal. Life had been one glorious, ever-changing adventure. And then... And then her mother had died. Laura's sense of adventure had died with her.

So had her father's joy in life, Laura thought. He buried himself in his work, caring about nothing else. Even his daughter. Since she was thirteen, he had more or less left her on her own. He hadn't abandoned her exactly. He had seen to it that she was well cared for and well educated. And they still had a deep bond that could never be broken although months would go by without her hearing a word from him.

Most of his letters were matter-of-fact accounts of his research projects, but his most recent one had deeply troubled Laura because he'd claimed that he had made contact with a yeti. Professing to have befriended the mythical abominable snowman was bad enough, but her father had gone on to state that he planned to stay at his Jewel Mountain site throughout the winter. Once snows blocked the mountain passes, he would be stranded there, and Laura was determined to bring him back to civilization and reality before that happened.

Steve's eyes never left her face. He doubted that he could ever tire of watching her. But why had she looked so dreamily happy when the music started, then sad, then troubled? Would she ever reveal her secrets to him? Not likely. They were two strangers passing through Kathmandu, soon to go their separate ways. After tonight he would probably never see her again.

So he would make the best of tonight. "Let's dance," he said.

Laura didn't want to dance with him. She sensed that it would somehow be a dangerous thing to do. And the sensible thing to do would be to part with him right here and now. Yet when he stood up and opened his arms wide, she found herself floating into them. And when he pressed her closer, she didn't protest.

They danced through the shadows of the empty terrace together, to the cacophonous sound of the orchestra playing "Strangers in the Night."

Chapter Two

How right it felt to be in this stranger's arms, Laura mused. Her reaction bothered her, but she couldn't help herself from enjoying the sensation of his long, lean body pressing against hers. She rested her cheek against the solid comfort of his shoulder. He was well over six feet tall. She would have to stand on tiptoe, she estimated, to kiss him on the lips. She blinked away such a thought. But it kept coming back again.

He danced smoothly and was easy to follow. Laura began to relax as he guided her around the flagstone floor. His rhythm meshed with hers. Some men were too stiff, some too showy when they danced. But Steve moved just right to suit her. She recalled that she and Jerome could never quite fall into step comfortably. Dancing had not been a pleasure for him, only a duty. Steve seemed to enjoy it, though. He had an innate grace, and his body flowed with the music naturally, without strain. He moved with the ease of a big mountain cat.

They kept their own beat, since the Nepalese band occasionally lost track of theirs. And the simple melody escaped them after every few bars or so. Every time they struck a sour note, Steve laughed. Laura felt the vibration of it in her chest. He had a deep soft rumble of a laugh that she found thrilling.

The trouble was she found everything about him thrilling—his voice, his eyes, his build, the very smell of him. She'd never felt such an immediate physical attraction to a man before, and it troubled her more than pleased her. Now wasn't the right time or place to have such a melting experience in a man's arms. But Steve was slowly massaging the small of her back as they danced, and she sighed.

"Does that feel good?" he asked softly.

She silently cursed herself for letting that little sigh escape. "Very relaxing," she replied as coolly as possible, and tilted back her head to look him in the face.

That was a mistake. His glittering gaze held hers, and she found his eyes so mesmerizing that she had the uncomfortable feeling that she was in his power completely. To prove to herself that she wasn't, she pulled back from him.

"What's wrong?" he asked.

She attempted a laugh and told him the truth. "For a moment there I felt as if you were trying to cast a spell on me."

He smiled back, amused by her fancy. "Do you believe in magic, Laura? I certainly don't."

She shook her head. "Neither do I."

That settled, he pulled her close again, but this time he wrapped both his arms around her waist, and she had no choice, it seemed, but to lift her own and entwine them around his neck. Now their bodies were pressed length to length, and every muscle movement held a shared intimacy. He bent his head to place his cheek against hers, and the slight bristle of his beard made her tingle all over.

She held her breath to contain another sigh of pleasure. As much as she distrusted Steve's physical effect on her, she

still felt safe in his arms somehow. This contrast of senti-
ments confused her. She blamed her jumbled thoughts and
chaotic emotions on exhaustion. Worry and long hours of
travel had taken their toll on her mind and body. Without
realizing it, she snuggled even closer to Steve.

"Are you falling asleep on me, Laura?" she heard him
whisper.

Her eyes flew open. Perhaps she really had been taking
a little catnap against this big sleek leopard of a man! She
realized that the music had stopped, although he still
swayed her back and forth in his arms. Without the music
their movements were far more intimate and sensual. How
long had they been dancing to silence? she wondered. And
why hadn't she even noticed?

"It's definitely time for bed," she told him. And then she
blushed over how he might interpret that statement. It
wasn't intended as an invitation.

"Let's go see if your room is ready yet" was all he said.

It wasn't. Once again the desk clerk offered elaborate
apologies to Laura. Steve interrupted him to demand action instead. The clerk assured him that the entire staff was
doing their best to be accommodating, but his profuse politeness was like a stone wall that could not be penetrated.
Laura tugged at Steve's sleeve, pulling him away from the
desk.

"It's useless to badger him," she said.

"But I wasn't badgering. I was simply demanding an
explanation."

"You won't get one. My room will be ready when it's
ready, and that's all there is to it. Patience is probably the
most valuable virtue you can have in Nepal."

"So I'm learning," Steve muttered. "But I dislike waiting around for something to happen."

"Well, you don't have to wait around with me."

"I don't mind being with you." He took her hand and
patted it, as if to assure her that he didn't. "Listen, here's
an idea. Spend the night in my room." He held fast to her

hand when she tried pulling it away. "That's not a proposition, Laura. I'll sleep in yours when it's finally ready. I'm not a bit tired myself. I adjusted to the time change weeks ago."

He really was quite kind, she decided. At the same time she was reluctant to accept. She didn't want to feel obligated to him. "No, thanks," she said. "Switching rooms back and forth will be too confusing. I'm sure I'll be settled in mine shortly."

"Suit yourself." He released her hand and began pacing the small lobby, checking his watch at short intervals and occasionally glaring at the clerk for good measure.

The clerk smiled back passively, but Steve was managing to drive Laura a little crazy with his restless impatience. "Oh, for goodness' sake, if you're going to pace like that, let's go for a walk," she finally suggested.

"Do you feel up to it? You were snoozing against my shoulder just a little while ago," he reminded her, then chuckled. "First time I ever had a woman literally fall asleep *on* me."

"I have amazing recuperative powers," she assured him.

And so they headed out the lobby door and into the night. It was past ten, and the streets were dark and deserted, except for a few open ricksha stands. Laura automatically took Steve's arm as they walked along the twisting unpaved lanes. The glimmer of cooking fires from open doorways and the flicker of candles in shrines and temples marked their way.

Steve began whistling "Strangers in the Night," true to the band's rendition, note for sour note. And as if to accompany him, dogs bayed from rooftops and alleys, filling the humid air with their plangent howling.

"Day or night, there's never any peace in this city," Laura commented in a raised voice.

Steve stopped whistling. "I wonder where all the cows that roam the streets during the daytime go at night?" he said.

Laura had no idea where the sacred cows of Kathmandu went at night. It was a question that had never occurred to her as a child, but she was sure her father would have had the answer. He had always known the answer to everything. She felt a poignant concern for him at that moment and wished she could express it to Steve. But that wouldn't have been prudent. Her father had urged her, in his letter, to tell no one of his yeti research. And that had been the only sensible thing he had written!

Steve squeezed her arm. "I'm always curious to know what you're thinking when you get quiet like this. But if I asked, I know you wouldn't tell me."

She took a few careful steps in the darkness. "You haven't given me much information about yourself, either. I assume you're an American, but I don't even know that for sure."

"Born and bred in the Green Mountains of Vermont!" he declared.

"Ah, no wonder you came to Nepal on vacation. You have an affinity to mountains."

"They attract me, that's for sure. I'd like to climb as many as I can before I get too old, because no two are alike."

"Like snowflakes," Laura said.

Steve's smile flashed in the night. "No, like women. Each new terrain offers exciting possibilities for exploration." He brought Laura's hand to his lips, sliding her knuckles across them.

The warmth of his mouth sent a shiver up her spine, but she kept her voice expressionless. "Some men claim that once you've climbed one mountain, you've climbed them all."

"I've heard some women claim the same thing," he replied. "But I don't believe that's true. Do you, Laura?"

"I've had limited experience in that sport," she said, her voice sharp in the soft, moist night. "Some people don't climb mountains just because they're there, you know."

Steve laughed softly. "You think that's what I do."

"I get the impression you're an adventurer, Steve. That you're after any thrill you can get."

"Wrong," he objected. "I'm very selective. Life's too short to waste on cheap thrills. And I never waste my time."

With me you are, she wanted to say. But she held back because she wasn't as certain about that as she would have liked to have been.

"We're going to get lost if we keep meandering like this," she said instead.

He squeezed her arm again. "Don't worry. I have an infallible sense of direction in the dark. It's like a sixth sense I was born with."

Once again she compared him to a leopard, stalking his prey in the night. But that was just a fancy. He was just a man who happened to be too attractive for her own good.

"Let's go back," she insisted.

Without another word he turned around with her, and they retraced their steps in silence. The heady scent of night-blooming jasmine drifted their way, and Laura breathed it in deeply. At the same time she stumbled in a rut on the road, and Steve gripped her arm tighter to steady her. They stopped.

"Are you all right?" he asked.

"Weak ankle," she said. "Sometimes it turns on me."

"You're sure you didn't twist it."

"No, no. I'm perfectly fine."

"Yes, you are," he said, his voice husky. "You're perfect and very fine. I've been wanting to tell you that all evening, Laura." He pulled her closer to him. "And there's something else I've been wanting to do all evening."

So the moment had finally come, she thought, realizing that she had been wanting it to happen all evening, too. A part of her remained objective as she turned her face up to his. It seemed inevitable that they should kiss. She had a burning curiosity to know what he would taste like, and she licked her lips in anticipation.

Slowly, slowly he lowered his face to hers. Her heart began to beat faster. The dogs howled in the distance, and the scent of jasmine hung in the air. A sliver of moonlight slipped through a thin break in the clouds. She took note of all this, still objective, as she waited in that long moment of time before their lips touched.

But when his mouth covered hers, all her objectivity dissolved, along with her reservations concerning him. She had never been kissed so completely, with such an overpowering demand that she respond. Yet with such compelling tenderness, too.

It was the unexpected tenderness of his kiss that seeped into her soul and made her want him. She lost herself in it, clutching him tightly as her limbs grew heavy, her muscles lax. She held on to him for the dear life of her, digging her fingers into the hard flesh of his back, silently urging him to deepen their kiss more. And more.

Laura could no longer smell the jasmine or hear the dogs or notice that clouds once again blotted out the moonlight. Nothing existed for her but this kiss, this man, this moment. She didn't even notice when the clouds broke and the rain poured down, drenching them. It didn't dampen her desire in the least.

It was Steve who finally pulled away. Blood pounded in his ears as the rain pounded on his back. He was only dimly aware of it. He felt drunk, thickheaded, immobile. Kissing Laura had shaken him to the core. He gripped her arm, trying to get a grip on himself, too.

"Come on," he said. "Let's make a run for it back to the hotel."

She didn't speak for a moment, and when she did, she sounded confused. "Why run?"

"Haven't you noticed that it's raining, Laura?"

She looked up and laughed, then wiped the rain from her face. "So it is. Don't worry. I won't melt."

But she already had, he thought. She had melted in his arms like warm, sweet honey. All he could think of was getting her back to the hotel as quickly as possible. That was the only clear thought in his pounding head. He wanted her. Badly. Her kiss had been filled with passion and promises.

He pulled her along through the heavy rain until she protested that he was walking too fast.

"We can't get any wetter than we already are, Steven," she pointed out breathlessly.

He apologized and shortened his pace. He liked the way she called him by his full name. On her lips it sounded intimate rather than formal. The hotel lights were in view now, a dim, hazy glow through the sheets of rain. They would be alone soon, he thought. *Soon, soon, soon* pounded in his brain with each step that brought them closer.

When they entered the lobby, Laura immediately felt self-conscious. Her wet knit dress clung to her body like a second skin, and she crossed her arms over her breasts. The bell captain rushed to them, clutching his hands, clicking his tongue, shaking his head in dismay.

"The rain has caught you!" he exclaimed. He began making apologies for the weather, as if the hotel and he were somehow responsible for it. "But I have good news, all the same," he concluded after his long discourse. He bowed to Laura. "Your room now ready, memsahib. We have transported your bag to it already."

Laura wished he had informed them of this right away, rather than waste time commiserating over their misfortune. She felt clammy now and had begun shivering.

Steve shared her irritation. "Well, don't just stand there chattering while we drip puddles on the floor, man!" he said in an exasperated tone. "Give the lady her room key so she can go dry off."

The bell captain stepped back, pulling in his chin. "That is not my function, sahib. I greet guests but not give them keys. That is desk clerk's function, and he is now having tea away. You will have to wait for his return, I fear."

Steve took a long deep breath and when he spoke, his voice was low, even and dangerous. "The lady will not wait one minute longer. Can't you see that she's cold and uncomfortable? Now, give me her room key before I lose my temper."

The threat of that happening seemed to do the trick. The bell captain ran to the desk and snatched a key off the board. When he handed it to Steve, he looked terribly offended to have been forced to perform a task not in his job description.

"Thank you," Steve said in a kinder tone. "I'm sure everything will be fine now."

That seemed to mollify the man. "We aim for pleasing," he said. "Go third floor up. Room is all ready and waiting."

Steve tipped him and ushered Laura into the elevator, an old-fashioned contraption run by a wizened little fellow wearing a gold turban. As it rose at a snail's pace, Laura glanced at Steve and noticed the tense muscles in his lean face as he stared straight ahead over the turbaned head of the elevator operator. She felt the same tenseness in her stomach. She longed to be alone with Steve. The ride seemed endless.

The elevator stopped with a jerk, and the operator folded back the door with a white-gloved hand. He bowed as they exited, impassively taking in their rain-soaked appearance.

"This way. Room seventeen," Steve said after checking the number engraved on the big silver key. "Seventeen," he repeated when they stopped in front of the red door displaying those brass digits. "My lucky number."

"Is it?" Laura said in a noncommittal tone. As much as she had longed to be alone with him only moments ago, she doubted the wisdom of it now.

They stood without speaking, gazing into each other's eyes as they listened to the groan of the elevator sinking down to the lobby again.

Laura cleared her throat. "I must look like a drowned rat," she said, pushing back a lanky strand of wet hair.

What a stupid thing to say, she chided herself. But she didn't know what *to* say to him now. They were strangers again. The mood had been broken. The deep, soulful kiss they had shared was now only a memory.

"No, you don't," Steve said in reply to her comment. "You look like an adorable wet little seal." He slid his hand down the side of her clinging black dress, along her rib cage and the curve of her waist. "A sleek, sexy seal with big silver eyes."

His words charmed her. He leaned closer to her, so close that if she moved even a fraction of an inch, her breasts would touch his chest. But she didn't move. She froze. She knew that he was waiting for her to invite him in. She saw the longing in his tawny eyes. Desire made them hard as sparkling topaz. Did big dangerous cats eat up little seals? she found herself wondering.

"I'll unlock your door for you," he said.

"No, wait." She stilled his hand before he slid the big key into the lock. "We have to talk. I mean, about that kiss..." She intended to explain to him that she hadn't meant to lead him on with her intense response to it, but her voice drifted off when he began to stroke her again, soothing her with his light caresses.

"That kiss?" he repeated. "Would you like another one, Laura?"

He didn't wait for an answer. He didn't have to. She had already turned up her face to him with the unthinking naturalness of a flower tilting up to the sun. Her lips parted expectantly as her eyes slowly closed, and she shivered in anticipation of the pleasure of it.

Her shiver vibrated through Steve. She was wet and cold, he thought, but he knew he could warm her up soon enough. He covered her waiting, soft little mouth and plundered it, pushing her against the door with his taut hard body, pressing his chest against her breasts. No tenderness now, only hot, driving need. He wanted her to yield to him. Completely.

And she would. He knew that. He could feel her desire pulling him in with the force of a tidal wave. She was his now. He was claiming her because she wanted to be claimed. He could taste passion on her tongue. He could feel the heat of it through her wet dress and his shirt. She belonged to *him*. So he kissed her without holding back, exploring the intimate recesses of her mouth, pressing harder against her with urgent male greed.

Pinned against the door, her body went limp under his persuasive hands as he fondled her breasts through the thin fabric. How supple she was, he thought, how willing. Her nipples were hard, hot buds. She moaned, and desire sparked all of his senses, making them sharp with need for more of her, for the feel and smell and touch of her.

But this was crazy, making love to her in a hallway when they had a bed and privacy just beyond the door. He tore his lips from hers and smiled when he saw the dazed expression on her flushed face. She continued to lean against the door for support, and he heard her breath come hard as her breasts rose and fell beneath the soaked fabric of the dress that he imagined peeling off her very slowly but very soon.

"You'll let me in, won't you?" he whispered.

She made no reply, but her limpid gaze told him everything he needed to know. When he put the key in the lock, he saw that his hand was shaking. It amazed and pleased him that she could shake him up like this. He had never wanted a woman more.

"My Laura," he sighed, turning the key. He laughed softly because she hadn't moved. Still dazed from his kisses, she continued to lean against the door, and the sight of her golden skin and black dress against the red background stirred him even more. He would always remember that image, he thought. Always.

He pulled her into his arms and threw open the door. They stepped inside the dark room, and he felt along the wall, searching for a light switch. He didn't want darkness when he made love to Laura. He wanted to see every inch of her, see every changing nuance on her expressive face as he gave her more and more pleasure. He knew it was going to be wonderful. They were meant for each other on this wonderful rainy night in Kathmandu. And just as these thoughts raced through his mind and his heart sang with anticipation, there came a bloodcurdling scream from inside the pitch-black room.

Keeping a protective arm around Laura, Steve managed to find the wall switch. He flicked on the light, but illumination made nothing clear. It did reveal the producer of the horrible screech, however. She was cringing in the bed, pink satin covers pulled up to her chin. But what the hell was this strange woman doing in *Laura's* bed?

Laura took a few steps toward the woman, speaking softly, soothingly. "Please stay calm. We won't hurt you. There's been some mistake. I'm sure it can all be explained."

Her calmness impressed Steve. He appreciated a levelheaded approach to a crisis. And he certainly considered this a crisis. He'd been expecting bliss once inside the red door, not chaos. Laura's attempt to assuage the woman had failed, and now she threw off the satin quilt and began jumping up and down on the bed, her silky blue nightgown flapping, her gold bracelets and necklaces clinking, her long black braid swinging.

Four more women with dark braids and bright silk gowns rushed into the room from a side door. At least that was the number Steve counted before they fell upon him, and then he was sure there were at least four hundred of them poking him, pinching him, pulling his hair. He didn't mind all that so much as their earsplitting shrieks. "Laura, go get help!" he shouted over them.

She ran out of the room, leaving him to fend for himself. He had to laugh at the absurdity of the situation. His attackers were tiny and delicate and could do him no real harm. His only fear was that he might inadvertently hurt one of them in an effort to extract himself from their clutches. "Ladies, ladies, take it easy," he pleaded.

The hotel manager finally arrived on the scene, none too soon as far as Steve was concerned. He was a short man in a dark suit and only added to the bedlam at first, his own voice high and piercing as he spoke to the woman jumping on the bed. At last she stopped her frantic acrobatics and clapped her hands sharply three times. The four women attacking Steve stepped back and gave her their full attention. Steve took this opportunity to make his escape. Guests from other rooms poked their heads out of their doorways and stared at Steve as if he were some sort of monster. The hotel manager joined him in the hallway, slamming the door behind him with a sigh of relief. He took out a snowy white handkerchief and wiped his brow. "Most unfortunate," he said.

Steve looked at the gold numerals on the door and shook his head. Seventeen hadn't turned out to be his lucky number after all tonight. "Yeah, most unfortunate," he agreed glumly. He wondered where Laura was now. Probably still trying to find help.

The manager put away his handkerchief and began wringing his hands. "The maharani is most deeply upset."

"I got that impression," Steve muttered.

"She is a most important Indian princess, and I tremble to think she is displeased during her stay at our fine hotel."

Steve noticed that the manager was indeed trembling and felt a little sorry for him. "Would you like me to go back in and try to straighten things out with her?"

"You are an exceedingly brave man to offer to do that, Mr. Slater. But I think that we should leave well enough alone. I explained to her that you are a reputable guest here, not some murderous thief in the night."

"Thanks for the good reference."

"But how did such an intrusion occur on your part, Mr. Slater? Not that I am inferring it was intentional."

Steve had to smile at the manager's utter politeness under such strained circumstances. "Certainly not intentional," he said. "A mix-up in keys." He handed over the one he'd been given.

"Ah, now I understand," the manager said in a mournful voice. "When I came in this evening, the bell captain complained to me that the desk clerk had been negligently away from his post, and he had been required to give you Miss Laura's key. But I thought nothing of it, assuming it was the correct one. Unfortunately it wasn't." He took out his handkerchief and wiped his brow again. "And not only the maharani, but the daughter of the esteemed Dr. Prescott has been inconvenienced. A double tragedy!"

Steve's eyes narrowed. He showed no other sign of surprise at discovering that Laura was Prescott's daughter. He didn't want to get the manager's guard up. "Do you know Adam Prescott personally?" he asked in a casual tone.

"Oh, yes indeed. He and his wife and little Miss Laura used to be regular guests here. But Dr. Prescott has not been back for a very long time."

"I suppose he's involved in his research." Steve paused. "On Jewel Mountain, right?"

"Yes. He is an expert on snow leopards, I am told."

"Does he study any other type of animal up there?"

"This I do not know, Mr. Slater. I know about hotels, not wild creatures."

"Seems to me you got a wild creature staying in room seventeen."

The manager looked confused for a moment, and then giggled appreciatively. "Ah, yes! The maharani, you mean. She can be very excitable. I hope the incident did not upset you too much."

"At the time I found it rather upsetting," he said with wry understatement. "But now I wonder if things didn't happen for the best." He needed time to consider this new information about Laura being Prescott's daughter. He could use it to his advantage if he chose to. And as he was contemplating this, the elevator doors slid open and Laura stepped out, accompanied by both the desk clerk and bell captain. They all crowded into the narrow hallway.

"Oh, there you are, Mr. Chumbi," she said, remembering the manager from days long ago. "I went to your office looking for you just now." She glanced at Steve. He appeared to have survived his attack by the tiny Indian women, looking tousled but no worse for wear.

"You must have missed me by moments," the manager told her. "One of the other guests called to complain of the ruckus, and I hurried right up here. But all is calm now. Your room is the one across the hall, number eighteen. A lovely room with a view."

"Yes, so I explained," the desk clerk spoke up. "And I gave the lady the correct room key this time." He tossed a look of disdain in the bell captain's direction. "*I* would never make such a foolish mistake."

This comment caused the bell captain to defend himself and state that *he* would never leave his post for tea. The desk clerk shot back something in Nepali, and a heated argument commenced. The manager silenced them both with a few sharp words and sent them on their way back to the lobby.

"I should fall down on my knees in profuse apology to you," he told Laura, his eyes brimming with sorrow.

"Please don't! There's no need to be upset about all this," she told him. "All's well that ends well."

She gave Steve a swift sidelong glance. He hadn't spoken a word but kept staring at her with narrowed eyes. She wished that he would stop staring at her so hard.

The manager would not let the matter rest. "I take full responsibility for what happened," he said. "You see, I was away from the hotel all day because of a family celebration. If I had been here to greet you on your arrival, you would have been given a room right away and none of this misfortune would have happened, Miss Laura."

Then she would never have struck up an acquaintance with Steve, Laura thought. Was it luck that she had? Or misfortune? She stole another quick look at him, standing there so silently, and her initial wariness of him returned. It upset her to realize that she had shared such passionate kisses with a man she didn't really trust.

Mr. Chumbi finally bid her and Steve good-night, leaving them alone in front of room eighteen. Not quite alone, Laura noticed. Guests from other rooms were observing them from half-open doors.

"Well, good night," she said, offering Steve her hand.

He stared down at it and arched a thick eyebrow. "I thought we'd gone past the handshake stage."

"I'm afraid we skipped over it entirely," she replied in a soft voice, acutely aware of the many eavesdroppers lurking at their doors. "And I think it would be wise to back up. Our... relationship was developing too fast for me."

"You sound relieved that it was unexpectedly called to a halt."

"Yes, I am," she told him frankly, meeting his eyes. "I'm not in the habit of allowing strange men to make love to me. I know that's probably hard for you to believe after the way I carried on with you, but—"

"I believe you, Laura," he interrupted. "And I take it as a compliment."

She felt relieved that he was being so understanding. She hadn't known what his reaction would be, but she sensed that he was a man who did not easily take no for an answer.

"I'm sorry, though, that the mood was broken so abruptly," he continued. "We were making great progress together."

"It was a very interesting evening," she said lamely.

He smiled at her choice of words. "As interesting as they come," he agreed.

She wanted nothing more at the moment but to kiss him one last time. But she didn't dare make a move to satisfy her desire.

And neither did he. Instead, he took the hand that she had offered and shook it. "Good night, Laura."

"We don't even know each other's last name," she said wistfully.

Something flickered in his eyes, but he remained silent.

"And we'll probably never see each other again," she added.

"Sure, we will," he said brusquely. "Let's have breakfast together tomorrow morning. Is seven too early for you?"

"No, that's good." Her heart felt lighter. "How long do you plan to stay in Kathmandu?"

"That depends on you, Laura."

His reply touched her. "Really? You would change your plans because of me?"

Again a flicker in his eyes. "Yes, but we can talk about that tomorrow."

"Tomorrow," she repeated. She turned from him and unlocked her door. He was gone before she could turn back to him again. The elevator creaked as it took him away.

"Well, that's all, folks. I hope you enjoyed the show," she called down the hall.

She heard a number of doors slam shut before she closed her own.

Chapter Three

Laura dressed carefully the next morning—as carefully as she could, considering her limited wardrobe. Except for her black dress, she had brought only rough clothes suitable for trekking. The dress hung drying in the bathroom now, still damp and shapeless and most likely ruined. She smiled as she brushed her hair, remembering how Steve's eyes had lit up when he'd first seen her in it last evening.

Only last night? It jolted her to realize that she'd known him for less than twenty-four hours. He'd been in her thoughts constantly since they'd parted. When worries about her father weren't disturbing her sleep, dreams about Steven were. Such sensual dreams!

Still, she was thankful that their lovemaking hadn't progressed any further. It made her uncomfortable to think about what would have happened if the fiasco with the maharani hadn't occurred. Yes, you have every right to blush now, Laura, she chided herself when she felt the heat rise to her neck and face. She had never taken a stranger to bed with her and never intended to.

But she had never met a man like Steven before, either. She recalled how compelling his deep-set eyes were, and how the timbre of his voice made her heart chime. She remembered with the utmost clarity how his face had looked in the lantern light: the hollows beneath his cheekbones, his strong jawline and stubborn chin, the curve of his finely molded lips. His smile tantalized her—a wry tilt of his lips that seemed to be all-knowing. It was the world-weary smile of a man who had seen it all and could not be surprised by anything, only slightly amused.

Rather than tantalize her, his smile should make her cautious, she realized as she sucked in her breath to tuck her white cotton shirt into the waistband of her jeans. She still knew nothing about the man except that he came from Vermont. And for all she knew, he could have made that up. She paused as she slipped a scarf through the belt loops of her jeans. Why did it occur to her that he would lie about it? Did she believe, deep down, that he really was some sort of undercover agent? But that was just a little game they had played. Another uncomfortable thought occurred to Laura. Had Steve been playing with her even when he was kissing her with such passion?

No, she couldn't believe that. His lovemaking had been genuine. Surely she could trust her feminine instincts on that score. She had never felt so desirable as she had in his arms. And she had adored every moment of it.

Even now she melted a little inside, remembering the thrill of his hungry mouth during their heated embrace. As hard as she tried to, she could not stop thinking about it. His passion had seared her and left its mark. And he seemed to truly care about her. Why else would he tell her that he would change his plans and stay in Kathmandu for as long as she did?

How delicious it would be, she thought, to spend long days and nights with Steve, exploring the city, exploring each other. But that was impossible. No matter how tempted she was to linger here with him, she would have to begin her trek to Jewel Mountain as soon as possible. If all went well today, she could start tomorrow. And she would leave Steve behind because her devotion to her father came first. She wasn't going to let some stranger with potent kisses sidetrack her.

And she wasn't going to let herself get carried away with his kisses again, either, she promised herself. She hadn't been herself last night. She'd been in a state of exhaustion. It all really did seem like a dream to her—the dance, the moonless walk through the city, his strange amber eyes.

She retied the scarf around her waist. She brushed her hair some more. It was a little past seven. He was waiting for her in the dining room. So why was she stalling? Because she feared that she would be disappointed seeing him in the daylight? Or did she really fear that she would want him even more than she had last night?

Adam Prescott's daughter. He was meeting Adam Prescott's daughter for breakfast. Steve couldn't believe his luck. He hadn't decided whether it was good luck or bad luck, though, as he waited for her at the same terrace table where they'd had dinner.

Obviously Laura had come to Nepal to visit her father. All Steve knew for sure was that the recluse scientist had a research site somewhere in the Jewel region. He'd been counting on hiring a guide who could locate it, but now the lovely Laura could lead him straight to his goal.

The lovely Laura. It would make things a lot easier if she weren't so damn lovely, Steve thought. Then what they'd shared last night wouldn't have happened, and he wouldn't be in the quandary he was in right now.

He'd paced his room until the small hours of the morning considering the possibility of not telling Laura who he was or what he was after. He could tell her he wanted to accompany her on her journey just to be in her charming company. She would believe that. He'd made his attraction to her pretty clear last night—about as clear as a man could be. Not only would she believe him, but the chances were good that she would also accept his offer to come along. She'd made it pretty clear herself that the attraction was mutual. A smile eased up Steve's mouth. About as clear as a woman could be.

His groin tightened with the memory of how she'd responded to him with such passion when he kissed her. She hadn't held back at all. His arousal grew as he recalled her soft flower mouth opening to him, drinking in his kiss. She'd been ready and willing to become his last night, and he was sure they would have awakened in the same bed this morning if he'd unlocked the right door.

Using the willpower he was so proud of, Steve forced himself to stop dwelling on Laura's kisses and concentrate on the problem at hand. Laura would be arriving momentarily, and he had to decide how to proceed with her.

The easiest solution would be to lie to her. Not that it would be a complete lie, Steve told himself. He truly did want to remain in Laura's company for a while longer. He wanted to kiss her again. He wanted to make love to her. He began dwelling on the taste and feel of that sweet honey mouth of hers again. Damn! Why was it so hard to concentrate? He rubbed his tired eyes, regretting all the sleep he'd lost last night.

When Steve lowered his hand, he saw Laura coming toward him across the flagstones. He loved watching the way she moved, appreciating the snug fit of her jeans. Her shiny blond hair was pulled back into a ponytail, which made her big eyes look even more wide set. It occurred to him that Laura was the Lady Luck he'd been waiting for all these days. She probably had a guide and porters lined up to take her to Jewel Mountain. And all he had to do was convince her to take *him*.

"Nice morning, isn't it?" he said when she sat down across from him.

"Yes, so fresh after last night's storm," she murmured.

Steve smiled. Was she remembering what he was about last night's storm? He couldn't tell. Her eyes were lowered as she studied the menu, which she seemed to find fascinating reading.

"It hasn't been this clear for days," he said. "Look at that magnificent view."

She raised her eyes and took it in, still avoiding eye contact with Steve. The terrace overlooked the red tiled roofs and golden temple spires of the city. And beyond that, the Himalaya Mountains shimmered in the morning sunlight.

"Isn't the tallest peak we can see from here Jewel Mountain?" he asked casually.

Laura didn't take the bait. "Could be," she said with a show of uninterest.

So she was still holding out on him. Steve tried again, hoping that she would reveal her destination without his having to ask her outright. "I'd like to climb Jewel one day. They say the going's rough."

"I'm sure it's not as difficult as Everest," Laura said. And that was all she had to say on the subject. The waiter came, and she ordered toast and tea and papaya.

Steve drank his scalding black coffee and watched her nibble on toast for a while. He liked watching her eat. He liked watching her do anything. She had small slender hands, but they looked capable, too. Clever hands, he thought, with short shiny fingernails.

"You're very quiet," he commented.

She put down her teacup and smiled shyly. "I feel self-conscious with you this morning."

"You didn't last night," he reminded her. He saw her cheeks pinken and enjoyed being able to make her blush.

"It's because I didn't last night that I probably do now," she admitted. "And it doesn't help to have you watching me so closely."

"I can't help it. You look so good to me. Morning becomes you."

She gave out a little laugh. "I was wondering how we would look to each other in the harsh light of day." She reached across the table and touched his hand. "Morning becomes you, too, Steven."

Maybe it was the sweet way she said that. Maybe it was the way she called him Steven. Or the light touch of her hand on his. Whatever it was, Steve decided to level with her. No matter how tempting it was to trick her into taking him to her father's research site, he couldn't do it. He had too much regard for Laura to deceive her. And he also regarded his own integrity too much. It always came down to that with him—his own personal sense of right and wrong. He liked to think of his conscience as a trusty pilot light, burning low and constant, ready to flare up when he needed to call upon it. So he called upon it now.

"Listen, Laura, I know who you are and why you've come to Nepal," he said, getting right to the point.

She took her hand from his, and he saw apprehension creep into her clear gray eyes like a shadow. "How could you know anything about me?"

"I'm a journalist, Laura. My last name is Slater, and I work for *Globe* magazine. I'm working on a story right now that happens to involve you."

"So you lied when you said you were here on vacation."

"Not really. I mean, that's why I initially came to Nepal, but—"

"You *lied* to me," she repeated more forcefully, cutting off his explanation.

"Technically I'm still on vacation," he insisted. "But when a Sherpa I met on Everest told me about a respected zoologist who had recently made an amazing discovery, I decided to investigate it for myself." Her eyes were darkening like storm clouds now, he noted. "It seems this scientist has been studying a creature believed to be mythical," he continued. Her face had paled, making her eyes look even darker. He wished that she would say something. "But of course you know all about this, don't you, Laura? That's why you've come to Nepal. You're on your way to visit your father."

"And you were lurking in the hotel lobby waiting to spring on me!"

"I had no idea who you were when you arrived," Steve protested. "How could I possibly know you were coming here? Hell, I didn't even know Adam Prescott had a daughter."

She considered this a moment. Her expression remained antagonistic. "All right, maybe you didn't know I was coming here, but you found out who I was soon after I arrived, didn't you? Everyone at the hotel knows who I am. And then you didn't waste any time getting...friendly with me."

"But I didn't ask about you. I had no reason to. My only motive for getting to know you was my attraction to you. The moment I laid eyes on you, I thought you were the most fascinating, lovely—"

"Oh, spare me the sweet talk now!" she interrupted. "It won't work anymore. I'm only sorry that I behaved like such a fool with you last night."

"Laura, listen to me." He placed his hand on her arm, but she stared down at it with such repulsion that he immediately removed it. "I didn't know who you were during our evening together. Whatever I said, whatever we shared, had nothing to do with the fact that you're Adam Prescott's daughter."

"You expect me to believe that?" She didn't wait for an answer. "How far were you going to go with your little seduction act?"

"It wasn't an act," he said evenly, keeping his temper reined in. "What do you take me for?"

"What do you take *me* for? An idiot? You wanted to use me to get to my father. Your ethics as a journalist leave a lot to be desired."

"You're not judging me fairly, Laura. I'm trying to be honest with you."

"Why don't you try a little harder?" she suggested in a sarcastic tone. "Why don't you come right out and tell me what you want from me."

"Your trust, for one thing."

"Don't make me laugh." She looked as if she were ready to cry, however.

"Laura, please listen to reason. If I intended to lead you on, why would I tell you that I want to write a story about your father?"

"Why didn't you tell me last night?"

"Because I didn't know who you were last night, dammit!" He was losing his patience and took a deep breath. "I only found out your last name after the room mix-up. The manager told me. You could have knocked me over with a feather."

Her glare told him that she would have liked to knock him over with something a lot heavier. "I'm not buying it, Slater. You've known who I was all along, and after your failed attempt to get me into bed, you decided to change your tactics with me."

Failure was not one of Steve's favorite words. "If you don't mind me saying so, Laura, you seemed to enjoy the attempt."

She obviously did mind his saying so. She threw down her napkin and stood up abruptly, scraping her chair against the flagstones. "Goodbye, Slater. I'm sure we won't be seeing each other again."

He caught up with her before she made it to the terrace steps and grabbed her arm to halt her. "We'll be seeing each other again, sweetheart. You can depend on it."

She jerked her arm from his clutch. "Don't sweetheart me, you big phony."

He ignored the insult. "We're both headed for Jewel Mountain. So we might as well go there together. It's a long, hard trek, and you shouldn't attempt it on your own." His tone softened. "Let me come with you. I've had a lot of mountaineering experience and I'll watch over you.

I'll make sure you arrive at your father's camp safe and sound."

"You're all heart, Slater." Her voice trembled with contempt. "Such an unselfish offer."

"No, a practical one that will benefit both of us."

"The way I see it, you have everything to gain and my father and I have everything to lose. There's no way I'm going to bring some nosy journalist to his research site. His work demands privacy. Now, get out of my way and out of my life."

He saw the obstinacy in her face and stepped aside. The moment he did, she scurried down the terrace steps without looking back. Did she really think she could get rid of him so easily, he wondered as he watched her flee. Did she think accusations and insults would dissuade him? Well, then she had a lot more to learn about Steve Slater. And she would learn soon enough, he thought, his expression set with an obstinacy to equal hers.

Good riddance to Trouble, Laura thought as she hurried away from Steve. She blamed herself for asking for it, for being so susceptible to his insincere lovemaking. She felt mortified by her own stupidity and weakness, and all the loving responses that he had aroused within her had turned sour with regret and self-recrimination.

Her only comfort, which she clung to, was that she had been discreet concerning her father. She'd given away nothing about his latest research project or his site location on Jewel Mountain. She was sure Slater would never be able to find it on his own. Then she recalled the stubborn set of his chin, the intensity in his eyes—signs of a man who had indefatigable persistence. Perhaps he would eventually locate the site on his own, but by then Laura hoped she would have convinced her father to leave the mountain with her for the winter. That would leave Slater with no one to interview—unless he managed to hunt down some yetis!

Did he actually believe they existed, and that her father had made contact with them? Or was he one of those ruthless journalists who ruined the reputations of famous people for the sport of it? Her father's fame as a zoologist had been hard earned and deserved, and Laura wasn't going to let Slater have the chance to make a laughingstock of him.

She looked over her shoulder to make sure Steve wasn't following her, then walked briskly down the same twisting streets she had strolled through last night with him. But now the city teemed with activity, a vibrant hodgepodge of colors and sounds and smells. Laura did not slow her pace until she reached the large bazaar in the heart of the city. The streets were crammed with people, and the little shops in the ancient brick buildings were crammed with wares. Vendors hawked fruit and vegetables and grains from baskets clustered around Hindu shrines and temples. Cows wandered freely, obstructing pedestrians, rickshas and motor vehicles. Street urchins spotted Laura's blond hair from afar and ran after her, begging for candy and money. She gave them all the change she had on her and pushed forward into the noisy chaos, losing them.

The blaring sounds of honking horns contrasted with the sweet notes of bamboo flutes. A huge black bull blocked Laura's way at one intersection, and as she skirted around it she almost got plowed down by a fume-spewing bus. Women in colorful saris, balancing bamboo poles across their shoulders, darted past her in both directions. Goats and mangy dogs scavenged through garbage on the sides of the streets. A holy man dressed in a loincloth and orange paint chanted relentlessly.

Laura took all this in without pause. Kathmandu was just as she remembered it, and it smelled the same, too—a combination of fragrant spices, incense and malodorous decay. Above the swirling market scene rose the temple spires and tridents, and beyond them the majestic Himalayan mountain peaks.

Vendors from the tightly packed clusters of shops called to Laura as she passed—shouting *Hey, didi! Hey, lady!*—trying to interest her in gemstones, bangles, pottery and yak-hide boots. She ignored their calls and their colorful displays, intent on finding one particular shop. She began to doubt that she ever would. It had been a long time, after all, since she last visited Kaba Par. She had to trust her instincts to lead her to his door.

And they didn't fail her. The tiny umbrella shop appeared as if by magic in the middle of the market chaos. She peeked inside and through the dimness spotted dear Kaba asleep on his stool. Laura smiled. Not for Kaba, this hawking of wares. Either Fate led customers to his door or it didn't.

She went inside. "Kaba Par," she said softly.

He opened his eyes immediately, and a beautiful smile spread across his wide, weathered face. He touched his hands lightly together.

"*Namaste,*" he said, a Napalese salute to acknowledge the godliness within a person.

Laura responded with the same greeting. "Do you remember me?" she asked him.

"But of course I remember you, Laura Prescott."

She was pleased that he did, although a little disappointed at his mild reaction. Wasn't he the least bit surprised to see her? But then she remembered what her father had always said about Kaba—he could be surprised by nothing. He seemed to live in another realm entirely.

"How could you recognize me after all these years?" she asked him. "I was only thirteen the last time you saw me. I must have changed a great deal."

"Eyes never change," he told her. "They are the windows to your soul. And I always saw the beauty of your soul in your eyes, Laura."

She smiled. "The years haven't touched you at all, Kaba."

She wondered how old he was. His broad face betrayed neither age nor emotions—an unlined brown face with flat cheekbones and dark, slanting eyes. He wore his grizzled hair cropped short, and perched atop his finely shaped head was a flower-patterned *topi*, a fez that was the national headgear for Nepalese men. But Kaba was a Sherpa first and foremost, from a mountain village in the Khumba region of Nepal. Laura's father held the Sherpa in high esteem and considered Kaba Par to be one of the finest guides in the country. He had accompanied Dr. Prescott on many expeditions until he'd retired and set up his umbrella shop.

"How is your father?" he asked Laura.

"I'm not sure," she said. "That's why I'm here to see you, Kaba."

He patted the stool beside him. "Sit. We will talk about it."

She sat down and took her father's letter from her purse. "I received this from Dad a few days ago," she said. "Please read it and tell me what you think."

He waved the letter away. "No, no, that would not be right. Unless Dr. Prescott gave you permission to allow me the liberty, I could not intrude my eyes on his personal missive to you."

She should have expected that. She had come to Kaba because he was so discreet. "May I read a section of it to you, then?" she asked him.

That seemed to be more acceptable to Kaba, and he nodded for her to go ahead.

Laura unfolded the letter. "I won't be visiting you for Christmas as we had planned, Laura dear," she read. "I know you were counting on it, and I'm sorry to disappoint you, but my work must come first." Laura stopped reading and looked at Kaba. "His work always came first, so that part didn't surprise me." Kaba said nothing, so she continued. "Something has interrupted my regular schedule, however. Something so astounding that I have left off my snow leopard research to investigate it full-time."

"Indeed," Kaba said.

Laura looked at him closely. "You know about it, don't you, Kaba?"

He remained silent and his expression, as always, revealed nothing. So Laura read on.

"What I have to tell you now, Laura, must remain a secret between you and me until I'm ready to make my findings a matter of record. I have discovered—"

"Please do not go on," Kaba urged Laura in a quiet voice. "If you continue, you will be breaking your father's confidence."

"But he wouldn't mind if I shared this with you. He trusts you completely. That's why I came to you, Kaba."

"If Dr. Prescott wanted to share this with me, he would have," Kaba said. "But I will tell you what I have heard of him lately. There have been stories reaching my ears from other Sherpas. I have discounted them, but now I fear they could be true, and that is what has brought you here."

"What sort of stories?" Laura asked apprehensively.

"That Dr. Prescott has left his comfortable hut to go live in a cave with . . ." Kaba paused. "With yetis."

"In a cave. Dad's living in a cave now? He didn't mention that in his letter."

"You know how mountain stories can become exaggerated," Kaba said mildly.

But Laura was already picturing the worst—her distinguished father with wild hair and a long beard, dressed in a loincloth, living like an animal. Isolation could do that to a person. As a child she'd heard stories about wild mountain hermits baying at the moon, driven crazy from loneliness. And her father had been living alone for a long time. Too long.

"Have others seen these yetis Dad claims to have befriended?" she asked Kaba.

He sighed wearily. "Many a Sherpa has seen many a yeti. That's why the legend persists. Alas, none can prove such a claim."

"It seems Dad intends to. Or risk his life trying." She straightened her shoulders. "I'm going to visit him, Kaba. I have to make sure he's all right."

"But that's impossible. You cannot take on such an arduous journey alone. You will lose yourself."

"That's why I came to you, Kaba Par. You know the way."

"Ah, you want me to be your guide."

"Yes! Please take me to Jewel Mountain."

"But I retired years ago, Laura. I am no longer a young man. Also, I have my business to run." He gestured around his little shop, where umbrellas were piled in disarray all around them.

Laura's heart sank, but she could not argue. She had been selfish and thoughtless, she realized, to request his help. But Kaba Par was the only one she knew of to turn to. "Perhaps you could recommend a guide for me," she said in a small voice.

"I know many good guides," he said. "But none who would want to take on the responsibility of a young woman alone. Especially during the monsoon season. It is the worst time to travel."

"I know, but I must reach Dad before snows make the high trails impossible. I have such dreadful foreboding about him. I fear his life is in danger."

"Your life could be in danger if you persist in this endeavor, Laura. It is a very difficult trip."

"I can manage it," she insisted. "Don't forget, I traveled to Jewel Mountain with my parents and you many times as a child."

"But never in the rainy season. And never so high up the mountain as Dr. Prescott is now. Besides, when you were a child, he would carry you when the going got rough."

"Not often, he didn't," Laura protested with pride. "I carried myself most of the way on my own two little feet."

Kaba smiled at the memory. "Yes, you had plenty of spank."

"You mean spunk," Laura said. She would have smiled, too, but her heart was too heavy. Kaba would not be coming with her this time. "Will you help me organize a small expedition as soon as possible? A guide and a few porters. I want to bring my father some supplies in case I can't talk him out of spending the winter at the site."

"I will do my best for you, but I advise you to wait until the monsoon passes."

"I can't wait! There's something else I must tell you, Kaba. Two years ago, the last time Dad visited me in New York, I didn't think he looked well and finally nagged him into going for a checkup. The doctor told him his heart was weak, that he shouldn't put extra strain on it. Of course, Dad refused to believe him or follow his advice. But I worry about him constantly, living so high up the mountain."

"It is not good to worry so much about what you cannot control, Laura. Your father must follow his own destiny, and you must follow yours."

"I intend to," she said. "As soon as I'm sure he's okay."

Kaba sighed. "You have made up your mind, and there is no changing it. You are just like your father that way, Laura Prescott. This is not always a good way to be."

"It's the only way I know how to be, Kaba."

"So then you should understand why Dr. Prescott must be the way he is, too. You cannot take him away from his mountain."

"At least I can try to reason with him. I would like to leave tomorrow if possible."

"I would go with you, but I cannot leave my shop," he said. "This is my busy season."

"I understand," she said, and even managed a smile. As a child she had adored Kaba Par, and now she still had a deep fondness for him, even though he had let her down. "You won't be getting much business today, I'm afraid," she said to make polite conversation before she departed. "It's a sunny day. Perhaps the monsoon rains have passed."

"No, too early for that by a week or two. No matter how sunny the day begins, the clouds always blow in again, the rain always falls down. This is the way it is during monsoon season."

And as if to prove his point, it began to rain again, lightly at first, but then in torrents. People poured into the shop to purchase umbrellas. Kaba Par sold five of them to grateful tourists in less than ten minutes without leaving his stool.

When there was a pause in trade, he slid off his perch and bustled about the shop, straightening up the tangle of merchandise and completely ignoring Laura. She took that as a sign that she was being dismissed and stood up, too. She was a few inches taller than the Sherpa.

"I'm staying at the Kathmandu Hotel. Will you please contact me there if you find a guide for me, Kaba?"

He made no reply but continued to rummage through his wares. "Aha!" he said at last, extracting a purple umbrella. "This is the very one I was searching for. It is difficult to acquire a *chhatris* with a bamboo handle nowadays. People seem satisfied enough with the plastic ones." He shook his head over this sad fact, then handed the umbrella to Laura. "This will be the most important piece of equipment on your journey, Laura Prescott. A good *chhatris* keeps the rain off your neck and the sun off your back and can be used as a staff on difficult mountain paths. Take it with my best wishes. A gift."

"Thank you, Kaba." She accepted the umbrella, assuming it was his way of saying goodbye.

But when she went out the door, he followed her, slammed it shut and padlocked it.

"Hey, mister," a burly man called from across the narrow street. He held a soggy newspaper over his head. "I need to buy one of your umbrellas."

"So sorry," Kaba told him. "My shop is just now closed."

"Well, open it again for a minute," the man urged. "Heck, I'll give you fifty bucks for one."

"How willing people are to overpay for what they think they cannot do without," Kaba said to Laura. "Go up the street to another shop," he told the wet, impatient man. "I will be selling no more umbrellas for a good while to come. You see, my young friend here and I are embarking on a long journey together. She needs me as her guide."

The man walked away, grumbling to himself, obviously not overjoyed with the shopkeeper's explanation.

But Laura was. She gave the Sherpa a heartfelt hug. "Thank you, thank you, Kaba!"

He extracted himself from her arms, maintaining his impenetrable reserve. "Do not thank me, Laura, until I safely deliver you to your father."

Someone else had also offered to do that earlier, Laura recalled with a tinge of bitterness—someone she distrusted as much as she trusted Kaba Par. But she would not think of Steven Slater again. Making this firm resolution, she snapped open her new umbrella. Kaba joined her under its protection, and they walked down the street with matching steps.

The purple umbrella, a bright beacon among the black ones, made it easy for Steve to follow Laura at a safe distance. He wondered who the little guy she'd hitched up with was. He would find out, he assured himself with supreme confidence. He always found out what he wanted to know.

Before giving himself a mental pat on the back, however, he felt a swift kick in the pants was what he deserved. He wasn't happy with the way he'd handled himself with Laura at breakfast. Maybe he shouldn't have told her the truth after all. Why did the truth usually make things more difficult? Because people rarely wanted to hear it—that's why, Steve answered himself. It made them uncomfortable.

Yet Steve still felt compelled to search out the truth and report it, no matter how unpopular it made him with those who had reason to avoid it. As foreign correspondent for *Globe,* he had reported the unsavory truth about corrupt regimes throughout the world. Steve was always the first to shout, loud and clear, when the emperor wore no clothes, and he took great satisfaction in doing so.

His nomadic life-style had been getting to him lately, though. He was beginning to question if his constant quest for the true story was a way to avoid settling down. It was tough to form permanent relationships when you had no permanent address. The closest thing he had to a home was his battered suitcase, he thought wryly.

He could change that if he wanted to. He'd been offered an influential editorial position at *Globe* before he took off for his vacation, and although he hadn't accepted it, he hadn't turned it down, either. He needed time to mull it over. Could he be happy behind a desk, directing others to go after the truth? Surely he would miss the excitement of the chase. On the other hand, he didn't want to miss out on having a life of his own. He wanted more to show for it than a battered suitcase, a filled passport and some journalism awards.

Funny he should think about all this while following Laura's purple umbrella. But meeting up with her yesterday had made him acutely aware of his need to have more in his life. He'd enjoyed being in her company a little too much. She'd made him realize how lonely he'd been lately. That didn't sit right with him. Steve considered himself a loner, not a man who could ever feel lonely.

He slowed down his pace, realizing that he'd been walking faster and faster and getting too close to Laura. That's the one thing he had to avoid doing from now on, he cautioned himself. He couldn't allow himself to get too close to Laura in any sense. It would jeopardize his objectivity when writing about her father.

He didn't understand why he was so determined to interview Dr. Prescott. Animal research wasn't his usual beat. But the idea of a prestigious scientist investigating the abominable snowman tantalized him. His sharply honed instincts told him that there was a big story waiting for him on Jewel Mountain. And he couldn't think of a better way to spend the rest of his vacation time than following it up. So he continued following Laura, making sure now to keep his distance.

Laura parted with Kaba Par in the Thamel section of Kathmandu, in front of one of the many shops there that sold trekking equipment. Kaba had helped her purchase the supplies they would need for the trip, which were to be delivered to him later that day. Kaba had also managed to hire four porters and a cook. He'd had to use all his persuasive powers to convince them to take on such a long journey during the wet season, and Laura knew that she could never have done it on her own.

Still, she had another hurdle to overcome, and Kaba couldn't help her with this one. She made her way to the Ministry of Home Affairs, hoping that Mr. Devi, another old friend of her father's, still worked there. She asked for him when she arrived and after a short wait, she was ushered into a large office. The man behind the teak desk stood and gave her a welcoming smile.

"How may I be of service to you?" he asked in a clipped British accent.

"Oh, there must be some mistake," Laura said. "I requested to see Mr. Devi."

"But I am he."

Was her memory playing tricks on her? The Mr. Devi she recalled was elderly and rumpled, while this man was elegantly dressed in a pale tropical suit and appeared to be no more than thirty. She noticed how his dark, sultry eyes took her in from head to foot with an interest that was more than official.

"Ah, perhaps you had expected to see my uncle," he said. "He retired last year, and I took his post at the ministry. Sorry to disappoint you."

Laura tried not to show how truly disappointed she was. She had been counting on her father's friend to cut through some red tape for her. "I'm here to get a trekking permit to Jewel Mountain," she told the new Mr. Devi.

"That's a restricted area, I'm afraid." He stroked his smooth, round chin as he continued to size her up with a great show of appreciation. "Why would such an attractive young lady as yourself wish to go to such an isolated spot, if I may ask?"

Well, of course he could ask, Laura thought irritably. That was his job, wasn't it? She didn't care for his unctuous manner, but she smiled anyway. "I would like to visit Adam Prescott. He's doing research work there."

"Yes, I know. Dr. Prescott has the government's special permission to study one of our national treasures, the snow leopard. He has done much to aid conservation and the protection of endangered species here in Nepal. But he does not like his work disturbed, and since we also consider *him* a national treasure, we respect his need for privacy."

"You don't know how pleased I am to hear that, Mr. Devi," Laura replied, handing him her passport. "But I'm sure Dad won't mind me disturbing his work with a surprise visit." She wasn't as sure about that as she sounded, however.

Mr. Devi examined her passport. "But of course, Miss Prescott! I will do my very best to expedite matters for you."

He called in a subordinate and ordered him to fill out a trekking permit for her posthaste.

"I hope you will forgive my initial reluctance to give you permission to travel to the Jewel region, Miss Prescott," he said after asking her to sit down and offering her tea. "But we do not allow just anybody to go there."

"No apology needed. I'll be sure to tell Dad how careful you are about screening visitors to his research site." Laura paused and considered what she was about to do. Then she went ahead and did it. "There is one person in particular whose visit would be unwelcome."

"And who might that be?"

Laura took a deep breath. "A journalist named Steven Slater."

A frown creased Mr. Devi's forehead, disturbing the smooth perfection of his moon-shaped face. "Yes, I know him." He riffled through some papers on his desk. "I have a report on him somewhere. Ah, yes, right here." He skimmed the sheet of paper and tossed it aside. "A bit of a troublemaker, this Slater chap."

Hearing that didn't surprise Laura. "What has he done?"

"Oh, nothing *illegal*." Mr. Devi seemed disappointed. "I suppose he could claim he was just doing his job. Got kicked out of China a few months ago while he was investigating some uprising or other. Probably trying to get himself another Pulitzer Prize." Mr. Devi sniffed.

Although his tone had been scoffing as he discussed Steve, Laura couldn't help but be impressed. "Slater received a Pulitzer Prize for Journalism?"

"That's what it says in the report." Devi shrugged it off. "I didn't think too much of him when I met him last week. Too brash. Too sure of himself. Came here for the same reason you did, Miss Prescott. He wanted a permit to travel to the Jewel region."

Laura stiffened. "And did you give it to him?"

"Not yet. His application is still under consideration. We have to be careful who we let into that area because it borders Tibet. We don't want to have problems with China." His dark dewy eyes took on a focused sharpness. "Tell me, Miss Prescott. Why would Slater be interested in interviewing your father? I find that most puzzling. I was under the impression that he reported on more earthshaking events than animal research."

"Oh, who knows." Laura kept her tone casual. "Maybe it's a slow month for uprisings. He told me he came to Nepal on vacation, and maybe he figures that if he did a story on my father, he could write off his travel expenses."

"Yes, that's a possibility." But Laura heard doubt in Devi's voice. "So you've met Slater?" he asked her.

"Just yesterday. He's also staying at the Kathmandu Hotel."

"I take it you didn't much care for him, either."

She didn't know how to honestly answer that question. She had cared for him far too much last night. And today she despised him for leading her on. "I don't trust him," she finally replied.

"Really?" Devi raised sleek eyebrows. "Why is that? Do you think he would write something harmful about your father?"

Laura had underestimated Devi, she realized. He was more clever than she'd supposed. She had to derail him off the right track as quickly as possible.

"Here's what I think, Mr. Devi." Sensing he liked intrigue, she leaned forward and lowered her voice. "I think Slater might not be interested in writing about my father's snow leopard research at all." Well, that was true enough!

"You mean it could be a ruse?" Devi drawled out the word, apparently liking the sound of it. "Hmm. That's an interesting premise, Miss Prescott." He tapped his manicured nails against the desktop. "From the Jewel region Slater could easily slip back into China. Now it all makes more sense to me."

Laura relaxed a little. But she didn't let up. "I'm sure Chinese officials would be rather upset if he managed to get back into the country by way of Nepal."

"And I would be held responsible because I issued the permit," Mr. Devi declared, looking nervous about it.

"You also have the authority to refuse issuing one," Laura reminded him.

"And believe me, Miss Prescott, I plan to use that authority. Without a permit Slater won't be able to get past the checkpoint in the area. If he wants to see Jewel Mountain, he'll have to do it from a plane."

Having effectively blocked Steve's passage to her father's site, Laura sipped tea with Mr. Devi and waited for a pang or two of guilt to come. None did. All she felt was sheer relief as she imagined a plane taking Slater far, far away.

"Might I have the pleasure of your company at dinner this evening?" the ministry official asked her.

The gleam in his eye told Laura that he hoped for more pleasure than dinner, but she still accepted his invitation. She knew she could handle Mr. Devi. He didn't have the unsettling effect on her that Slater did. Or *had*. That was over now. The plane she imagined taking him away became smaller and smaller in her mind's eye.

"Why not dine at your hotel?" Mr. Devi said. "The Kathmandu serves the best food in the city."

Laura agreed to his suggestion. She didn't mind if Steve saw her there with Devi. Let him guess that she'd had something to do with keeping him out of the Jewel region. In fact, it would give her a perverse pleasure for him to know that.

When Laura left the Home Ministry, she felt satisfied with all she'd accomplished there. She had her trekking pass. And Slater wouldn't be getting his. All this had been managed in less than an hour. And during that time, the rain had let up. Surely a good omen, Laura thought.

Since everything was set for her trip the next day, and she didn't want to return to the hotel and run into Steve, she decided to stroll through the city a while longer. She recalled a temple she had been fond of as a child because of all the monkeys that congregated around it. Curious to see if they still did, she set out to find it.

She let her subconscious guide her along side streets that took her farther and farther away from the city bustle. She eventually came upon the temple as easily as she had located Kaba Par's shop. And sure enough, she could hear the monkeys chattering even before she entered the enclosed courtyard. She smiled when she saw them swinging from vines and trees, scampering over the golden roofs of the three-tiered structure.

Because it was off the beaten track, the temple attracted few visitors, and Laura had it all to herself for the moment. Except for the monkeys, that was. She sat down on a stone bench and watched them, letting her mind wander back to the past.

Her parents had brought her to this temple. They'd shown her exotic and fascinating sights all over the world. It had never occurred to Laura that her life was quite different from other children's. Secure in the warmth of her parents' love, she'd never had trouble adjusting to strange environments. Her mother had tutored her during their long stretches of time living in isolated regions, and she'd happily played with the local children, learning their language and adapting to their ways.

It wasn't until after her mother died and her father sent her back to so-called civilization that Laura had trouble adapting. She'd been an outcast at the boarding school she'd attended until she'd learned how to act and talk and dress like the other girls. It had been a painful experience, one she'd vowed never to repeat. Since then she had always done her best to fit in, although deep down she still felt like an outsider.

Lost in her musing, Laura forgot to keep her guard up around the monkeys. One of them took advantage of the situation and snatched her purse from the bench. Laura leapt up and chased after him as he ran across the courtyard with it. He climbed up a tree and perched on a branch, looking down at Laura with a taunting monkey grin. She stared up at him with frustration. The purse contained everything that mattered most to her at the moment—her passport, her trekking permit, the letter from her father.

She tried to cajole the monkey down with soft calls and kissing sounds. He responded with a maddening monkey chatter. And from behind her, Laura heard a deep human laugh, equally maddening because she knew whom it belonged to. She whirled around to face Steve Slater.

Chapter Four

"Well, don't just stand there snickering. Do something, Slater!" Laura damanded.

How imperious she sounded, Steve thought. Not that it bothered him. In fact, he sort of liked it.

"What do you expect me to do, Laura?"

"Climb up and get my purse back for me, of course."

Steve looked up at the high tree branches, arms folded across his chest. "Why don't you climb up yourself?" he suggested mildly. "I'll stay down here to catch you in case you fall."

"Thanks for nothing," Laura muttered, then proceeded to follow his suggestion, hoisting herself up to the lowest branch with impressive agility.

"You'll never reach him," Steve said. "And if you do, he'll just swing from the vines. Can you swing from vines, too, Laura?"

She ignored him and continued climbing. The closer she got to the monkey, the higher up he went.

"You're going to break that pretty neck of yours if you keep climbing," Steve warned her. "Come down from there. I have a plan."

She threw him a haughty look from her elevated vantage point. "What sort of plan?"

"I'm not going to shout it up to you and let *him* overhear. Come back to earth and I'll tell you."

"This better be good, Slater."

She climbed down more slowly than she had gone up, less surefooted now that she'd had a moment to consider the possibility of falling. Steve enjoyed the view from below. "Take your time," he advised.

When she came within his reach, he grabbed her by the waist and swung her to the ground. He was reluctant to let go of her, but she pushed his hands off her waist and stepped away from him.

"What's this great plan of yours?" she asked.

Her cheeks, he noted, were flushed. From exertion or his touch? he wondered. Exertion, most likely. Her glare made it clear that she loathed him and the only reason she could endure speaking to him was because she needed his help. She had looked at him in quite a different way last night, he recalled. Desire had made her gray eyes luminous. How beautiful she'd been, the sheen of rain on her face, her lips parted for him. But now her expression was hostile, her luscious lips clamped shut.

"Keep your eye on the monkey," he told her. "Don't lose sight of him. I'll be back in a minute." He left her standing by the tree.

Laura waited, and more than a minute passed. More than a few. It occurred to her that leaving her staring up at a jeering monkey and never returning could be Slater's idea of a practical joke. But he did come back shortly, holding two big hands of bananas.

"Had to find a fruit stand," he told Laura. "I figure we can lure that fellow down with some goodies."

He waved the bananas at the monkey, who stared at them intently but remained still as a statue.

"Maybe he's waiting for you to peel him one," Laura suggested dryly.

"I think he wants us to leave the offerings and go away."

"Great. Then he'll have the bananas *and* my purse. This isn't such a great plan."

"Got a better one?"

As Laura was trying to come up with one, the monkey began making his way down, slowly, cautiously, twitching his tail and swinging Laura's purse. Then he stopped and froze again. Meanwhile, other monkeys began moving in, beady eyes equally intent on the bananas Steve held.

"We're being surrounded on all sides," he said in a theatrical whisper.

"They bite, you know," Laura informed him. "They have very sharp, nasty fangs."

"Then I better put down these bananas before one of them mistakes my fingers for a hand."

Laura groaned. "Your joke is as bad as your plan."

"I'm not ready to give up on it yet. That's my philosophy, Laura. Never give up."

"Frankly, at the moment I'm not much interested in what makes you tick. All these monkeys are making me nervous."

"Yeah, they look awfully hungry, don't they? Like they would kill for a piece of the action."

"I wish you hadn't expressed it quite that way."

"Not to worry, Laura. I've revised my plan. I'm going to put down the bananas, and when I do, jump aside."

"Happily!"

"When these critters swarm in, my guess is our purse snatcher will leave his perch and come join the party. One of us will grab the purse off of him when he does. Got that?"

Laura nodded.

"Ready?"

"Ready."

"Be careful not to get bitten in the fray," he advised.

"I'll be careful."

"And above all, never lose sight of our thieving friend," he added.

Steve threw down the fruit, and the monkeys swarmed around it. They were hard to tell apart except the one who was sporting a fine leather purse. Steve got to him first and grabbed the strap. A tug-of-war ensued, with much spitting on the part of the monkey and much swearing on the part of the man. In the end the man won, but just barely. He raised the handbag above his head like a victory flag.

Overjoyed, Laura ran up to him and was about to give him a congratulatory hug. Then she remembered how much she disliked him and distrusted him and held back.

"Thank you. Well done," she said stiffly. She put out her hand for her bag, but he continued to hold it above his head.

"Don't I get a better show of thanks than that after risking my life for you, Laura?"

"Don't exaggerate."

"Listen, that little monkey was one vicious adversary. He could have gone for my jugular."

"Well, he didn't. May I have my purse back now?"

"On one condition, sweetheart."

No doubt he was going to demand a kiss from her, Laura thought. Her heart began to pick up its pace. Not that she wanted to kiss him again. But if she had to meet his silly demand in order to get her purse back, she would force herself. One kiss before they went their separate ways. She tilted her head expectantly.

But he didn't ask for a kiss. "Let me accompany you to Jewel Mountain," he asked instead.

Her heart slowed down as it dipped. Of course that's what he wanted. That's all he'd ever really wanted from her. "First you're a scheming Romeo, and now you're attempting extortion," she said. "You've got the morals of a...of a monkey, Slater."

Her accusations made Steve bristle, and he was tempted to throw her purse back into the squealing primate fray. But that would only prove her assessment of him to be correct. Which it wasn't, dammit.

"Just thought I'd ask again," he said, tossing her the handbag. "Too bad you're too stubborn to appreciate the advantage of taking me with you."

She sniffed at that. "You're the one who wants to take advantage."

"You never know when you might need me. What about today? You'd still be chasing a monkey up a tree if I hadn't come along," he pointed out.

She looked at him with silver eyes as sharp as blades. "You've been following me around all day, haven't you?"

"You've been a busy little bee," he replied. "Who was that man in the fez cap you hitched up with?"

"None of your business."

"He looked like a Sherpa to me. Correct?"

She ignored him and hurried to the bench to get her umbrella before it was stolen by a monkey. Steve accompanied her.

"And you must have gone to the Home Ministry for a trekking permit, which means you had to deal with Devi," he persisted. "You looked pretty satisfied with yourself when you came out. Did that officious bureaucrat give you one?"

Laura smiled.

"He did, dammit!" Steve said. "And he's kept me waiting for over a week."

"Mr. Devi doesn't go around giving out permits to just anyone," Laura said snidely, enjoying herself. "They try to keep unsavory characters out of restricted areas of the country."

"Is that what Devi called me? Unsavory?" Steve laughed. "Those are just the words that pompous jerk would use."

"Actually, those are *my* words to describe you," Laura admitted. "Mr. Devi and I didn't waste too much time discussing you." True enough. They had settled his fate in less than five minutes. "But you've wasted a lot of time shadowing me all day. What good did it do you?"

"I demonstrated how helpful I could be when you ran into trouble, didn't I?"

"Yes, when it comes to monkey business, you're in your element, Slater. But I already knew that about you."

"You don't know me at all," he replied in an even voice. "Every assumption you've made about me is wrong. I've been straight with you from the very beginning."

"Oh, really? Well, I think slinking around following somebody is pretty crooked. And I know enough about you to make some accurate judgment calls. So forget about trying to persuade me to take you to my father's research site, Slater. You're the last person on earth I would bring there."

"Okay," he said. "I'll forget about it."

That had been far too easy, Laura thought. She walked away from him before he could try another tactic. He followed her as she headed to the temple.

"What made you come here today?" he asked her.

"It was one of my favorite spots in Kathmandu when I was a child," she replied, not looking at him but staring up at the pagodas.

"You must have been a pretty sophisticated little girl."

She didn't understand that remark. What was so sophisticated about liking to watch monkeys play?

"I find the carvings fascinating myself," he added.

Carvings? For the first time Laura noticed them on the struts supporting the pagodas—hundreds of writhing couples in every conceivable erotic position. Her parents had certainly never brought that to her attention!

"Excellent craftsmanship, don't you think?" Steve went on. "I can understand your avid interest in them."

"I wouldn't call it avid," Laura murmured, averting her eyes from the figures and then looking back at them. They *were* fascinating.

"Embracing tantric gods," Steve said. He sighed dramatically. "Making love is as close to nirvana as we mortals can get on earth, don't you agree?" When she didn't answer, he bent his head closer to her ear. "Two bodies become one. Ego is lost. Mutual pleasure is everything."

She tore her eyes from the erotic depictions. "I never noticed these carvings as a child, but I do know that a lot of temples have them for protection against lightning. The belief is that the chaste goddess of lightning finds the subject matter shocking and won't come near any temple displaying such art."

"That poor chaste goddess doesn't know what she's missing," Steve said, pressing his chest against Laura's back.

She shifted her body away from his, although a part of her still longed to lean against him. "Be careful. She may strike you down if you don't take her seriously."

It began to rain again. Steve looked up at the sky, smiling. "But I'm protected by the temple."

"Then you'd better stay here." Laura opened her umbrella and walked away.

"Hey, how about sharing your umbrella with me?" he called to her.

She turned back to give him one last disdainful look. "I'm never going to share anything with you, Slater."

She hurried away, leaving him standing under the curving pagoda roof. In the trees all around her the monkeys twittered. Laura had the upsetting sensation that they were laughing at her.

"You are an exceptionally pretty young lady, Miss Prescott, but I'm sure you've had that observation made to you many times over," Mr. Devi told Laura over dinner on the terrace that evening.

"Not all that many times," Laura replied. And never with such stifling formality, she silently added. She would have told Devi to call her by her first name but feared that he would interpret that as too friendly a gesture on her part. Men in this part of the world sometimes misconstrued an American woman's natural informality.

Still, she wished Mr. Devi would loosen up a bit. She also wished he hadn't dressed so formally. His dinner jacket made her feel uncomfortable, since she was dressed in a turtleneck and jeans. She didn't explain to him, however, that the one dress she'd packed had been ruined in the rain the night before. He would have to take her as is. And he didn't seem to be having any trouble doing that. His eyes brimmed with admiration, and she sensed that he was racking his brain to come up with another elaborate compliment to pay her. She headed him off at the pass.

"My looks aren't all that exceptional, and it embarrasses me to have someone remark on them," she said.

"Your modesty is as endearing as your beauty," Mr. Devi replied.

"You're too kind," Laura said flatly.

Another thing she wished was that he hadn't insisted on being seated at this table. It was the one she and Steve had shared for dinner and breakfast. Not that it should make any difference to her. But somehow it did, even though she wanted to forget that she and Steve had shared anything at all.

And she would forget about him soon enough, she assured herself. She figured that a hard day or two on the mountain trail would diminish his impact on her considerably. Meanwhile, Mr. Devi wasn't making the slightest dent in that department. Not from lack of trying. She'd never had a more solicitous dining companion. She smiled at him politely.

Steve paused at the terrace entrance. Why the hell was Laura having dinner with that moron Devi? And at *their* table, no less. She'd done this to spite him, he decided. Well, he wasn't going to let it bother him, or at least he wasn't going to show that it did. He ambled across the flagstones and took a table to the side, where he could keep an eye on them without being too obvious about it.

"In case you haven't noticed, that chap Slater has put in an appearance," Mr. Devi told Laura sotto voce.

She had noticed, all right. She felt a tingling sensation all over. "Well, I suppose he has to eat like everybody else," she said with a great show of indifference.

"He's really not like everybody else, though," Devi said. "Have you noticed that about him, Miss Prescott? Not that I mean to imply that he's special. Only that he thinks he is. I find his arrogance extremely abrasive."

"I suppose he can be charming when he puts his mind to it." Laura bit her bottom lip. How had that slipped out?

"Charming?" Devi frowned. "No, I can't see that particular trait in him at all. I don't think the Chinese government found him charming. He seems to stir up trouble wherever he goes. We don't need that sort in Nepal."

"I'm sure he'll leave once his trekking permit is denied," Laura said.

"If he doesn't, he should be asked to. Politely, of course. I may suggest that to those higher up." Devi raised his eyes to the ceiling, then leveled them back on Laura. "Nepal has an image to protect, after all. Tourism is our major industry. Slater has a reputation for destroying public images of all sorts."

That was exactly what Laura feared. If Slater wrote a story about the renowned Dr. Prescott living in a cave trying to prove the existence of the abominable snowman, he would not only become a figure of ridicule, but he would probably also lose the grant money he needed to continue his legitimate work. But that wasn't going to happen, she assured herself. She wasn't going to let it.

"I can understand your concern, Mr. Devi," she said. "Perhaps it would be wise to make sure Slater left Nepal as soon as possible."

Steve wished he could overhear what Laura and Devi were talking about. He didn't like the idea of Laura getting chummy with such a self-serving stuffed shirt. At least she wasn't wearing that sexy black dress of hers. For all their chivalrous affectations, men like Devi couldn't be trusted. Laura had been smart to cover up from neck to ankle. That didn't stop Devi's eyes from crawling all over her, though.

"Would you reconsider and have a glass of this excellent wine I ordered?" Mr. Devi asked Laura for the second time. He'd mentioned how excellent it was the first time, too.

"No, thanks," she said again. "I'm starting early tomorrow and want to be fresh for the trek."

"How long will it take you to reach your father's site?"

"According to my guide, Kaba Par, that all depends on the weather. If we don't get too much rain, we should get there in less than three weeks."

"I admire you for such a strenuous endeavor, Miss Prescott. Indeed, I admire you in every way. You have all the fine qualities a man looks for in a young lady." He sighed. "But alas, one comes across them so rarely. You are like the perfect pearl one happens upon once in a lifetime. And a discriminating man, such as myself, recognizes the genuine article when he spots it. And you, Miss Prescott, are the genuine..."

But Laura had stopped listening to Mr. Devi's drivel. Her attention had been captured by a little drama taking place at Steve's table. The maharani, followed by her four female companions, had entered the terrace and made a beeline straight to Steve. She looked a lot more dignified than she had the night before, when they'd accidentally intruded into her room. Her black hair was twisted into a satin coil, and she wore an elegant indigo sari edged in gold.

Many gold bangles dangled from her slender wrists, and white orchids decorated her glossy hair. Her big eyes were outlined in black kohl, and she sported a vermilion *tikka* on her forehead. She looked splendid and held her chin high, like a woman who knew she did. What in the world could she be discussing with Steve? Laura wondered.

Steve stood up when the maharani stopped at his table, half expecting to get a slap across the face for his effort to be polite. But what he got instead was a warm, gracious smile.

"So we meet again, Mr. Slater," she said. "Not under such awkward circumstances this time."

"My apologies for that, princess. A mix-up in room keys."

"So the manager explained to me."

"If I'd known you spoke English so well, I would have done the explaining myself. But you were screaming so much you probably wouldn't have heard me."

"Perhaps I overreacted a bit," she allowed. "A woman traveling alone can't be too careful."

That's exactly what he'd told Laura, Steve recalled, when he'd found her asleep on the hotel sofa. Her face, he remembered, had looked so angelic in repose. He glanced at her now and was glad to see that her eyes were wide open and staring at him and the maharani. He turned his attention back to the maharani.

"You weren't exactly alone, princess. You had an earnest squad of bodyguards." He bowed to the four women surrounding her. "Nice to see you again, ladies. You look more like butterflies tonight than tigresses."

Apparently the maharani didn't care to share the spotlight. She clapped her hands and dismissed the women. They fluttered off.

"I feel quite safe with you alone tonight, Mr. Slater," she said. "May I join you for dinner?"

It was an unexpected request, but Steve showed no surprise. He wondered, though, what this pretty princess was up to...or after. It would be fun to find out, especially with Laura looking on. He gave her a little wave, and she turned away quickly.

"I would be honored to have you join me," he told the maharani. He seated her with elaborate care, making sure her silk sari didn't get caught between the wrought-iron table and chair.

"It surprised me to find you dining alone this evening," she said. "I expected you to be with your little American girlfriend."

Steve smiled, hoping that Laura had overheard that putdown. The maharani's voice was high and shrill enough to carry. "Miss Prescott isn't my girlfriend," he said. "We're two strangers passing through Kathmandu. Like ships in the night." He hoped Laura heard that, too.

"There are no ships in Kathmandu," the maharani said. "Nepal is a landlocked country. And a rather dull one, to my way of thinking. So I would not mind sharing dinner and...whatever with a handsome man such as you."

So that was it, Steve thought. The princess was bored and looking for action. Maybe he should introduce her to Devi. Then he and Laura could go off and settle their differences in the moonlight. But that was just wishful thinking. It would take more than moonlight to get Laura to trust him again.

He felt the maharani's little slippered foot slide up the side of his leg. She didn't waste any time. He usually liked that in a woman. But as lovely as this one was, he couldn't focus on her. His eyes and mind kept drifting to Laura. And why the hell was she letting Devi hold her hand like that now?

"I really don't put much stock in palm reading," Laura was telling Mr. Devi, finding such an obvious seduction ploy tiresome. She didn't want to hurt his feelings, though, and continued to allow him to hold her hand in the grasp of his slightly damp one.

"I see you have a warm heart and a trusting nature, Miss Prescott."

"Yes, sometimes too trusting," she admitted, eyes darting in Steve's direction again. He seemed to be having a good time with the princess from India. Of course, last night any observer would have thought he was having a good time with her. Was he putting on an act for the princess, too? It was hard to tell with such a dissembler.

Devi gave her hand a little tug. "Your interest seems to waver at times," he said with a slight edge to his ever-so-polite voice.

Laura looked back at him. "I'm sorry."

He released her hand. "No need to be. If you don't believe in palmistry, so be it. Your father must have taught you to have faith in only what can be proven scientifically."

That was exactly what her father had always professed, which made Laura all the more anxious about his so-called yeti research. He'd always proclaimed yetis to be the figment of mountain people's imaginations. He had never put any stock whatsoever in the persistent rumors of their existence.

"Be sure to tell your famous father that I am a great admirer of his," Devi told her.

She promised him that she would.

"He'll no doubt be delighted to see his lovely daughter."

She shifted uneasily and made no reply. She had no idea what her father's reaction to her visit would be. Through the years he had become a stranger to her. And she missed him terribly. She missed the loving father she'd once known, not the elusive recluse he'd become since her mother's death.

Mr. Devi talked on. "Would you be so kind as to tell Dr. Prescott how I facilitated your journey to him?"

"Yes, of course I will."

"Your father is highly respected in Nepal. His good reference could greatly help one who..." Devi paused to smile ingratiatingly. "One who modestly wishes to advance his career in government. A letter from your father to my superiors at the Home Ministry would be most appreciated."

So that's why Devi had been playing up to her all evening! For the second night in a row a man had tried charming her in order to get to her father. Devi was no better than Steve Slater. But his ploy didn't bother her half as much. It didn't wrench her heart the way Steve's had. This man only made her want to laugh. Instead, she remained polite.

"I can't promise you a letter of recommendation from my father, Mr. Devi. He knew your uncle well, but I don't believe he's ever met you."

"Actually, no. I've never had the pleasure of his acquaintance. But I do know *you*, Miss Prescott. And if you could put in a good word for me, it would mean a great deal to me. I find you such a delightful, interesting, beautiful—"

"Enough!" Laura said. "You've made your point, Mr. Devi. Really you have." She felt relieved when the waiter appeared with the check. This interminable dinner had come to an end.

A short while later Steve watched Laura bid Devi goodnight with a no-nonsense handshake and exit from the terrace without him. Good! He excused himself from the maharani's company and went to talk to Devi, who had stayed at the table to finish the bottle of wine.

"Has approval for my trekking permit come through yet?" Steve asked the official without preamble.

Devi didn't hide his irritation when he looked up at Steve. "I don't discuss such matters outside my office, Mr. Slater."

"You don't have to say a word. Raise your right hand if the answer is yes. Your left if it's no."

"Are you trying to be amusing?"

"No, I'm trying to find out if my damn permit has been approved. What's the holdup?"

"This is neither the time or place to go into it," Devi said. "Come to my office during the posted hours."

Steve sat down at his table instead. "Let's pretend, just for a minute, that we're in your office right now, okay? And all you have to do is tell me if I can plan to leave for Jewel Mountain tomorrow."

"Oh, tomorrow is out of the question."

"The next day, then?"

"Also out of the question. And every day after that."

Steve's eyes narrowed. "Are you trying to tell me, in that obtuse way of yours, Devi, that I'm never going to get a permit?"

Devi took a sip of his excellent wine and smacked his lips. "It doesn't seem likely. It would disturb certain individuals if you did so."

"One certain individual by the name of Laura Prescott, you mean?"

"I must admit that she expressed misgivings about your presence in that restricted area."

"Since when does Laura Prescott have authority to say who can and who can't go to Jewel Mountain?"

Devi rolled his narrow shoulders. "She doesn't, of course. But *I* do, Slater. And I would not wish to displease such a delightful young lady."

Steve groaned. "Oh, give me a break. Your job has nothing to do with pleasing or displeasing women, no matter how delightful they are. So stop blathering like a pompous ass and start talking like an official, Devi."

"Very well. The *official* reason your pass is being denied is because you can't be trusted in that area of Nepal, Mr. Slater. It's too close to the Chinese border, and we don't want to aid and abet your illegal return there."

"But I don't want to get back into China, dammit! I covered the story I wanted to there. I'm a journalist, Devi, not a revolutionary."

Devi patted his plump lips with his napkin. "One or the other, they both mean trouble. I advise you to leave Nepal as soon as it is convenient for you to do so, Mr. Slater. And perhaps you could find it convenient to leave bright and early tomorrow morning."

"What does that mean? Are you kicking me out?"

"I'm merely suggesting that you go someplace else. That's not an official order." Devi smiled. "As of yet."

"Then let me tell you what you can do with your suggestion."

Mr. Devi raised his hand and shook his finger at Steve. "Don't be crass, Mr. Slater, although I'm sure it's difficult for you not to be. Miss Prescott didn't seem very impressed with your demeanor, either."

Steve's laugh was short and harsh. "Well, that's too bad if it didn't impress her."

He was sorely tempted to pick up Devi's bottle of wine and pour what was left in it down his pleated shirtfront. But he didn't give in to the temptation. After last night he didn't want to cause the hotel manager any more trouble. So he walked away from Devi's table without making a scene.

When he rejoined the maharani, he could tell by her sour expression that his demeanor didn't please her any more than it had Laura.

"I'm not used to being left alone and ignored," she told him.

"You could have always clapped your hands for company."

His coolness seemed to warm her. Her expression turned sweet. "But it is only your company that I desire, Stevie."

She had started calling him Stevie after the first course. He realized that he should have nipped it in the bud, but he was too busy keeping tabs on Laura to pay much attention. The maharani nudged her little sandaled foot against his leg again.

"Let's forego dessert," she said.

"Fine with me." Steve was bored with her company and sneaked a peek at his watch. Laura had left the terrace ten minutes ago.

"We can have dessert in my room," the maharani told him. She licked her brightly painted red lips so lasciviously that Steve looked away, embarrassed for her. "You will see me to my room, won't you, Stevie?"

How could he refuse? "I'd be happy to escort you, princess."

When they went into the elevator, he inhaled her potent perfume, and all he could think about was how fresh Laura's skin had smelled from the rain. He remembered how pumped up his heart had been during their ride to her room, how excitement had raced through his veins. He had wanted her so much.

And now, in the same elevator, he stood with the woman who had destroyed the passion between him and Laura the night before. This woman had made it clear, on no uncertain terms, that she was his for the asking. Life was filled with amusing little ironies like this, Steve mused. Except he didn't find this one so amusing. There had been a time in his life when he'd found one beautiful woman as satisfying as another. But not anymore. Playing the field had left him with an empty feeling deep inside, and this emptiness could only be filled by someone special.

Lost in thought, he didn't notice when the elevator stopped. The maharani pulled his arm. "Aren't you getting out with me?"

He looked at her. She really was extremely attractive, with flawless skin and almond-shaped eyes. "Yes, of course," he said.

She led him to her door, the same door he had led Laura to last night. Number seventeen. His lucky number.

"Where's your entourage, princess?"

"My what?" She gave him a puzzled smile.

"Those four little ladies with sharp nails and pinching fingers who attacked me the last time I entered this room."

"Oh, my servants, you mean." She laughed. "Not to worry, Stevie. I dismissed them. They will leave us alone." She lowered her eyes demurely. "And I promise you I won't scream for help when you enter this time."

He recalled that her hair, uncoiled, was very long. Her braid had reached the small of her back. He imagined how it would look streaming down loose around her slender body. But another image superimposed itself in his mind—Laura leaning against this red door.

"Sorry, princess, but I can't come in. There's something important that I've got to take care of tonight."

"More important than me?" Her tone was one of disbelief.

"I'm afraid so. It's . . . a matter of life and death." Well, that might have been stretching it a bit, but he couldn't come right out and tell her he wasn't interested in what she had to offer. As much as Steve believed in the truth, he held his tongue when words were best left unspoken. Not too often, but at certain times. Like this one.

"Life or death?" The maharani didn't sound too impressed. "Very well, Mr. Slater, I bid you farewell."

He waited politely while she unlocked the door. The moment she slammed it in his face, he went across the hall to Laura's door and knocked.

"Who's there?" she asked after a moment.

"It's me, Laura."

"Me? That could be anyone."

"Come on, Laura. You know who it is. Open up. I have to talk to you."

"But I don't have to talk to you, Slater."

"Do you want me to make another scene in the hall? I promise you it'll top last night's fiasco."

"Another extortion attempt," she grumbled. But she opened the door. "Well, what is it?"

He smiled at the sight of her. He could tell that she'd just scrubbed her face. Her pert little nose was shiny, and there was a smudge of cream on her chin. She looked delightful to him. "I missed you tonight."

"You hardly know me. How could you miss me?"

"Beats me, but I did. Can I come in?" He didn't wait for a reply but entered her room, softly closing the door behind him.

She pointed the hairbrush she was holding at him like a gun. "No more funny business, Slater."

"Is that what you call what we shared last night? Funny business?" Steve shook his head. "Where's your sense of romance, Laura?"

"My common sense got the better of it. So stop pretending last night meant anything to you." She began to brush her hair with vehemence. "I know now that it didn't."

Steve listened to the crackle of her hair as she brushed it, and said nothing for a moment. He knew the futility of trying to convince her that he'd been sincere. He could show her, though. He could take her in his arms and kiss her with a passion she would have to believe. But everything had changed between them since he'd discovered who she was. Of all the women in the world, why did he have to get emotionally involved with Prescott's daughter?

"How did your evening with Devi go?" he asked her.

"Turns out he wanted the same thing you did, Slater."

"He wanted to make love with you?" Steve roared indignantly. "I hope you told him to go to hell!"

Steve's outrage surprised Laura, but she continued to brush her hair without pause. "That's not what I meant. Devi wanted to get to my father through me. Just like you did. Maybe I should get used to men trying to use me."

"I never tried to use you, dammit!" Steve grabbed the brush out of her hand and threw it on the bed. He stood so close to her that she could feel his hot breath on her face. "I wanted you. It was as simple as that."

And did he still want her? All Laura could see in his eyes now was anger. She glared back at him. "No, it wasn't that simple. You had an ulterior motive."

"Why do you insist on believing that? Are you afraid of passion, Laura? Are you putting this barrier of distrust between us to keep me at arm's length? Well, it won't work, sweetheart." He pulled her to him. "Kiss me," he demanded. "Open your mouth to me again. Let me taste you."

She gave not an inch. Her expression and mouth remained closed. He released her.

And Laura released her breath. That had been a close one, she thought. She had almost weakened and done what he'd demanded. But she could not allow this man to destroy what she valued most in herself—her absolute self-control. She had proven to both of them that she was still the master of it.

"You win this round," he said, stepping away from her. "But only because I let you."

She forced a laugh. "You let me? The decision not to kiss you was all mine, Slater. Why don't you go across the hall and visit your new friend, the maharani?"

"She doesn't interest me."

"Oh, really? Then why'd you let her play footsie with you all evening?"

Steve smiled. "You must have been keeping close tabs on us."

"Her tactics were so obvious they were hard to miss."

"At least she didn't try to read my palm."

"Seems you were keeping tabs, too, Slater."

"It was stupid to be at separate tables instead of enjoying each other's company."

"No, last night was stupid," Laura said. She'd enjoyed his company far too much.

She went to the bed and retrieved her hairbrush. It was made of silver, with an intricately worked design, a gift from her father when she'd turned sixteen. He had sent it to her at school—another birthday he'd missed. She patted the back of it against her palm a few times, waiting for Steve to state his reason for coming.

He stared at her with unblinking amber eyes. "You've been plotting against me with Devi, haven't you, Laura?"

"I expressed my concern about you going to Jewel Mountain, if that's what you mean."

"That's exactly what I mean. You used your feminine charms to influence some two-bit official. That's foul play, sweetheart."

"Whatever charms I have weren't called into service. Mr. Devi had misgivings about you before I even met him."

"Which you took advantage of, I'm sure. You batted those big eyes of yours and pleaded with him to keep big bad me away from your daddy."

Steve's tone was light, his posture relaxed, there was even a little smile on his face. But Laura sensed the undercurrent of anger beneath the surface and became a little frightened by his absolute stillness as he watched her. She nervously resumed brushing her hair.

"You interfered with my work, Laura," he continued. "That's something I don't tolerate."

No, she wasn't going to let him frighten her. Not that he'd made the slightest menacing move. "Well, Dad doesn't tolerate having his work interfered with, either," she retorted. Her own voice, she was sorry to note, wasn't as steady as his. "Leave him alone, Slater."

"I can't. I smell a story. A good one."

"After another Pulitzer Prize, are you?" she asked sarcastically.

"I don't give a damn about prizes. Getting the story right is the only thing that matters to me." He headed for the door. "I wish you a safe journey, Laura. Take care." He opened the door, blew her a kiss, and then he was gone.

Gone. At last he was out of her life for good, Laura thought. Hadn't that been exactly what she wanted? Then why did her heart feel deflated? Shaking off the sinking sensation, she began packing her bag with more energy than the simple task required.

Chapter Five

"You have beaten the sun up today," the night clerk said when Laura appeared in the empty lobby with her duffel bag the next morning.

"What sun?" she asked him. It had been raining since midnight—ceaseless, heavy, depressing rain.

She was dressed for her journey in clothes she'd purchased the day before. Beneath her slicker she wore a long loose cotton shirt and baggy Nepalese trousers called *suruwal*. Her running shoes looked a bit ludicrous with this getup. But jeans, she knew, would be considered improper feminine attire in the remote areas beyond Kathmandu, where Western civilization had little cultural influence.

After settling her account with the clerk, she went out into the dark and waited for Kaba Par under the hotel awning. Tension knotted her stomach muscles. Tension and fear. For all her surface self-assurance, deep down she was afraid the trek might be too much for her. She jogged daily, so she felt that she was in pretty good shape, but running on city streets and climbing steep mountain trails were not the same type of exercise.

She reminded herself that she'd made this trek as a child and had considered it a lark. But the weather had never been this bad, and the destination never as high up. More importantly she'd had both her parents along to protect her then, to help and encourage her. Now she was on her own. She couldn't expect Kaba Par to coddle her. He was her guide, not her nursemaid. She had resolved never to complain to him about anything.

A Jeep came around the corner. Laura waved and forced a brave smile as Kaba pulled up, jerking the rented vehicle to a gear-grinding stop.

"You drive, memsahib," he told Laura. "I am far better at walking."

She threw her duffel bag in back with the supplies and got behind the wheel. "Since when am I memsahib to you, Kaba?"

"Since this moment, the beginning of our journey. I am now officially your sirdar, and the porters will expect such formality."

But she didn't feel comfortable hearing that form of address from him. "In front of the porters call me memsahib if you think that's best, but in private please still call me Laura," she said.

"Very well," he agreed.

"Well, then, we're off!" she cried with false cheer as she stepped on the gas.

It took them six hours to reach Theltho, a small village at the end of the waterlogged, nearly impassable dirt road. After Theltho no road existed at all.

Kaba Par had grumbled about Laura's poor driving all the way there. She had done her best to avoid the many ruts in the road, but with such low visibility, she had missed spotting more than a few. Now Kaba, still grumbling, got out of the Jeep and walked away in search of someone to drive it back to Kathmandu.

Laura had never seen Kaba in a bad mood before. She wished she could blame it on the weather but knew that wasn't the reason. She could only blame herself. She had asked Kaba for a favor that he couldn't refuse, but he didn't really want to be going on this trek. He'd looked so comfortable snoozing on his stool in his cozy umbrella shop. She should never have asked him to be her guide. However, he was the only one she knew who could bring her to her father, so she had imposed on his good nature and sense of duty.

She hurried after him as he headed toward an openfronted shack that served as the village teahouse and held her purple umbrella over his bent head.

"I'm sorry, Kaba Par," she said. "I'm sorry I came out of the blue and disrupted your peaceful life."

"If only you had followed my counsel, we would not be here during such wretched weather. And I worry that you will continue to disregard my counsel."

"No, I won't! I'll go along with anything you say during our trip. You know best. As expedition sirdar, you'll always have the last word."

He stopped in his tracks and looked at her closely. "Is that a promise, Laura Prescott?"

"Yes. I promise to always follow your counsel during our trip, Kaba."

He smiled at her for the first time all morning. "I am glad we settled this between us."

They went to the teahouse and waited for the bus delivering the porters and additional supplies to arrive. They were served weak hot tea in thick cheap glasses, and when Kaba urged Laura to add a few lumps of coarse sugar and some buffalo milk to her tea for energy, she did so, although she loathed the taste of buffalo milk. But she had promised to heed his advice.

The rickety bus eventually arrived and stopped in front of the teahouse. Laura's heart leapt into her throat when she spotted a tall, lanky man with dark hair get out. But when he looked her way, she saw that his eyes were blue, not tawny, and he was a mere boy. A tourist, she guessed, here on school holiday. Her poor heart was still beating wildly, and she felt foolish about getting so worked up over nothing. Except for his height and the dark hair, the boy didn't look at all like Steven Slater.

Kaba Par introduced her to the five men he had employed for the expedition. Each of the four porters looked like a good, dependable man. The cook, on the other hand, didn't. His fierce appearance intimidated Laura. He was larger and burlier than most Sherpa, with a shaved head and a severe expression. She could tell he didn't like the idea of having a woman expedition leader. She appreciated it now when Kaba called her memsahib and showed her the utmost respect.

It took a long time for Kaba to distribute the supplies and gear among the porters, making sure everyone received equal weight. He carefully packed their baskets, which they would carry on their backs, secured by tumplines around their foreheads. Even though Kaba had been so painstaking about it, they still complained about the weight, but in a cheery, singsong way that wasn't meant to be taken too seriously.

Meanwhile, the cook busied himself finding additional fresh provisions in the village. Pickings were slim, but he managed to hunt up some eggs, bananas, guavas and a chicken. He put the chicken in a wooden cage, which he balanced on his sleek head. His inventiveness won Laura's approval. But she hadn't won his by a long shot. He responded to her smile with a harsh glare.

It was midafternoon by the time the expedition party was ready to leave the village. Laura felt disappointed about getting such a late start. Kaba said that it was for the best. He knew an ideal campsite less than four hours away, and he wanted Laura to take it easy for the first few days to slowly build up her leg muscles. She told him that she had strong legs because of her jogging, then had to explain to him what jogging was. He found it amazing that people ran for recreation.

The rain was only a drizzle when they set off. The trail they took followed a swollen river, and the pedestrian traffic along it was heavy. People streamed past them from the opposite direction, many of them carrying small animals on their backs. Kaba told Laura that they were Hindu mountain people headed for a big religious festival in Kathmandu, where the animals would be sacrificed. A small goat bleated piteously as it went by Laura, as if it knew its fate.

A group of women in bright shawls, brass ornaments in their nostrils, examined Laura closely when she stepped aside to make way for them on the path. They pointed to her shoes and giggled. She wondered if their laughter meant approval or disdain.

This was a tired old habit of hers, worrying what people, even passing strangers, thought of her. She'd grown terribly conscious of her appearance when she'd gone to school in the States. Before that she'd never given it a second thought, and that must have been all too obvious. The other girls had laughed at the way she'd dressed and worn her hair. They'd called her Monkey Girl, and at age thirteen that had cut her to the quick.

But now she was an adult who ran a successful catering business, and she knew that she should have outgrown her insecurity long ago. It was a flaw in her personality, Laura realized. One that her ex-fiancé had shared with her. When she'd insisted on rushing off to Nepal a week before their scheduled wedding date, Jerome's major concern had been what people would think. He'd given Laura an ultimatum. If she insisted on going, the wedding would not be postponed—it would be called off for good. So here she was, and that was that. For once she hadn't cared what he or anyone else thought.

But that wasn't quite true, was it? Laura had to be honest with herself. Wasn't part of her concern about her father caused by worry over what people would think when they heard of his bizarre interest in yetis? Well, somebody had to worry about protecting his fine reputation. Her father had never given a hang about it himself. All he cared about was his work.

In a way Slater reminded Laura of her father—both men were intense, headstrong individualists. But her father had ethics, which Slater sorely lacked. His deception still hurt Laura. If only he had been up-front with her from the beginning and told her of his intentions to interview her father. Instead, he had wormed his way into her heart. How he must have been laughing to himself when she'd responded to his kisses with such fervor! He'd made her want him, but all he'd really wanted from her was to be taken along to Jewel Mountain. She found that humiliating, but she wasn't going to dwell on it now. It was over and done with.

She concentrated instead on the lush tropical vegetation of the lowlands as she walked. The flowers all around her glowed bright in the mist. Frangipani, hibiscus—flowers her mother had been so fond of. She could feel her mother's loving spirit in them. She began humming a happy little tune her mother used to sing, and her own spirits lifted. Kaba glanced over his shoulder and smiled at her. Everything was going to be all right, Laura thought. The trek would go smoothly, and she would find her father in good health. He would be delighted to see her and agree to return home with her. They would celebrate Christmas together, after all. And when he returned to his mountain site in the spring, he would have forgotten all about his yeti fascination and would resume researching animals that weren't figments of his imagination. Cheered by such optimistic thoughts, Laura hummed all the louder.

By the end of the afternoon, however, she wasn't singing anymore. Although the climb wasn't steep as of yet, it was consistently uphill, and she felt the strain in her legs.

She shifted her rucksack against her sweaty back. It seemed to grow heavier with each step she took, and the weight of it dug into her flesh. She was almost grateful for the rain. In this hot, humid climate of the foothills, strong afternoon sun would have been hard to take.

Kaba Par continued a steady pace in front of her. Although he carried a rucksack that was much heavier than Laura's, and he was many years older, he seemed to glide without the slightest effort. So Laura forced herself to stop thinking about how heavy her rucksack felt and enjoy her surroundings instead. The gray river flowed below her, and along the hills the terraced rice fields looked like iridescent emerald steps leading up to some magnificent kingdom.

Because of cloud coverings, she couldn't see the snow-capped peak of the mountain that was their goal, and Laura had difficulty believing they would ever reach a cooler climate. She'd taken off her slicker, and perspiration soaked her thin cotton shirt. She longed to take a short break, but couldn't bring herself to tell Kaba that. He'd told her that this would be an *easy* walk, and if he knew that she'd already begun to tire, he would conclude that he'd been right all along, that the trek was going to be too difficult for her.

And so she continued in silence. The trail brought them to a clearing on high ground, with a spring nearby. Kaba told Laura that this was where they'd be camping for the night, and she hoped her face didn't reveal the great relief she felt that their trekking was over, at least for the day.

It began to rain more heavily as they waited for the porters to catch up. Standing under her umbrella in the dimming light, dead on her feet, Laura found it difficult to maintain a cheery front. Good-natured as Kaba was, he had little use for small talk and seemed content to remain silent beneath his own big black umbrella. Laura experienced a deep sense of isolation as the only sound she heard was raindrops drumming on her purple one.

But when the porters and cook arrived, they made camp with a flurry of activity and chatter. Kaba directed them to set up Laura's tent first, then urged her to go inside it to keep dry. She lay on her sleeping bag, exhausted, until one of the porters brought her a mug of tea and a plate heaped with lentils and rice. She attempted a conversation with him, but he shook his head to demonstrate that he understood neither English nor Nepali. Laura tried a few Sherpa phrases she recalled, but he still shook his head, and she realized that he felt awkward in her presence and just wanted to be gone.

She ate alone in her tent, feeling a bit like a pariah as the men outside talked and laughed. Having nothing better to do after finishing her simple meal, she changed into dry clothes and crawled into her sleeping bag. Kaba stopped by to check on her before turning in himself. She told him she was comfortable and bid him good-night. But then she lay in the dark a long time, her eyes wide open, feeling miserable and lonely. Was this what she had to look forward to for many days to come?

She began worrying about her business back in New York, although she really had nothing to worry about. She had a competent staff who could handle the upcoming events that were scheduled, and the major one that month—her own wedding—had been canceled.

Perhaps this would be a good time to have a cry over Jerome, she thought. But the tears wouldn't come. Maybe it hadn't hit her yet, that she and Jerome were through. She tried conjuring up his face in the darkness. Another man's face kept blocking it out. She shut her eyes tight, but the image of Steve Slater still floated behind her lids in vivid Technicolor until she fell into a deep, dreamless sleep.

Laura awoke the next morning to the sound of rain beating down on her tent. It was a sound that gave her little inspiration to arise and face another soggy day of trekking. As she was trying to get up the energy to do just that, a big hairy arm protruded through her tent flap. At the end of this arm was a beefy hand encircling a steaming mug of tea. From the guttural growl that accompanied the intrusion, Laura guessed it was the cook. When she took the mug from him, his arm disappeared.

Not the most pleasant way to start the day, she thought as she sipped the sweet milky brew. But by the last swallow she had stopped feeling sorry for herself and was ready to take on the challenge, even though every muscle in her body ached and she had blisters on both big toes.

They trekked through giant rhododendron forests that morning, then up a stony path that aggravated Laura's blisters. But whenever Kaba looked back to see how she was doing, Laura smiled at him. Sometimes she even managed a jaunty wave. They stopped for a midday meal when they came to a mountain pasture. Rice and lentils again. Kaba joined Laura under a tree and ate with her.

"When is our master chef going to cook up that chicken he carries on his head?" Laura asked him as she picked at her mushy food.

"This evening," Kaba replied. "We will stop early today and indulge in a feast."

That sounded good to Laura. "What's the cook's name, by the way?"

"Cookie."

Laura laughed. "But what's his real name?"

"He goes by that name only."

That didn't sound so good to Laura. "Why won't he divulge his real name? Does he have something to hide?"

Kaba Par waved away such ominous conjecture. "Cookie has served me well on past treks. You must trust my judgment, Laura."

"But I do!" she assured him. "It's just that Cookie doesn't seem to have the most pleasant disposition."

"He does not care about surface pleasantries, this is true," Kaba allowed. "But so often surface pleasantries are meaningless. I judge a man by his eyes, and our cook had good ones. Just wait until you taste his chicken stew. Then you will know his true nature."

"I can hardly wait," Laura said, putting aside her tin plate of mush.

"You finish your *dal-bhaat*," Kaba commanded. "You need a great amount of nourishment each day to keep up your strength. This is most important advice."

Laura picked up her plate again and continued to eat, but not with much enthusiasm. She was too fatigued to be hungry. The heat and constant rain took a lot out of her, more than she'd expected it would.

Her guide patted her back when she'd finished the last bean and grain on her plate. "You have been listening to me very well, Laura. You have so far kept your promise."

"I never break a promise, Kaba."

"It will be more easy for you when we go up higher to cooler regions. And the rains will eventually abate."

"Will these rains bring snow to the high passes, do you think?"

"It is a possibility. If so, we will have to turn back. Has Dr. Prescott enough provisions to last him through the winter?"

"Oh, Kaba, I don't know! He didn't mention anything about provisions in his letter, and I'm terribly worried that he'll get snowed in without food."

Her guide patted her back again. "Worry is so useless, Laura. Your father knows how to take care of himself very well. In all the years he has studied wildlife in Nepal, he has always made it up and down the mountains without mishap."

"But his heart isn't as strong as it used to be. And what if this yeti discovery he claims to have made is just an illusion?"

"All of life is an illusion," Kaba replied mildly.

But Laura had no patience with his convoluted philosophy now. "Tell me honestly and directly, Kaba. Do you think Dad has . . . lost his mind?"

"But I cannot answer such a question. I have not seen Dr. Prescott for a long time."

"Then tell me this. Do *you* believe that yetis exist?"

"Yes," he said. "I wouldn't be a true Sherpa if I didn't."

She should have expected that answer. His belief came from legends he'd heard since he was a child. "Trouble is, Dad isn't a Sherpa," she said.

Kaba smiled. "Perhaps in his heart he is."

During the afternoon the going became rougher, all up and down. It seemed to Laura that they were making little headway and would never reach higher altitude. Tough as the steep upward climbs were, she preferred them to the knee-wrenching descents back into the humid valleys. Going down caused her poor blistered toes to jam into her shoes, and her thigh muscles throbbed as she tried to maintain her balance.

Thick clouds made it impossible for her to see very far below or beyond, and she felt closed in, as if wrapped in a cocoon of wet heat. The temperature rose each time they descended into a valley. The trails oozed mud.

Laura felt her spirit suffocating. But then she passed a stand of cotton trees that looked as if they were on fire in the rain because of their huge red blossoms. Their beauty gave her the inspiration to go on.

"We will camp when we reach the top of the next crest," Kaba told her.

It was the steepest climb all day, and as soon as Laura accomplished it the rain ceased, as if to reward her. The porters cheered over the break in the weather, and even Cookie smiled. He took out the battered pots and pans he carried in his basket and rubbed his meaty hands together, crooning to the caged chicken.

Kaba told Laura that she could bathe in a pool beyond the campsite before the evening meal, promising her absolute privacy. He had been diligent about this from the beginning, his own personal modesty motivating him to ensure hers. Laura appreciated this more than any of his other kindnesses. She took a towel, soap and a fresh change of clothes out of her rucksack and headed in the direction of Kaba's pointed finger.

She found the pool with no difficulty by following the sound of a waterfall. The water came foaming down the high rocks from the melting peaks above. She washed her hair under the fall, then lolled in the warm deep pool beneath it, floating on her back and staring up at the gray sky.

A large bird hovered above her. Laura estimated his wingspan to be over eight feet. A lammergeier, she recalled from childhood nature lessons her father had given her. He'd given her a great deal of time and attention when she was young, but after her mother's death, when she'd needed him more than ever, he'd become remote. She forgave him for that, although she never understood it. Why had he sent her away when they could have been such a comfort to each other after such a great loss to both of them?

After Laura had bathed and dressed, she strolled toward the edge of the ridge and looked down. A curtain of clouds hid the valleys below. After all the hard climbing, she would have appreciated a good view for her effort. Still, the pride she felt in herself was enough of a reward. She had kept up with Kaba, she hadn't complained and she sensed that she was going to make it through this long journey just fine.

She had been in need of a good challenge, she realized. Perhaps she had gotten into too deep a rut back home. After the initial tough years getting it established, her catering business now practically ran itself—or rather, she'd hired good, responsible people to run it for her. Jerome was also a caterer. They'd met at a convention. And they'd planned to combine their two businesses once they married. Getting married had seemed like such a convenient, practical thing to do. After all, they'd had so much in common.

But not really, Laura thought. Jerome had had such a conventional, proper upbringing. He'd always gone to the right schools, known the right people, done the right thing. And she'd thought she wanted the safe, normal, predictable life he could give her. Until less than a week ago, she'd been sure that's what she wanted. But now that it was lost to her, she felt no regret. She wasn't even angry with Jerome for giving her an ultimatum. Perhaps deep down she had wanted that to happen. It had made things so simple, the break so clean.

Her feeling of relief instead of regret puzzled Laura. Jerome suited her so perfectly, or at least she had thought so until now. He had given her a sense of steadfast security, exactly what she'd always wanted from a man. She had no use for unpredictable adventurers—men like Steve Slater, for example. But oh, those amber eyes of his! They had thrilled her to the core.

She wondered where Slater was now. Off to his next adventure, his next story, his next woman, no doubt. When a man like him couldn't get what he wanted, he didn't hang around too long, she was sure. He just went after something else.

She had hoped to forget all about him after a few days on the mountain trails. And she almost had, she assured herself, except for a few stray thoughts now and then. But his wild, glittering eyes were hard to forget, especially at times like this, when she was completely alone. It was so peaceful here, so quiet.

And then she heard it—the sound of someone whistling. Someone was whistling "Strangers in the Night"! No, it couldn't be. Laura shook her head. She was letting her imagination get the better of her. Still, the whistling persisted. The sound came from below the ridge. She peered down, standing as close to the edge as good sense allowed. She could barely distinguish a tall figure of a man through the clouds, making his way up the pass. Were both her eyes and ears playing tricks on her? But then she could no longer hear the whistling because of the blood pounding in her eardrums.

She felt dizzy and stepped away from the edge. She took a few deep, calming breaths. When she looked back down, she could see Steve more distinctly. He was much closer now. He marched like a man who knew exactly what his goal was and how to reach it. His lanky frame emanated a male force that seemed to her indefatigable. He would reach the campsite in no time, she realized. She turned away from the edge and ran back to warn Kaba of the oncoming invader.

But when Laura arrived at camp, Steve was already there, talking to Kaba. She hurried up to them, breathless, eyes blazing.

"I always like the way you look with your hair wet, Laura" were his first words to her.

"What the hell are you doing here, Slater?" were her first words to him.

Kaba smiled benignly. "Such an abrupt way to greet an old friend, memsahib."

"This man—" she stabbed a finger in Steve's direction "—is no friend of mine. If he told you he was, he's a liar."

"You always call me the sweetest names, Laura. You seem to be holding up pretty good. Just as feisty as ever."

"Oh, she has both strong legs and strong heart," Kaba said.

"Good teeth, too," Steve added.

Kaba looked a little confused over that remark.

"He's just using you as a straight man to make me the butt of his joke," Laura told him. "This man has come to make trouble, Kaba."

"That was not the intention he expressed to me, memsahib."

"Did he tell you he intends to write a story about my father?"

Steve spoke up for himself. "Of course I did. I was as straight about it with Kaba Par as I was with you."

Laura rolled her eyes to the heavens. "May the goddess of lightning strike you down for lying." But since the goddess did not come to her aid, she had to deal with him herself. "You're not joining up with this expedition, Slater. So you might as well turn back right now."

"At least let him stay for the night," Kaba said.

"No. I don't want some..." She paused to come up with the right word. "Some *predator* in our camp during the night."

Steve's smile came slow, as if the description suited him just fine. He needed a shave, and the dark shadow of beard along the hollows of his cheeks made him look dangerous. He was sweaty and scruffy and even more attractive to Laura than she remembered him. His deep-set eyes never left her face. She felt a warm melting within her, and a hot resentment, too. He had no right to look at her in such an intimate way.

"But it is too late for Mr. Slater to find another suitable place to camp," Kaba said. "It will be dark soon. Surely we cannot turn him away."

"Oh, very well!" Laura said, frustrated. "It seems we're stuck with you for one night, Slater."

He bowed to her. "I accept your gracious hospitality. Where can I wash up?"

"There's a pool back there." She waved her hand in the direction.

"Why don't you walk me to it?"

"You'll find it easily enough. I did." She didn't want to be alone with him. Not ever again.

"Come with me," he insisted. "You and I need to have a little talk, Laura."

"No, we don't. The answer is still no."

His smile became even broader. "Doesn't that depend on the question, sweetheart?"

With that he walked off to find the pool. Laura glared at his back until he disappeared into the trees. Then she noticed that Kaba was staring at her with amused interest.

"Sorry if I sounded so inhospitable, Kaba, but that man can't be trusted. I'm amazed that he tracked me down. Of course, he knew the general direction I was headed, and he must have just gotten lucky and taken the same trail."

Kaba said nothing.

"He's the most determined man I ever met," Laura added, shaking her head over it.

"I'll go tell the porters to put up his tent."

"He can do it himself, Kaba. There's no reason the porters should have to go through extra work for him. After all, he's not part of our expedition party. He's just stopping for the night."

Again Kaba said nothing. He hurried off to speak with the porters.

The rain held off all evening, and Laura, Steve and Kaba ate dinner outside their tents, on folding stools around the kerosene stove. Cookie ladled out chicken stew from a big dented pot. He served Steve first, Laura noticed. She sensed that Cookie now considered Steve the expedition leader and was greatly relieved to have a man instead of a woman in that position. The porters also appeared more at ease with Steve around. Even Kaba Par seemed delighted with his company. Which made Laura odd woman out, so to speak. She was the only one who resented Steve's presence.

Kaba and Steve were discussing how life had changed in the Himalaya Mountains since Westerners had started trekking them.

"Too many tourists come for adventure here," Kaba said. "They do not understand how to coexist with nature. Sacred forests are cut down for fuel. There is pollution where there was once beauty. This upsets the spirits that protect the land."

Steve nodded his agreement. "The problem is that man has always disturbed the balance of nature. It's in *our* nature to do so. Thanks to progress, no area of the world can remain isolated anymore. Even remote mountain regions are reachable."

Laura gave him a pointed look. "At least the government is making an effort to keep outsiders from entering the Jewel region."

"For the time being, perhaps," Kaba said. "But there is no guarantee that it will be protected forever. When a country is as poor as Nepal, it is difficult to turn away tourist money. We have come to depend on it. Even I!" He sighed. "I make a living selling umbrellas to hapless tourists caught in the wet embrace of the monsoon."

"Hey, it's an honest living," Steve said.

"Yes, but it feels good to be back in the mountains again. I have missed them, and it pleases me to be a part of them again. We will be passing through much beauty on our way to Jewel Mountain, Mr. Slater."

Laura was glad to hear that Kaba found pleasure from this journey. It made her feel less guilty about asking him to take it. But it bothered her that he had directed his remark to Steve, as if he would be coming along with them. Surely Kaba hadn't meant to imply that. She had made it clear to him that she didn't want Slater along.

"This stew is delicious," Steve said, finishing up his with gusto.

Cookie was immediately at his elbow. "More, sahib?" he asked.

"Only if there's enough."

"Plenty enough," the cook assured him. As he took Steve's bowl for a refill, he actually grinned.

"Nothing like having a good cook along on a trek," Steve said. "Sure beats eating beef jerky and dried fruit."

"Well, enjoy it tonight," Laura told him. "You'll be back to your regular rations tomorrow."

"But I just carried enough food to take me this far," Steve replied in a carefree tone.

"How unfortunate for you," Laura said. "You're going to get mighty hungry on your return trip." She reconsidered. "But I couldn't send even *you* away without food. We can spare some rations for Slater, can't we, Kaba?"

"Yes, indeed," her guide replied. "I made sure to bring enough for Mr. Slater, too."

Laura wasn't sure that she had understood him correctly. "But why did you do that, Kaba? You had no way of knowing..." She observed the sheepish look on Kaba's face and suddenly understood perfectly. "Now I get it. You knew that Slater would be joining up with us, didn't you, Kaba? You and he planned it all out together before we left Kathmandu!"

Kaba shifted uneasily and didn't deny it. Steve continued to eat heartily, a little smile on his face.

His smirk enraged Laura. "What did you do, Slater? Bribe my guide into taking you along?"

Steve stopped smiling. And Kaba slowly raised himself from his camp stool and walked away, back stiff.

"You can accuse me of anything you want, Laura, and I'll just ignore it," Steve told her in a low, even tone. "But you sure as hell shouldn't accuse a man like Kaba Par of taking a bribe."

His reprimand was unnecessary. Laura had realized the stupidity of her words the moment they had slipped out of her mouth. Heat rushed to her face, and she jumped up from her stool, knocking it over in her haste to go after Kaba.

"Kaba, wait!" Laura entreated when she caught up with him. "Please let me apologize to you."

He didn't refuse her request. When he stopped to face her, Laura couldn't make out his features in the descending darkness, but she could feel his hurt.

"Oh, Kaba, I didn't mean what I said!"

"Then why did you say it, memsahib?"

His coldness made her shiver. "Because I wasn't thinking straight at that moment. I know you would never take a bribe, Kaba. I know that in my heart, but stupid words came out of my mouth. And now I'm begging for your forgiveness.''

"You have it," he replied after a moment, and patted her back.

Tears of relief sprang to her eyes. "Now you see what a troublemaker Slater is, don't you? He's been here for only a few hours and has managed to cause a rift between us."

"That was your doing, not his," Kaba pointed out gently.

"But he has such a terrible effect on me! And even though I hurt you so thoughtlessly, Kaba, I still deserve an explanation, don't I? Why did you arrange to have him meet us two days into our journey?"

"I felt that two days would be enough time for you to appreciate his company."

"Appreciate his company?" She attempted a laugh, but it came out more like a sob.

"Mr. Slater will be your companion and protector during our trek. He will make the going easier for you."

"No, he won't! If you knew him as well as I do, you wouldn't regard him so highly."

"Perhaps I am able to see his worth more clearly than you can, Laura. We had a long talk when he visited me at my home the day before we left Kathmandu. Mr. Slater impressed me as a man of character and strength. And he expressed a deep concern for your welfare."

"But he doesn't care about me at all," Laura protested. "You don't understand, Kaba. He just wants to interview my father."

Kaba shrugged. "Dr. Prescott does not have to speak to him if he does not wish to."

"But you see how persistent Slater is. I don't want him bothering Dad. Remember the letter he sent me? He doesn't want anyone to know about his yeti research at this time."

"But Mr. Slater already does know about it. There is no way you can stop him from finding your father. If we do not take him to Jewel Mountain, he will surely find another way of getting there. As you say, he is a persistent man. So why don't we include him in our expedition and make use of his able-bodied presence? When the trail becomes more difficult, you will be happy to have his strong arm to lean on."

"Never," Laura said with deep conviction. "I will never ask Steven Slater for help."

"Then he will give it to you without your asking. That is the sort of man he is."

"But how can you know what sort of man he is, Kaba?"

"His eyes, of course. Indeed, he reminds me much of your father, a man of equal determination. Dr. Prescott can hold his ground with Mr. Slater. There is no need for you to be concerned about that, Laura."

Frustrated by Kaba's inability to see Slater's true nature, Laura looked toward the campsite, where she saw him standing with the porters by the stove, a tall silhouette towering above the others in the group. He had no right to be there, and she deeply resented his intrusion. She turned back to Kaba.

"I don't want Slater traveling with us," she stated firmly.

"But I do." Kaba's voice was soft but equally insistent. "I think it would benefit you if he came along. And you promised me that you would follow my counsel at all times, Laura Prescott."

"I made that promise to you without knowing that you planned to have him join up with us."

"And are you breaking it now that you know?"

"I'll go along with everything else you decide on this trip, but not this."

"Then you do not trust my good judgment."

"Only as far as Slater is concerned."

"There can be no exceptions, memsahib. Either you trust me, or you do not. And if you do not, I will not be your guide."

So it had come down to this, Laura thought. Either Slater would accompany them, or Kaba would refuse to take her any farther.

"I have no choice in the matter, then," she said. "I need you, Kaba."

"But I am no longer a young man, Laura. You cannot depend on me entirely. What if some misfortune or illness made me unable to continue?"

She touched his arm. "Please don't even say such a thing."

"But we do not know what the future holds for us. Please understand that it is in your best interest that Mr. Slater come with us."

She didn't believe that it was, but she understood that Kaba was only thinking of her and didn't hold it against him. Slater had somehow managed to win his trust, and that made her resent the interloper all the more.

Laura walked back to the campsite with Kaba. Steve was still standing with the porters and cook. They all looked toward her when she approached. She kept her face an impassive mask.

"Mr. Slater will be joining our expedition," she announced in a clear, strong voice. Without glancing at Steve, she left Kaba to translate her short statement and went inside her tent.

Alone, she allowed herself a bitter smile. There was something she knew that Kaba obviously didn't. Slater didn't have a trekking permit. He would be detained at the first police checkpoint they reached in the Jewel region. So even though she would have to endure his company for a while, she would be rid of him before he reached his goal. That was her only comfort now.

Chapter Six

"How long do you intend to give me the silent treatment?" Steve asked Laura as he followed her on the trail the next morning. She made no response so he resumed whistling "Strangers in the Night."

His off-key rendition was as abrasive to Laura's ears as the sound of fingernails scraping against a chalkboard. She had to fight back the urge to scream at him to stop. But she'd resolved not to utter one word to him for as long as he remained part of the expedition. Until they came to a checkpoint, that was. Then she would gladly bid him goodbye and good riddance.

But that could be days, even weeks away. Could she stand hearing him whistle that long? They'd only been hiking for an hour, and he'd already managed to drive her quite mad. Laura imagined that hell must be marching up a mud-slogged trail with a whistling demon close at her heels. To make it all the worse, they were alone. Kaba had gone a good distance ahead, and the porters, as usual, had fallen behind.

Steve had hoped Laura would thaw a little now that they were alone. Conversation would have made the time pass more quickly for both of them. Even an unpleasant conversation would have broken the tedium of climbing this narrow trail through pine forest. But no, she wouldn't open her mouth. She wouldn't look over her shoulder and give him so much as a glance.

Stubborn, he thought. Not a pleasant trait in a woman. Or in a man, either, for that matter. He didn't consider himself stubborn in the least. Tenacious, perhaps, when he'd set a goal for himself, but certainly not stubborn. He believed in making the best of a situation, and wished Laura shared that belief. What good was refusing to speak to him doing her? He would whistle until she broke, he decided, although his lips were getting a little sore.

What Laura resented most about Steve's whistling was that he persisted in that one particular tune. It was the song they had danced to in Kathmandu, and she felt that he was taunting her with it, reminding her of the way she'd lost her head over him that night. She was sure she could feel his hot breath on her neck as he whistled, so she turned up the collar of her shirt.

Steve wished she hadn't done that. He'd been enjoying the way her ponytail swished against her smooth neck as she walked. Now the ponytail caught on her collar, breaking the swishing rhythm. Even more regrettable, the collar hid the only expanse of her lovely skin that was visible to him now. He decided to attempt conversation again. Maybe he could goad a response out of her.

"Where'd you get those godawful baggy pants?" he asked her. "That cute little bottom of yours is completely hidden from view." He saw her back stiffen, but she didn't say a word. "You looked great in that black dress the other night," he continued. "But I guess I made my approval pretty obvious at the time."

At least you pretended to, Laura silently replied.

"Are you going to wear those baggy pants throughout our trip?" Steve continued. "Hope you packed those tight jeans of yours. I'd appreciate it if you wore them tomorrow and gave me something to admire from back here. Will you do that for me, Laura?"

The man had nerve, colossal nerve, Laura thought. But she wasn't going to let him get to her. No way.

"I don't think that's asking too much," he persisted. "It would really give me something to set my sights on." He paused, waited—nothing. "If there's one thing I admire in a woman," he went on, making sure to drawl out his words. "It's a nicely rounded, firmly packed, sweetly curving, well proportioned, adorably perky, sensually undulating—"

His insinuating words were cut off when Laura stopped and turned to face him so suddenly that they had a head-on collision. Steve grabbed her around the waist and steadied them both before they tumbled down the steep trail.

"Were you about to say something, sweetheart?" he asked her.

She had. She had been about to tell him off. But the close call of a fall had shaken her. She didn't show it, though. She pushed away from him and turned her back to resume climbing. At least she had stopped his inane dialogue without uttering a word.

But not for long. "Now, what was I describing before you interrupted me by almost knocking us both down the cliff, Laura? Oh, yes, a certain portion of your anatomy now sadly hidden from view. Luckily I have a good imagination. Up, down, up, down—poetry in motion."

Steve smiled at the way her back became more and more rigid with each word he uttered. He enjoyed teasing her. He'd enjoyed their brief clutch even more. He liked holding her, even when she was angry with him. He hoped, though, that she wouldn't stay angry with him for too much longer. It was beginning to wear on him.

But he was used to sticking around where he wasn't wanted, he reminded himself. He'd spent his whole life doing that. He'd grown up with a stepfather who couldn't stand the sight of him, so he'd developed a tough hide.

It came in handy in his profession. When a journalist's presence was welcomed, that often meant there wasn't much of a story to be uncovered. So Steve usually went where he was most unwelcome. That was part of the challenge, part of the excitement of getting a good story.

Still, it hurt a little to have Laura despise his company so much now. Not enough to make him turn back, though. Hell, no. He could outlast Laura Prescott's resentment. And he would do his best to eventually wear her down.

So he decided to stop teasing but keep talking to her. Even if she never responded, it beat dead silence between them.

"I'll be glad to get out of this thick forest," he said. "I can't stand feeling closed in. Maybe that's why I'm always on the move. For the past year or so, I don't think I've spent more than two weeks in one place."

Or with one woman? Laura was tempted to ask. But she wouldn't give him the satisfaction of hearing her voice. She didn't mind hearing his, however, now that he'd gotten off the subject of her physical attributes. It was much more pleasant than listening to his infernal whistling, and she hoped he would continue talking about himself. This section of trail had become tedious, and she wouldn't mind learning a little more about him since she was stuck with his company anyway.

"I sometimes wonder how people can stand to live in one place all their lives," he went on. "Like the small town I come from. I found it so stifling there. Couldn't wait to get out. But you like being in a rut, don't you, Laura? At least that's what you told me the other night."

Laura was surprised that he remembered anything she'd said to him.

"Well, you're out of your rut now," he said when she didn't respond. "How does it feel? Scary or liberating?"

Both, Laura thought. Less than a week ago her life had been all planned out. She would marry Jerome and settle into a comfortable suburban life-style with him. But today she was climbing Asian mountains, and her future was unsettled. It had all happened too quickly, and she had no idea what would happen next. Anything was possible.

"I'm surprised you're not married, Laura," Steve said, as if her own thoughts had drifted into his. "I would think you'd welcome the security of marriage if being in a rut is what you really want."

Marriage doesn't have to be a rut! she protested silently. But of course a man like Slater would consider it one.

"And I'm sure a bright, pretty woman like you has had plenty of proposals," he added. "How old are you, by the way?" He didn't expect an answer to that question. He estimated her age to be in the mid-twenties, so he added a few years just to get her goat. "About thirty, I'd guess," he said, then chuckled when she stumbled on some stones in the path.

Laura had to really fight back the urge to set him straight on that score. He'd added a good five years to her age! Oh, he really was a devil. But she gritted her teeth and kept true to her vow of silence.

"Or maybe younger," he added, admiring her self-control. "Whatever your age, I'm surprised you haven't tied the knot with someone by now."

Tied the noose around some poor man's neck, did he mean? That's what his tone inferred. Laura wished Slater would go back to talking about himself and leave her out of his monologue entirely.

"Personally I believe in the institution of marriage," he declared. "For some people, anyway." His tone sounded grim. "The family unit is the cornerstone of civilization, after all. Mommy, daddy, kiddies. A house with a nice yard in back. A two-car garage. A living room with new match-ing furniture.''

That all sounded very nice to Laura. Except for the new matching furniture. She and Jerome had planned to col-lect antiques. A Chippendale sofa. An Oriental rug. An Edwardian side table. Tiffany lamps. They'd discussed furnishings with almost the same intensity as they'd dis-cussed how perfectly suited they were for each other. Re-calling these conversations now, as she hiked up an unknown path, Laura realized how boring they had been to her. No! That wasn't true at all. At the time she had found them fascinating. It was only Slater's disparaging tone that had made her think otherwise.

"People like me, though, we don't settle down," he told her. "It's in our blood to keep on the move. When I'm in one place, I'm already thinking about the next one I want to be. Somewhere I haven't been before. A story I haven't covered yet. That's what keeps me going. That's what keeps me alive."

Why was he telling her all this? Steve asked himself. He wasn't even sure she was listening to him. But still he felt this great need to communicate with Laura.

"I almost got married once," he confessed. "I met her at a protest rally." He laughed. "I don't even remember what we were protesting at the time, only that she and I were on the same wavelength. Until she began talking about that house in the suburbs and swings in the backyard for the kiddies. I started getting this suffocating feeling, as if somebody were actually strangling me."

Laura listened intently to his words. As much as she longed to turn around and look at Steve, to see the expres-sion on his face, she kept her back to him.

Like talking to a closed door, Steve thought. He wanted to grab Laura by her stiff shoulders and make her face him. But he resisted the impulse and gave up trying to make a dent in her stubborn silence. He felt hurt by her rejection of his company and opted for silence himself. For the next mile or so, the only sound either of them made was that of their trudging footsteps hitting the trail.

And during that time Laura missed hearing his deep, resonating voice behind her. Resisting the temptation to turn around and look at him became more of a strain on her system than the climb. When they left the forest and reached a small village, she was relieved to see Kaba sitting on a stone wall built around two trees. He waved and beckoned to them.

"Did all go well for you during your walk?" he asked them.

"Yeah, Laura's great company," Steve said. "She chirped away like a little bird the whole time."

"Slater is being flippant, as usual, Kaba. I felt no obligation to keep up a conversation with him."

"Really?" Steve said. "I hadn't noticed." He backed into the stone wall and dropped his pack on top of it, using it for the purpose it was designed.

Laura had to give Slater credit for carrying his own tent and equipment instead of having the porters do it for him. He was a man who made sure to carry his own weight. When it was off his back, he stretched like a big cat.

"Well, I'm glad you are getting along so well," Kaba said, either not understanding that they hadn't been, or understanding only too well. "When the porters arrive, we'll have our midmorning meal here. How fortunate that the rain has held off. If this continues, we will make good progress today."

"Could be that the bad weather has passed for good," Steve said.

Kaba looked up at the dull gray sky. "Let us be thankful for any respite we get and not expect more."

"Well, it sure would be nice to see the sun for a change." Steve smiled at Laura. "But I guess I'll have to be content with your sunny disposition, sweetheart."

Kaba laughed softly as Laura glowered at Steve. "You rest together here while I gather information from the villagers about the trail ahead of us." He slid off the stone platform. "*Chautara* were built to give weary travelers a place to rest. The two trees the wall encircles are a pipal and a banyan, representing man and woman. See how well they grow beside each other? In perfect harmony." He gave Laura and Steve a benevolent smile and left them alone.

Laura hoisted herself up on the wall and leaned against one of the trees. Every muscle in her body complained to her, but she tried not to pay attention. Until her body got used to so much exercise, she would have to live with the aches and pains. She had a long afternoon of hiking in front of her, and more of the same after that. Much more.

Steve continued to stretch, touching his toes and doing deep knee bends. Laura wished he would stop. His movements kept pulling her eyes in his direction. His lanky body had a compelling power and grace to it. Every inch of him was lean, hard muscle.

"You should do some stretching, too," he told her. "You don't want to get any more uptight than you already are."

Ignoring both his advice and his wisecrack, Laura delved into her rucksack and took out a bag of trail mix. She'd only had tea and a few biscuits since arising, and that seemed like days rather than hours ago. Kaba felt it best to get an early start each day, and a hot breakfast would have taken too long to prepare. So in the old trekking tradition, they always hiked in the cool morning before breaking for their first big meal of the day.

Laura nibbled on the trail mix without offering Steve any. This made her a little uncomfortable, since her natural inclination would have been to share. Soon she had the opportunity to do just that. Like magically sprouting mushrooms, children's heads began popping up along the wall. Laura smiled for the first time all day and gestured to these village children to come sit with her on the wall. Two of the bolder ones immediately accepted the invitation. She passed around her bag of dried fruit and nuts and began talking to them in Nepali.

A few feet away Steve watched her. And when she laughed at what one of the children said, it was like the sound of silver bells to him. It was nice to hear her laugh again. She put her arm around the little boy sitting next to her, and a tiny girl toddled up to the wall and pressed her cheek against Laura's leg. Another child ran her fingers through Laura's blond hair.

Seeing Laura surrounded by children, enjoying their company, made Steve feel good for some reason. He couldn't figure out why it should, though. Laura's stubborn refusal to talk to him all morning had made him more and more aggravated with her. But now his aggravation dissolved. He found the scene charming. The children were adorable, and Laura's immediate rapport with them captivated him. He smiled at her.

Happy with her new companions, Laura forgot herself and smiled back at Steve. Their eyes locked, and they shared the pleasure of the moment as the children chattered and giggled. And for that brief time, Laura felt her heart go out to Steve, as it had so easily once before. But she reined it back in again with a hard mental yank. She quickly looked away from him and back to the children.

But Steve had seen the chink in her armor and attempted to take advantage of it. "Why don't we call a truce, Laura?" he asked over the sound of the children's clear, light voices. As he waited for her reply, the little girl who had been hugging Laura's leg walked over to him with the bag of trail mix and offered him some.

The child's simple, gracious gesture disarmed Laura completely. It suddenly seemed foolish and petty to continue ignoring him.

"All right, Slater, a truce," she agreed. What good did it do to refuse to speak to him? Holding her tongue had been more a strain on her than on him, anyway. "But I still don't want you along," she added to make sure he knew she hadn't capitulated.

He bent down to take a nut from the bag and chewed on it thoughtfully for a moment. "Maybe you'll have a change of heart," he said. "Maybe there will come a time when you'll have reason to be glad I hitched up with you."

Laura doubted that would ever happen but didn't refute him. She didn't want to argue with him anymore. It took too much out of her, and the trip was difficult enough. It would be easier to try to get along with Slater until his luck ran out and he was forced to turn back by officials.

"Please have some more trail mix," she said with sweet cordiality. "And be careful not to choke on it."

Kaba waited until after Laura and Steve had finished their meal of porridge and fried potatoes before telling them the bad news.

"Unfortunately all this rain has washed away the bridge up ahead, so we will be forced to take a slight detour," he said.

"How slight?" Laura asked him.

"Oh, a few miles or so."

"How few, Kaba?" she persisted, aware of the Sherpa reluctance to impart unpleasant information.

"Ten," he admitted. "Or maybe more."

No doubt more, Laura thought grimly. "Oh, well, if we have to, we have to," she said with more spunk than she felt.

"You mean we'll have to circumvent the river," Steve said. He wasn't too thrilled with the news, either. He always liked to go forward.

"Yes, we will be taking a path through a low-lying jungle. I had hoped to avoid that particular area during the wet season."

"Why? Because it'll be so muddy and hot?" Laura asked.

"That, too."

"What else?" She smiled to encourage him to tell her the worst.

But he only lifted his shoulders and smiled back. Then he glanced at Steve and shook his head.

That's when Steve guessed what Kaba was so concerned about, but he figured what Laura didn't know wouldn't hurt her. Not yet, anyway. He just hoped she wasn't too squeamish.

"Did you pack plenty of salt, Kaba?" he asked.

"I will go check with Cookie to make sure." He hurried away before Laura could ask him any more questions.

"Why such a sudden concern about salt?" she asked Steve.

"You got me."

"But you're the one who asked Kaba about it," she pointed out impatiently.

He shrugged. "I just thought our morning meal was pretty bland, didn't you? I like my fried potatoes with lots of salt on them."

"You're not going to tell me what's up, are you? You and Kaba are plotting against me again."

"Never against you, Laura. You know Kaba would never do that."

"But I'm not so sure about you, Slater."

"Hey, I thought we were friends again."

"We're on speaking terms again. That's all." She paused. "And we were never friends."

"I thought we got pretty friendly one rainy night in Kathmandu," he said in a caressing tone. "You remember that night, don't you, Laura?"

She didn't answer him. She got up and walked away from him instead.

Steve smiled to himself. He'd effectively put a stop to her asking him any more questions about what he and Kaba didn't want her to know yet.

They resumed their journey a short while later. It began to rain lightly, and when they entered the humid jungle area Kaba urged Laura to put up her umbrella.

"But it's only misting," she said.

"It is always best to be prepared for a downpour," he told her.

"Oh, all right," she said, although she thought Kaba was becoming a little too bossy. But it could be that he sensed a heavy storm about to break, so she put up her umbrella.

"I will go back and hurry up the porters," he said. "Mr. Slater, you will look out for the memsahib?"

"Yeah, I'll get her through this patch," he said.

"I don't see why either of you have to look out for me," Laura grumbled when Kaba left them. "I think I'm doing just fine on my own."

"You'd do better if you picked up your pace," Steve said.

"Don't you start bossing me around, too, Slater. Kaba is the only man who can get away with that." She heard a soft, heavy plopping on her umbrella, but it didn't really sound like raindrops.

Steve moved in front of her. She noticed that he'd put on a battered baseball cap and his canvas jacket was buttoned to the neck, although it was hot and humid in this tropical forest. The plopping sound on her umbrella increased.

"Come on," he urged, grabbing her hand.

Bone weary, she balked. "What's the rush?"

And then she knew. She saw the black leeches falling from the trees and onto Steve's shoulders. Her umbrella was no doubt crawling with the slithering little beasts.

"Run!" Steve said.

He didn't have to ask her twice. He kept a tight hold of her hand and pulled her through the leech-infested area, crashing through the thick vegetation. They didn't slow down until they had cleared it and reached high ground again.

For once the porters didn't lag too far behind and when they too ran out of the jungle, Laura was aghast to see that their bare legs and arms were streaming with blood because leeches had attached themselves to their flesh.

"Oh, my God!" she cried. "We have to do something to help them, Steve."

"Check yourselves," Kaba said. "I'll see to the porters." He took a bag of salt out of his rucksack and applied it to the leeches on his men to disengage them.

Laura glanced down and saw a leech slither down her pant leg. She dropped her umbrella and brushed it off before it could worm its way into her shoe.

"Nasty little buggers, aren't they?" Steve said as he slipped off his backpack. "They hang on the trees and drop onto you when they detect your body heat." He removed his jacket and shook leeches off of it.

"There's one on your arm!" Laura cried.

"So there is," he said casually. He took a bag of salt from his pocket and poured it over the leech. It fell off, but his arm continued to bleed where it had been bitten.

"Why won't it stop bleeding?" Laura asked him.

"They inject an anticoagulant. But it'll eventually clot."

Laura took off the red bandanna around her neck and wrapped it around Steve's wound.

"Thanks," he said, looking surprised by her simple kindness.

"No thanks needed," she said brusquely. "At least we got through with only one leech landing on each of us."

"Don't be so sure of that, Laura. The worst part about them is that they can crawl around your skin without being felt. I didn't even know that one was on my arm."

Laura stared down at the swarming mass of them on her umbrella. "You mean some could be crawling on me right now?" Her voice trembled, and she started to shiver at the thought of it.

"Stay cool," Steve said, grabbing her hand again.

He led her up a steep bank until they were out of sight of the rest of the party.

"Now what?" she asked him breathlessly.

His smile came slowly. "Now you strip for me, Laura."

She stared at him, motionless, openmouthed.

"Well, you want me to check you, don't you? Unless you'd prefer Kaba to do it."

That was an unthinkable alternative. Poor Kaba would die of embarrassment before she did. Her skin began to itch all over, and she decided that she could bear Steve's examination of her body more than she could bear the idea of leeches on it. She began unbuttoning her shirt. Steve's smile grew wilder.

"Don't you dare enjoy this, Slater."

He laughed at that. "How can I help myself?"

Her hands dropped from her shirt. "This is very awkward."

"Don't be too modest. Just get it over and done with. Take off every stitch you're wearing, shake it out and hand it to me."

She removed her shoes first, instead of her top. When she shook them out carefully, a leech tumbled out of one of them. She made a sound of disgust and began undressing a lot faster. Steve offered his arm for her to drape her clothes across. He kept a straight face now and made no comment as she revealed more and more of herself.

But his amber eyes danced with glee, Laura noted as she unhitched her bra. She threw it at him and he caught it midair, as if snatching a butterfly in flight. He let the silky slip of a garment dangle from his hand and raised questioning eyebrows. With a sigh of resignation, Laura pulled off her panties.

The sight of her naked body jolted Steve like a punch in the stomach, and he couldn't breathe for a moment. Every inch of her delighted him, and he had the notion that she was meant for him alone because he found her so perfect. She was built with a graceful economy of flesh, athletic yet supremely feminine. He tried not to stare at her small high breasts too long, or the golden triangle of her femininity. He wrenched his eyes from what attracted him so compellingly.

"Turn around," he said hoarsely.

She swiveled quickly on one foot. Yes, perfection, he silently pronounced. He longed to skim his fingers across the creamy expanse of her buttocks. Her succulent skin gleamed in the mist. She had a heart-shaped mole at the base of her spine. He would have liked to have bent down and kissed it.

"Well, don't just stand there and gawk, Slater. Tell me if I'm all right," Laura said sharply.

It brought Steve back to earth. Lovely and creamy smooth as Laura was, she had developed the personality of a porcupine whenever she was with him. "You made it through the jungle unscathed," he told her.

"That's a relief." She turned around and snatched up the clothing he held, avoiding his eyes as she hurriedly dressed.

When his hands were free, he began taking off his shirt. "My turn," he said. "Or rather, your turn to enjoy the show."

Her eyes ricocheted off his bare chest. She took his shirt from him and shook it out hard. "Don't flatter yourself. Seeing you naked is a duty, not a pleasure, I assure you."

"Don't be so sure until you've had a good look, sweetheart," Steve replied, unbuckling his belt.

But his bravado suddenly left him when he unbuttoned his pants. He'd never given much thought to stripping in front of a woman before. But this was different. This was Laura. And she was watching him now with a little smile on her face, as if she suddenly had the upper hand.

"Just get it over and done with," she said, repeating his words in a slightly mocking tone.

But then she had sympathy for him because she could tell he felt as uncomfortable about disrobing as she had. Big, bold man that he was, he seemed more like a shy little boy to her now. Her taunting smile turned tender as he shucked off all his clothes with awkward movements, frowning slightly in his haste.

She enjoyed the sight of him naked more than she knew she should have. He had a finely honed body. It was muscular without being muscle-bound, and his skin had a golden cast to it, as if the pulsing vitality within made him glow outwardly. Broad of shoulder, narrow of hip, his proportions pleased Laura. His dark mat of chest hair captured her interest for a moment as she imagined the way it would tickle against her cheek if she pressed her ear against his upper torso to listen to his heartbeat.

He shifted impatiently under her scrutiny. "Don't take all day," he said gruffly.

"Must be thorough," she replied, but she only allowed her eyes to snag on the section of his anatomy he was probably most sensitive about for a second.

She walked around him, taking in the masculine elegance of his smooth sloping back and firm backside. She found him pleasing from every angle. He was a fine specimen of a man; there was no doubt about it, but she had never doubted that in the first place. Indeed, that's what made him seem so dangerous to her. She feared her own attraction to him more than she feared the man himself. And if he guessed how desirable she still found him, she didn't think she would stand a chance of holding her own with him. She had to keep up her guard with him at all times. Just because a man had a good body, it didn't mean that he had a good character.

"You pass inspection," she said. She placed his clothes on a rock and walked away without looking back.

The expedition continued on higher ground for the rest of the afternoon without further mishap. Laura and Steve talked now and then to pass the time—inconsequential conversations about the weather and the terrain. The shared intimacy of seeing each other naked seemed to have made them more stiff with each other rather than relaxed. It seemed odd to Laura that she had felt more connected to Steve when she hadn't been on speaking terms with him earlier that day. At least then he had talked to her on a more personal level.

At dinner that evening Kaba told them that he was pleased with the progress they'd made, despite the detour. They had climbed steadily upward since then and would no longer have to travel through jungle valleys. Even though they were still in the throes of monsoon storms, he said, they had left the tropical climate behind them for good.

"And the leeches?" Laura asked. "Have we left them behind, too?"

"Yes," he replied. "No more jungle, no more leeches."

"Thank heavens for that! I just hope I don't have nightmares about them." She bid the two men good-night and went to her tent.

"You weren't holding out on her, were you, Kaba?" Steve asked the guide after Laura had left them.

"No, we have gone too high, I think, to be concerned about leeches anymore. But other unforeseen problems could lie in our path."

"For example?" Steve prompted.

"I would only be guessing, Mr. Slater. I know what to expect if we stay on the established trail, but we may have to veer off again, and then I know as little as you do of the terrain."

"We'll have to play it by ear if that happens," Steve said. He always liked doing that.

But Kaba did not understand him. "Play by ear?"

"You know, improvise. Don't worry, Kaba. I can be pretty inventive when I have to be."

"But I am not worried anymore, Mr. Slater, now that you have joined our expedition. You will safeguard Miss Prescott."

"I'll do my best to look after Laura, but I can only do so much, especially when she'd rather reject than accept my help. Besides, she impressed me today as a woman who can look after herself."

Kaba nodded. "She has made such an impression on me also. But I will always regard Laura as Dr. Prescott's little girl, you see. This was how I first knew her, and first impressions are lasting ones.''

Steve hoped they weren't too lasting, or Laura would never warm up to him, no matter what he did to win her trust from now on.

"I bet she was a stubborn little girl," he said.

"A bit willful at times," Kaba allowed. "But sweet natured. As she still is."

"I haven't seen the sweet side of Laura's nature for a while," Steve grumbled.

"Just so long as you know it is there," Kaba replied. "You will have the patience to wait for its return."

"Not me, Kaba. I'm the type of man who doesn't wait around for anything."

"If that is a boast, Mr. Slater, it is a very shallow one."

Steve made no reply, not sure if he'd been boasting or confessing to Kaba.

Unlike Laura, Steve had no fear about nightmares when he climbed into his sleeping bag that night. But he hoped dreams about Laura wouldn't disturb him too much. Even so, he allowed himself to dwell on the image of her standing naked before him as he waited for sleep to block out desire. He wanted her more than ever now. That part was simple and natural. But the rest became more and more complicated as each step brought them closer to her father.

Steve found himself wishing that he wasn't after a story. Then there would be no barrier between Laura and him. They could resume where they'd left off on that magical night in Kathmandu, when he'd become drunk on her honeyed kisses. Perhaps, even without a goal of his own, he would have accompanied her to Jewel Mountain just to be with her. But it seemed more likely that they would have gone their separate ways. He wasn't inclined to follow women. It went against his deep grain of independence.

It could have been different with Laura, though. But now he'd never know. He had his own reason for being here, one she was well aware of and despised. It kept them together and it kept them apart. No matter how hard you tried to simplify it, Steve thought, life always managed to become too complicated. The trick was to keep your emotions separate from your work, and he thought he usually did a pretty good job of that. He valued his objectivity as a journalist as much as he valued his independence. And he could not allow Laura Prescott to interfere with either.

But still—those luminous eyes of hers, that creamy skin and lovely body. Steve shifted restlessly in his sleeping bag. The hardest part of his arduous journey was going to be keeping his hands off Laura. No, she would make that easy for him. She'd made it clear to him that she wanted no part of him now. And that, Steve thought, was just as well.

It began to rain with a vengeance, as if the ominous clouds had held back all day only to gain strength for this powerful downpour. The rain lashed against Steve's tent, and he congratulated himself for buying such a good one in preparation for his Mount Everest vacation. He wondered how Laura was faring and had the impulse to go check on her. He stifled it. Knowing Laura, she would interpret any caring gesture on his part the wrong way.

So he stayed put and waited for sleep. The rain seemed to be coming down even harder now. Did the porters put up Laura's tent correctly? He'd observed that it wasn't as sturdy a tent as his. Could it withstand this downpour? The more he thought about it, the more Steve became convinced that he really should go check on her. Then he could sleep better, knowing she was all right. So he got out of his comfortable sleeping bag, left his snug tent and ran over to hers under the protection of his canvas jacket.

Laura was sleeping soundly when Steve poked his head into her tent. Startled awake, she screamed. He crawled in and covered her mouth with his hand.

"It's only me," he said. "No need to wake up the whole camp." He took his hand away.

"How dare you come barging in here like this?"

"I just wanted to know if you were okay, Laura."

"I should have expected this from you."

"Expected what? My concern for your welfare?" It didn't sound to him that that's what she meant, though.

"No, I should have known you'd come prowling around."

"I'm not prowling, dammit. You make me sound like some sneaky tomcat."

"Exactly. What did you think, Slater? That seeing you in the raw today would inspire me to invite you to spend the night? Well, forget it."

"I already have," he replied gruffly. "I have no intention of trying to make love to you during this trip, Laura. It's not in my game plan."

Laura didn't know if she found this more insulting than her initial assumption. His body and deep voice filled the tent, leaving little room for clear thinking. But whatever his plans were, she wasn't going to let him play games with her.

"So you just dropped by in the middle of the night for a friendly little chat, did you?"

"Your tone is beginning to grate on me, Laura. I came because it was raining so hard that I got worried about you."

For the first time Laura became aware of the rain beating down. But that was nothing new. It *always* rained. So she wasn't going to buy that flimsy excuse from him. She wished that she could make out his face in the darkness. "Listen, Slater, whatever you have in mind, it's not on my mind. So I'd appreciate it if you went back to your own tent instead of dripping water inside mine."

"That's right, Laura. I'm dripping wet. I went out in a downpour to check on you, and all I get for my trouble is reproofs, insults and suspicion. I knew you'd act this way, dammit."

"Then why did you come if you knew?"

"That's a good question, sweetheart. I think I'll go sleep on it." He backed out of her tent and slapped the flap closed.

Laura stared into the darkness. Damn that man—he was going back to sleep after leaving her wide-awake and confused. Should she feel guilty for acting so ungraciously? Well, of course she should if his motive had been selfless concern for her. *If*. How could she be sure with him? What if she'd welcomed his visit with a delighted little laugh? Would he be kissing her passionately now, despite his claim of not wanting to make love to her? And since when had he changed his mind about *that?* It had certainly been part of his game plan back in Kathmandu.

As she lay on her back, wide-eyed and blaming Steve for it, Laura doubted she would ever fall asleep again that night. She estimated that at least an hour must have gone by since his visit. And during that time she'd decided that he really had been concerned about how she was faring, and she'd been rude and too quick to accuse him of less chivalrous motives. She supposed she would have to apologize to him tomorrow. And he would no doubt give her a hard time about it. Well, at least she didn't have to face him until morning.

And then she felt a big drop of water splash on her forehead. She shifted her head, and another drop fell right in her eye. No, it couldn't be. The proprietor of the Kathmandu shop where she'd rented this tent had sworn on his mother-in-law's head that it was waterproof. She groped for her flashlight and flicked it on, then directed the beam around the top of her tent. She spotted not just one leak, but four.

Nothing to panic about, Laura told herself. She got up and rearranged her sleeping bag to avoid them. But as soon as she was reasonably comfortable again, another leak made itself known. Droplets bounced off her cheek and trickled into her ear. Laura felt the sides of the tent. They were soaked through. She estimated that by morning her sleeping bag would be soaked, too, unless she moved it to dry quarters. She didn't think Kaba Par would be too pleased to have her for a roommate. Which left one alternative.

Long moments passed before Laura accepted this as the only solution—long wet moments. Steeling herself, she got up, rolled up her bag and ran to Steve's dome tent.

She heard him snoring like a hibernating bear inside. She was about to call out his name but thought better of it. Why disturb him? She slowly unzipped the door to his nylon cave and crept inside. He still didn't stir. Good! She unfolded her bag and got into it, careful not to make a sound. At first his snoring bothered her, but she soon became lulled by the steady rhythm of the deep male sound and fell fast asleep beside him.

When Steve opened his eyes the next morning, the first thing he saw was Laura's golden head peeking out of her sleeping bag. This confused him for a moment. Was he still dreaming? He sat up and pulled the quilting away from her face. How adorable she seemed to him without that suspicious look she usually wore in his presence.

He kissed her cheek and she turned to him, eyes still closed, mouth slightly open. He studied her mouth for a while, until it nearly drove his crazy with desire. He lightly tickled her bottom lip with the tip of his finger. She wrinkled her nose and awoke.

The first thing she did when she saw him was put on her suspicious look again, Steve noted. Then she scraped her teeth across her bottom lip. "Did you just tickle my lip?" she asked him. She didn't wait for an answer. "It's not fair to tease a sleeping person."

"Would it be fair to ask this person what she's doing in my bed?"

"I'm not in your bed. I'm in your tent. Mine was leaking."

"Oh, is that so? I seem to recall your indignation when I came to inquire about exactly that possibility last night."

She took a deep breath. The time had come to apologize. "I'm sorry if I misinterpreted your motives."

"You sure did, Laura."

"I appreciate the use of your tent," she added, hoping to mollify him.

"Well, you didn't have to sneak into it. I would have let you in . . . maybe."

"I would have asked your permission but you were sawing wood, Slater. Do you always snore so heavily?"

"I never had complaints about it before. And I've never had a woman sleep with me without an invitation before, either."

"I slept beside you, not *with* you," she corrected him. "There's a big difference."

"Well, I think you should give me credit for not taking advantage of the situation."

"Hah! How could you? You were dead to the world."

"Yeah, but I'm up now, Laura." A smile eased across his wide mouth as he slowly, ever so slowly began unzipping his sleeping bag. "And you know what? I sleep in the nude."

"Well, I don't." Laura scurried out of her own bag and hurried out of Steve's tent, her baggy Nepalese pants flapping in her haste to get away.

"What's the rush?" he called after her. "Didn't you tell me that the sight of me in the raw left you uninspired?"

He chuckled to himself over her quick exit. Obviously Laura wasn't as indifferent to that sight as she professed to be. And however uninspired she claimed to be, she certainly didn't leave him that way. Waking up to her soft breathing and sweet scent had made his head reel with inspired ways to pass a private hour or two with her.

He felt a little chagrined that he hadn't been aware of her presence all night, however. He must have been more exhausted than he'd realized. He envisioned the headline. Slater Snores Away While Beautiful Laura Sleeps Beside

Him. About as hard to believe as the existence of the abominable snowman, he thought sardonically. But it had happened, clearly proving to him that anything was possible.

Chapter Seven

"Porridge ready, memsahib!" the cook called to Laura during their midmorning break.

"I'll be right there, Cookie," she called back, and wrung out the laundry she'd been washing in the icy stream.

They had been climbing higher and higher for two days, and the temperature change made her feel energetic. It was such a relief to have left the sticky humidity behind. The air at this higher altitude had the crispness of autumn in it, and the fir trees gave off a fresh spicy scent. Laura appreciated this new climate, and the best part of all was that it hadn't rained again since the storm. Still, ominous clouds followed the expedition party like unwanted visitors who refused to go away.

Like Steve Slater, Laura thought as she hung her underwear on tree branches to dry. They were still in unrestricted territory and hadn't come across any checkpoints yet. Unless the police turned him back, there was no way she could get rid of Slater. The porters idolized him, and

Cookie showed him the utmost respect, always serving him first and making sure he had seconds. And every morning Kaba conferred with him about the route they would take. For all intents and purposes, Slater had become the expedition leader.

Laura didn't like this, but she could understand it. The Sherpa men weren't used to taking orders from a Western woman. They felt much more comfortable looking to Steve for guidance. Laura was sure that he epitomized every quality they looked for in an expedition leader. Tall and rugged, tireless and optimistic, fair-minded and even-tempered, he no doubt met their expectations of what the Great American Adventurer should be. Even the dark beard he was growing fit the image. And how Laura wished he would shave it off!

She caught herself. What did it matter to her if Slater shaved or not? Still, she did miss the sight of his high, lean cheekbones. Without the beard his face was extremely attractive. She looped a pair of her panties over a branch. Even with the beard his face was attractive, she had to admit.

Why deny it? She was drawn to the man. He'd intrigued her from the first moment she'd set eyes on him in the Kathmandu Hotel lobby. Perhaps what drew her to him was the same thing that made her draw back from him—he represented danger to her. On the surface she recoiled, but a deeper part of her nature, a part she would just as soon keep buried, longed for the excitement his glittering eyes promised whenever he looked at her.

Not that Slater had been looking her way too often lately. Reminding herself of this, Laura snagged a sock on a sharp twig as she hung it. She should be grateful that he'd been ignoring her, of course. She should be even more grateful that it hadn't rained at night lately, and she hadn't had to go begging him for dry shelter again. Yes, she had a lot to be grateful for, didn't she?

"Here's your breakfast, memsahib."

That wasn't Cookie's gravel voice, but a more melodious baritone. Laura glanced over her shoulder to see Slater ambling toward her carrying two tin plates.

"I was just about to join the party," she said.

"Well, this certain party decided to join you instead."

That was a switch, Laura thought. He'd been avoiding her as much as possible these past few days, walking with Kaba or the porters instead. As much as she hated to admit it, the time had dragged without his infuriating company.

"Eat your heart out," he said, handing her a plate.

She looked down at the food and made a face. "I've had about all I can take of porridge and potatoes or lentils and rice."

"Yeah, I could go for a nice juicy hamburger right now." Steve sat down on a rock by the edge of the stream and, despite the yearning he'd expressed, began eating heartily.

His appetite never failed to impress Laura. She sat down beside him. "If I had my choice, I'd take a hot dog over a hamburger," she said.

"You would?" Steve pretended shock and dismay over her preference. "You know what I'd really like? A big bowl of spaghetti with white clam sauce."

"No, no, it has to be red sauce," Laura countered. "And forget the clams. Make it shrimp."

"Let's skip the main course and go on to dessert. A big fat wedge of warm apple pie with a scoop of vanilla ice cream melting on top of it. Oh, yeah!" Steve sighed over this reverie.

"Pecan pie," Laura shot back. "Apple pie is too mundane."

"You wouldn't call my grandma's apple pie mundane if you ever tasted it, Laura. It's like biting into a juicy piece of heaven."

This sparked Laura's interest. "You actually have a grandmother who bakes apple pies for you, Slater?"

"Well, sure. What did you think? That I was raised by wolves or something?"

"Not wolves, snow leopards," she replied.

"Why snow leopards? I bet you've never even seen one."

"I certainly have!" Laura said indignantly. "And more than once. On Jewel Mountain when I was a kid."

"Then you're lucky," Steve said. "Very few people ever have that opportunity."

"Yes, they're very elusive creatures. And solitary and unsociable to boot. The snow leopard is a loner."

"Like me," Steve said.

Laura nodded. "You have similar characteristics, but there's one feature in particular that I think you have in common."

"I once read that the snow leopard has a remarkably long tail, thick to the tip," Steve drawled.

A smile tugged at the corners of Laura's mouth. "That's not the feature I was thinking about, Slater. I was referring to the eyes. A snow leopard has piercing amber eyes. I looked right into a pair of them when I was a girl, and they made me shiver."

"And do my eyes make you shiver, Laura?"

She'd admitted too much to him already, so she didn't reply. They ate in silence for a while.

"So tell me about this apple-pie grandma of yours," Laura said to pick up the conversation again.

"She's over eighty and still going strong," he replied. He laughed to himself. "Still manages to chase me around the kitchen with her rolling pin when she thinks I'm being fresh."

"Good for her." It pleased Laura enormously to hear Steve talk about his grandmother with such warmth and fondness. It made him seem less alien, more accessible. "Do you visit her often?"

"Not often enough, according to her. But I try to make it back to Vermont now and then just to see her. She's the only relative I have much in common with, and we're not even related by blood. She's my stepfather's mother." Steve shook his head. "It's hard to believe such a kindhearted woman has such a bastard for a son."

"I take it you don't get along with your stepfather."

"That's an understatement, Laura. The man hated my guts."

"I'm sorry to hear that." Without thinking, Laura placed a comforting hand on Steve's shoulder.

But he shrugged it off. "There's nothing to be sorry about. Thanks to him, I left home as soon as I could and got a chance to see the world."

"What about your natural father?" Laura asked.

"Him I never knew." Steve threw his fork on his empty metal plate, and the clang of it resonated through the stillness. "Like me, he was a traveling man."

They fell silent again. Laura didn't ask any more questions. She could tell by the distant look in Steve's face that he considered the subject closed. So she picked up on a safe one.

"A ham sandwich on rye with mayo and lettuce," she chimed, continuing their dietary wish list.

"Mustard, not mayo," he contradicted. "But let's not argue about it, Laura. We haven't argued for days."

"That's because you've avoided me for days," she reminded him, trying not to sound too offended about it.

"I figured you would prefer it that way. I left you alone because I seem to rub you the wrong way."

"Not always," she told him.

"You mean sometimes I rub you the *right* way?" His teasing smile returned. "Yeah, I did manage to do that back in Kathmandu, didn't I, Laura?"

She looked him straight in the eye without blushing. "I wasn't myself that night, Slater."

"Who were you, then?"

"An exhausted traveler. I'd been up in the air for hours and wasn't thinking clearly."

"Oh, I get it." Steve tilted his head and regarded her with an amused expression. "You're saying it wasn't sexual attraction that made you kiss me like that. It was jet lag."

"Something like that," she murmured.

"Then jet lag is one heck of an aphrodisiac, sweetheart."

"Don't exaggerate, Slater. Nothing really happened between us."

"It could have."

"It didn't." She kept her voice firm, her gaze steady. "And it never will."

"Never say never, Laura," Steve cautioned. "Life is too unpredictable."

"Not mine."

Steve chuckled. "Even yours, little Miss Stuck-In-A-Rut. Or did you plan to be here now, eating porridge by a mountain stream thousands of miles from your comfy little home?"

"Actually I did plan to be away from home now." She paused. "On my honeymoon."

Steve's amused expression faded. "Weddings usually come before honeymoons, don't they?"

It was her turn to laugh. "Yes, that's the usual procedure. I intended to have one of those, too."

"What happened? Did you get cold feet? Or did the groom bail out at the last minute?"

"You have such a refined way of putting things, Slater, and you're so subtle, too. Is this your usual way of conducting an interview?"

"More or less. I don't waste time beating around the bush when I really want to know something. And what I want to know now, Laura, is why you're here with me instead of with the man you intended to marry?"

Laura didn't want to tell Steve about the upsetting letter she'd received from her father. That would only confirm the rumors he'd heard and make him more determined than ever to reach Jewel Mountain. She'd been careful never to admit to him that her father was investigating yetis, and she wasn't going to do it now when he was poking his nose into her personal business.

"Things didn't work out," she replied coolly. "Let's just leave it at that."

But of course he wouldn't leave it. "Are you still in love with him, Laura?"

Had she ever been, Laura wondered. Or had her relationship with Jerome been built on the passionless base of shared interests and goals?

"You're not," Steve decided for her when she didn't answer him. "If you were still in love with the man, you wouldn't have responded to me the way you did."

"Why do you keep going back to that?" Her tone was exasperated. "I wish you would forget all about our evening together. I certainly have."

"What part of it have you especially forgotten about, Laura? Our first kiss in the rain? Or when I pressed you against the door and you—"

"*All* of it," she interrupted. "Everything!" After making this adamant declaration, she left him to join the others.

Left alone so abruptly, Steve gazed at Laura's undergarments drying on the tree branches. As they fluttered in the breeze, they reminded him of exotic birds and flowers even though he'd never found white cotton underpants and thick woolen crew socks especially exotic before.

What had happened to disrupt Laura's wedding plans? he wondered. Knowing her penchant for keeping on a predictable course, he figured it must have been something extraordinary. Steve doubted the groom had been the one to call off the wedding. Any man would be a fool to let a woman like Laura get away once he'd committed himself to her.

So what caused this sudden change in plans? Had her father summoned her? Most likely that was it. Prescott had wanted his daughter to witness what he'd discovered, and she'd decided she couldn't pass up the opportunity of a lifetime.

Well, neither could he, Steve thought. He wasn't going to let this golden opportunity slip by, either. It would take a lot more than Laura's objection to his company to make him turn back now. And he'd deal with the checkpoints when he came to them. He didn't know how he would, but he trusted his resourcefulness. He'd always managed to overcome roadblocks to his desired goal in the past, and he would in the future. No sense worrying about it now.

He put aside concern about not having a trekking permit and thought about something else instead—Laura in a wedding gown standing beside some unknown man. It wasn't an image that made Steve comfortable, so he blinked it away. Whoever the guy was, he was out of the picture now, anyway. Steve was sure on that score. Laura didn't love the man she'd left behind. The same instincts that told Steve there was a big story waiting for him on Jewel Mountain told him that Laura wouldn't have responded to him the way she had if her heart was committed to another.

It didn't matter to Steve that she now refused to acknowledge the passion they'd shared. She didn't fool him or herself. They both felt it still simmering between them. But he'd resolved to let it remain on the back burner for the time being. As strong as the physical attraction between them was, this wasn't the right time or place for a love affair.

Steve knew that as well as Laura did. Her appraisal of him notwithstanding, he considered himself a man of principles. Until he got what he wanted from Prescott, he would take nothing from Laura. That's why he'd gone out of his way to keep his distance from her for the past few days.

He raised his face to the sky and frowned at the storm clouds crowding in at a slow but determined pace. If it didn't rain by this afternoon, it surely would by nightfall, he thought. Then Laura would be forced to share his tent again. That would sure make it difficult to keep his distance. But he always liked a good challenge, and having her asleep beside him all night would certainly be a challenge to his self-control. He could handle it, he assured himself. In fact, he looked forward to it. His frown changed into a smile.

Torrents. The rain came down in unrelenting torrents late that evening. Steve waited for Laura in his tent, impatient for her arrival. What if her stubborn pride made her stay in her own leaking tent? Then he would have to go out and drag her back into his. He didn't want to have to do that. He wanted her to come to him and admit she needed something from him now. That would give him a great deal of satisfaction.

So he waited...and waited...becoming more and more impatient with Laura for holding out. She couldn't hold out for too much longer, he knew. And when she did finally come, he would give her a hard time. He would make her *beg* for admittance into his dry haven. At last he heard her voice through the rain.

"Slater? Can I come in?"

He forgot all about giving her a hard time and quickly unzipped his tent flap. "You should have come sooner, before the clouds broke."

She left her umbrella outside and went in.

"I was hoping the storm would hold out until morning," she said, unfolding her bag beside his. The space was cramped, and when he tried to help her, they bumped heads. "Besides," she added, rubbing her head, "you didn't extend an invitation."

He laughed, rubbing his own forehead. "Did you expect an engraved one? You should know that you can bunk with me any time you please, Laura. Rain or shine."

"Only when necessity forces me to," she replied.

It wouldn't kill her to be a little grateful, Steve thought. Even so, he took another stab at being hospitable. "It's too early to go to sleep. How about a game of cards?"

"In the dark?"

"I'll light some candles."

"The only card game I know is bridge."

Steve groaned. "You want to learn how to play poker?"

"It's never been one of my aspirations. But I bet you're good at it."

"Oh, I am," Steve assured her, lighting the candles and taking a worn deck of cards from his backpack. "Got any money on you?"

"Sorry, not one rupee."

"It's no fun to play without risking something."

"I suppose you'll be suggesting we play strip poker next," Laura said.

"One of my favorite games in mixed company as a boy." He shuffled the cards. "But I've outgrown that sort of entertainment. I've already seen you in the buff, anyway, Laura. No surprises left there."

"You make it sound as if you were disappointed." She kept her voice light, unconcerned.

"No, I wasn't disappointed." He smiled at her. "I think you're very beautiful. The memory keeps me warm at night."

His words made her feel warm, too. "I wasn't fishing for a compliment."

"Yes, you were, Laura."

"Really I wasn't," she insisted testily. Did he always have to be so blunt? "And I'm too tired for games tonight. I think I'll go to sleep now."

"Have it your way," he said. "I'd like to stay up for a while. Will the candlelight bother you?"

"No, nothing will bother me." She took off her shoes and slipped into her sleeping bag. "Good night, Steve," she said, turning her back to him.

At least she'd called him by his first name for a change, he thought. That wasn't much, but it was something.

"Oh, and thank you," she added.

"For sharing my tent? Don't mention it."

"I meant thanks for the compliment." She kept her back to him. "But the fact that we find each other physically attractive is irrelevant under the circumstances."

"We? Meaning I have your approval, too?"

"Now who's fishing?"

He chuckled. "You're a difficult woman to be around, Laura. Before this trip is over, you'll end up driving me crazy."

"I was hoping to drive you *away*."

"No chance of that, sweetheart. Sleep tight now."

But Laura couldn't sleep at all, too aware of Steve's every movement in such close quarters. She heard him shuffle the cards again, then snap them down on his sleeping bag one by one. She guessed he was playing solitaire. She'd forgotten that she knew that card game, too. She had played it by the hour, alone in her room at boarding school during vacations when all the other girls went home to their families.

A short while later she heard Steve undressing. The sound of his pants zipper shrilled in her ear. She listened all the harder, trying to ascertain if he really slept in the nude, but couldn't be sure about it. She considered sneaking a peek but decided against it.

He snuffed out the candles, and she heard him get into his bag. After that the only sound was the rain pelting the tent. No snoring sounds from Steve. She wondered if he were asleep and longed to call out his name to find out. But she didn't.

Steve lay awake, listening to Laura listening to him. He could tell that she was still awake by her breathing. He ached to reach out and touch her. Hours seemed to pass before he finally dozed off.

When he awoke, dawn had broken and Laura was gone. He felt both disappointed and relieved. Her close proximity had been a strain on him. His body was tense from it, his nerves on edge. He didn't think he could take another rainy night under the same roof with her without further intimacy. He was no saint, after all, and he'd never had any aspirations to become one, dammit.

It turned out that Steve didn't have to worry about being canonized. The rain held off for the rest of the week, and Laura paid no more nocturnal visits to his dry tent. She never asked for his help on the trail, either. Or for anybody's help, for that matter. She got through some pretty rough sections just fine on her own, and Steve's admiration for her tough, independent nature grew with each passing day.

But as much as he respected Laura's self-reliance, he would have liked her to lean on him once in a while. He would have liked for her to acknowledge his male strength, or at least admit that having him along made the journey easier for her. She never did.

As he followed her now, on a narrow path along a river gorge, Steve marveled at Laura's surefooted progress. He'd sent Kaba ahead to scout out a possible check point now that they were nearing the Jewel region, assuring the guide he would watch out for Laura on this tricky section of terrain. But as usual, she didn't seem to need any looking after.

Laura couldn't remember ever being more frightened in her life than she was now. Heights didn't usually bother her, but the path she and Steve now traversed was no more than a foot wide in some places, cut into the solid rock face of the gorge cliff. She could hear the river roaring beneath them, but it was hidden from view by thick clouds. Laura was thankful for that. She didn't want to see how far she could fall if she lost her balance and tumbled down the steep ravine. But the clouds also swirled all around and above her, making her dizzy with the sensation of floating in space, in complete isolation.

She found great solace in the sound of Steve's footsteps behind her. She had gotten so used to having him around that she had to keep reminding herself she didn't *want* him around. She even missed sleeping with him and had caught herself gazing up at the sky in the evening, hoping for rain. And sometimes she would awaken in the middle of the night and feel so alone that she would consider creeping into Steve's tent even though the sky was clear, just to have his warm big body for company. She could never give in to such a temptation, though.

Right now her biggest temptation was to stop walking altogether. The path was too steep, too narrow, too dangerous, and she was too tired to go on. It was the fear of falling more than the actual walking that fatigued her. If she could only rest a minute, then perhaps she would regain the fortitude to go on. But no, she couldn't stop. If she did, she would be giving in. She forced herself to keep going, but took a false step and stumbled. She stopped and leaned across the rock face, trying to catch her breath. That false step had shaken her badly. She could have fallen thousands of feet.

"Easy, Laura," Steve said softly as he came up behind her and placed a steadying hand on her back. "Just stay there and rest a moment."

"I'm all right. I can go on." But her voice was weak and tremulous. The high altitude made it difficult to breathe. She was afraid to look over her shoulder at him, afraid even that small movement would cause her to lose her balance.

"Well, I could sure use a little break right now," he said in his low, soothing voice. "And I'd appreciate your company. It's damn lonely up here in the clouds."

"You're humoring me, aren't you, Steve?" His big, warm hand felt so good on her back, though.

"You've been pushing yourself too hard," he told her. "What are you trying to prove?"

"I just want to get to my father as soon as possible. And I want to clear this section as soon as possible, too—the sooner the better!"

He began massaging her tense shoulders as he stood behind her on the narrow path. There wasn't room for both of them abreast.

"The slower the better, you mean," he said. "It's reckless to hurry on a stretch like this, especially after losing your bearings the way you just did."

"It was just a little slip. I'm okay now." But she rolled her shoulders beneath his hand and sighed, hoping he wouldn't stop his massage.

He didn't. "Let's play another wish game," he suggested. "But not favorite foods this time. I'm too hungry. Let's talk about all the other things we miss since starting this endless trek. Like a big soft bed."

"Yes, a bed," Laura agreed in a voice filled with longing. "With fluffy down pillows and crisp fresh sheets."

"I miss reading a newspaper," he said. "I don't even know what's happening in the world right now. But what I'd really like, even more than a paper, is a hot shower."

"You can have your shower," Laura said. "I want a long soak in a deep tub." She sighed again, imagining herself slipping into it.

"With bubble bath?" Steve asked.

"Oh, yes. Lots and lots of bubbles that crinkle like crinoline when I move."

"And don't forget your rubber ducky."

"I don't have a rubber ducky, Steven." She bent her head so he could knead the base of her neck with his clever, soothing fingers. "I do have a big, fat loofah sponge that I'm fond of, though." She laughed. "Listen to me going on about a dumb sponge. Funny how you miss the little things you take for granted in life when you don't have them anymore."

"Do you miss the man you were going to marry? You haven't mentioned him yet, Laura. Unless he's one of those little things you take for granted."

"We were talking about things, not people," she replied, evading his question. She didn't want to admit that she didn't miss Jerome a bit.

Steve didn't pursue the subject. "I miss my typewriter," he said. "It's an old manual I've had for over twenty years. I bought it with money I saved up from a paper route when I was a kid. Two of the keys stick."

"Which ones?" Laura asked dreamily, just to keep him talking. The sound of his voice calmed her as much as his massage did.

"The *l* and the *p,*" he said.

"Those are my initials!"

"So they are." He chuckled. "Now I'll have to get a new typewriter or I'll never get you out of my mind after we part, Laura."

That comment silenced them both.

"We'd better get a move on," Laura said after a moment.

But Steve wrapped his arms around her and pulled her closer against him. She could feel the heat of him as they stood at what seemed like the edge of the world. Below, the river roared its presence; above, the cliffs loomed like hulking monsters, and the path ahead was cruelly steep. Clouds swirled around them like steam from a cauldron. Yet feeling Steve's energy, his life force, mingle with hers as he held her from behind caused Laura to experience a strange contentment that transcended her physical exhaustion and fear.

A clatter of hooves disrupted their peace. Laura felt Steve's body tense.

"What the hell is that?" he asked.

They found out in the next moment, when they saw a string of mountain goats coming down the gorge path from above, heading toward them with no room to pass. Steve pulled Laura backward, into a wider space where the rock face was hollowed out just enough for them to squeeze themselves off the trail. Huddled together, they hugged the cold rock wall as the tough little pack animals streamed by, brushing and butting against them and bleating belligerently.

Laura almost panicked, sure the goats would dislodge them off the path and into the abyss below. But Steve kept a tight hold on her and held his ground as the creatures moved past in a relentless flow. Their hooves scraped and skittered on the bare rock trail, but their balance was miraculous, considering they had saddlebags heavy with grain tied to their backs.

"They'll be past us in a minute or so," Steve assured Laura.

But they kept coming down the mountain—hundreds of them—a never-ending flow. A few small dogs were mixed in with the pack, barking madly to keep the herd moving. Intent on their duty as traffic managers, the dogs ignored Laura and Steve, or perhaps didn't notice them at all.

Eventually the shrill calls of humans could be heard above the barks and bleats and jangling of neck bells. Five packmen, dressed in rough woolen garments, appeared on the scene, bringing up the rear guard. They passed Steve and Laura without a word, but gave them dark, unsympathetic looks. This wild, raucous parade lasted a good twenty minutes, then ended as abruptly as it had begun. The scent of the animals remained in the air as peace returned.

The incident seemed so ludicrous to Laura that she began laughing. She laughed a little too long and hard because tears began streaming down her face. Dimly, through her fit of giggles, she realized that she was overreacting, perhaps even behaving a little hysterically. But this knowledge could not make her stop.

Steve's kiss did. His mouth stifled her uncontrollable laughter, and after catching her breath, she responded with an ardor that surprised her as much as the goat caravan had. How could she feel such passion after being frightened nearly to death only moments before? And yet desire, hot and mindless, cut through fear, through exhaustion, even through her deep-seated doubts about the man pressing against her, his body hard, his mouth soft and compelling. She melted against the rock face as she had melted against the red door in Kathmandu days ago, a lifetime ago. She still wanted him! And she didn't want him to stop kissing her. She only wanted more.

Steve had only meant to calm her down with his kiss, to distract her from her laughing fit. But now he was the one who was distracted, totally. He had not expected her to kiss him back with such torrid intensity. Her response astounded him. He had never had this with a woman before—this blazing craving whenever their lips met. It overwhelmed him, and all he wanted to do was take her completely. But attempting such a foolhardy act of passion would surely topple them over the precipice and into the abyss below. Using all the willpower he had within him, Steve wrenched his mouth from hers.

Still holding her to him, he leaned against the rock face until his head stopped spinning, his blood stopped racing. He'd never had problems with altitude before, but now he was dizzy and disoriented. He needed some time to collect himself before they went on. Right now he couldn't even walk.

"Are you okay now?" he managed to ask Laura around his thick tongue.

"My legs are all shaky." Her voice shook, too.

"That was a close call."

Laura nodded, knowing full well what he meant. They said no more but held on to each other until their breathing steadied and their senses stopped reeling enough for them to continue.

"You go first and I'll keep a tight grip on your rucksack in case you stumble again," Steve said.

"And risk falling off the cliff with me?"

"Yes, I'd risk that in order to save you."

She believed him. She didn't know why, but she did. Her heart warmed, expanded. But she shook her head. "No, Steven. Holding on to me will put you off balance. If you fell into the ravine with me, what good would that do either of us?"

"Neither of us is going to fall, Laura." His voice was resolute. He twisted his hand under the strap of her rucksack. "Now just take it one step at a time. Don't look right or left, and keep your balance centered in your belly."

They continued across the cliff. Sections of the ledge path had fallen away, making it even more narrow, but Laura kept her eyes straight ahead and concentrated on putting one foot in front of the other. As simple an act as this was, it took great courage on her part and she had to delve deep within herself to muster it up. But she couldn't let herself falter now that she had Steve's safety to consider along with her own. She didn't doubt that he would keep a tight grip on her strap, even if it meant his own downfall.

When they made it to the top, they both shrugged off their packs and collapsed with relief onto the grassy crest. Lying side by side, they panted and listened to the combined sound of their beating hearts. They turned to each other, faces flushed and perspiring, and shared a smile of sublime satisfaction, as if they had just made glorious love. Laura reached out and touched Steve's face, feeling the rough beard beneath her fingertips.

"Thank you for helping me make it up here, Steven," she said.

"Don't thank me. You did it all on your own without coming close to falling."

But she had fallen, Laura realized. Somewhere along the treacherous path she had fallen in love with him.

And Steve saw it. He saw the love shining in her wide gray eyes so brightly that it almost made him flinch. Love was the one thing he couldn't handle. He wanted passion from Laura, even friendship, but not a deep emotional commitment. Never that!

How vulnerable she looked to him now, the truth in her heart glowing in her eyes. He'd once told her that he could read her emotions on her face so easily, and now he saw something he didn't want to see. As much as he still wanted her, he knew that he couldn't touch her again without guilt, without future remorse. Hadn't he warned her enough, in so many ways? He was a loner, a traveling man, the wrong sort of man for a woman like Laura to care for too much.

"No, don't thank me," he said again.

Laura heard what he really meant. Don't *love* me. His face had closed to her, the small muscles around his eyes tightening. She felt the change in him. He'd withdrawn from her emotionally. The desire in his eyes had dimmed. Now that she was ready to admit how much she wanted and needed him, he no longer wanted her.

She took her hand away from his face, confused and hurt. She doubted that she would ever allow herself to touch him with such tenderness again. He didn't want from her what she most wanted to give him: *love*.

Without either of them uttering a word, it had been settled between them. She should be grateful for that, Laura told herself. Her moment of weakness had passed without consequence. Their silent communication—her total acceptance of him and then his withdrawal from her—had been so subtle that it could now be ignored. It had happened so quickly, so decisively.

She sat up and ran her fingers through her hair. "All right, I won't thank you anymore if you don't want me to," she said softly.

"It's just that I didn't do anything to deserve it," he mumbled. He sat up, too, and looked away from her, showing great interest in the sky. "It's clearing," he said after a moment. "See the sun breaking through over there?"

Laura looked where he was pointing and saw golden light filtering through the mass of clouds. But she needed a lot more than a few thin rays of sunshine to cheer her up now. Nevertheless, she forced a smile. "I haven't seen the sun since leaving Kathmandu."

Steve was relieved to see her smile. He knew that his silent rejection had hurt her, but he thought that better than accepting her love and hurting her much more in the end. He could never stay with one woman any more than he could stay in one place for too long. There was nothing he could do about it, no matter how lonely it left him feeling in the end.

As they sat together, with nothing left to say to each other, the sun parted the clouds with high-voltage energy. The unaccustomed brightness made them both squint.

They stood up, looked over the edge of the cliff and watched in amazement as the clouds split apart to reveal the panoramic view below and beyond them, a maze of valleys and glistening snow peaks. Waterfalls cascaded down the mountains across from them, and the cultivated terraces they had left far below glistened emerald and burnished gold. Closer to them the dark spruce and fir forests of the northern slopes looked wild and impenetrable.

The view was too stupendous to take in all at once. The majestic scale of the Himalayas far surpassed normal visual experience. Speechless, Steve automatically reached for Laura's hand, needing her warm human contact as he witnessed such awe-inspiring natural grandeur. In the distance Jewel Mountain, in all her icy, glittering grandeur, beckoned. But Steve kept a tight hold of Laura's hand, at that moment wanting to be with her more than caring about reaching his goal.

Laura squeezed Steve's hand in response. She forgave him for not being able to return her love. How small and insignificant her disappointment seemed at this moment. Who was she, after all, but one small creature in God's magnificent universe? She exalted in the beauty of this universe and felt her spirit soar.

But then there was a slight shifting of light, of clarity, and although the beauty remained to be seen, it no longer overpowered either of them. The mood was broken. Their hands slipped away. Laura sighed. Steve cleared his throat.

"Quite a sight," he said. A man of words, he was at a loss for them now.

Laura only nodded. Her momentary elation drifted away as swiftly as the clouds had. Although the sun had come out, nothing else had changed. Long days of trekking lay before her, and the man beside her remained a stranger.

"Kaba told me that it was a relatively easy walk from here to the village where we'll spend the night," he said.

"Might as well get going again, then." Laura picked up her rucksack and slipped the straps around her weary shoulders.

"I think you should rest here a little longer, Laura. We just finished a hard climb."

"But it's over and I'm ready to continue. I've taken it in stride." She hoped he realized that she'd taken more than the climb in stride. She even dared look him directly in the eye. "You sent Kaba ahead to see if there was a checkpoint in the village, didn't you?"

He wouldn't lie to her. "Yes. He agreed to scout it out for me and double back to warn me if there was one. Since he wasn't waiting for us here, I figure the coast is clear."

"But you're bound to run into one before we reach Jewel Mountain," Laura said. "What will you do then? I know you don't have a permit."

"Of course you know, Laura. You made sure I didn't get one."

She didn't deny it. "So what will you do?" she asked again.

"Whatever I have to," he replied. He turned away from her and shrugged into his own heavy load.

They fell into step, picking up the path just over the ridge.

"So how far is this village?" Laura asked him.

"According to Kaba, no more than five miles."

After the hundreds they'd already covered, that didn't seem like much to Laura. "A piece of cake," she said.

Steve laughed. "You're one hell of a trouper, Laura. I'll give you that."

That was about all he would give her, Laura thought. She been foolish to lose her heart to such a man. But she would find it again and put it back in place. Love was such an elusive emotion, anyway. Perhaps what she'd felt for Steve a while ago hadn't been love at all.

He moved in front of her when the trail narrowed through forest to push away branches and make her going easier. She could barely see the top of his head over his backpack and so she concentrated on his back and long legs instead. Love and lust were emotions that often got confused, she told herself. Maybe it was just lust she felt for him, pure and simple.

Well, not so pure. And not so simple. Until today she'd been able to separate her physical attraction to Steve from her deeper feelings. But now it was all muddled. She didn't just want him. She wanted to love him. And that inclination was so much harder to resist. Love paid no attention to good sense. Love had a power all its own. Laura was just beginning to realize that . . .

She tripped over a fallen tree branch and fell down with a crash.

Steve whirled around to see what had happened. Laura quickly picked herself up and brushed herself off.

"I wasn't watching where I was going," she muttered, not about to tell him she'd been watching the way his bottom half moved with such powerful grace.

"Are you okay?"

"Yes, I think so."

"Don't move until you're sure," he cautioned.

She disregarded his advice and went ahead. She didn't get very far. After three steps her left ankle screamed out its protest. She stopped in her tracks.

"Bad news, I'm afraid," she told Steve almost casually. "I seem to have twisted that weak ankle of mine pretty badly this time."

"That sure isn't good news," he agreed in the same composed tone.

But when they looked at each other, Laura saw deep concern in his eyes. And Steve saw pain in hers.

He knelt down and took off her shoe, then rolled down her sock and pressed gently. But not gently enough. A cry of protest escaped from her pale lips. "Not good at all," he said, his tone serious now. "It's already swelling. I wish we could ice it."

"Gee, you didn't notice a handy ice machine along the way, did you?" Laura's try at a joke fell flat because of the hitch in her voice.

Steve stood up and touched her cheek. "Don't worry, I'll take care of you." He took off his backpack and shuffled through it. "At least I can wrap your ankle good and tight to keep the swelling down," he said, pulling out an Ace bandage. He knelt before her again, stripped off her sock and twisted the bandage around her ankle. Then, with gingerly care, he slipped the sock back on and patted her foot. "You'll be all right, Laura."

"Sure, I will. In a few weeks!" She'd sprained the same ankle running last year and knew how slow the healing process could be. She might be able to hobble around in a few days, but certainly not hike. Tears of frustration welled in her eyes. "How stupid of me not to have paid attention to where I was going. Here I made it through a tough climb on a rock ledge, but can't manage a simple stroll through the woods."

"Don't blame yourself." Steve offered her his arm. "Try walking again. Lean against me and see if you can put any weight on your ankle.

She attempted a few steps, but the pain was too much to go on. "Maybe I can hop on one foot," she suggested gamely.

His expression became grim. "This is all my fault, dammit. I should have insisted that you rest a while longer before we continued. This might not have happened if you had."

"Oh, for goodness' sake, don't blame yourself, either. I'm not a child," she told him. Even so, she felt like bawling like a baby over this nasty turn of events. And she probably would have done just that if Steve weren't around to witness it. Instead, she kept a stiff upper lip although her bottom one trembled a bit.

"I know you're not a child, Laura," he said patiently. But he patted her back to comfort her anyway.

"Listen, you go ahead," she told him. "I'll wait here for the porters. The four of them will somehow manage to lug me to the village like a lumpy bag of potatoes." Another failed attempt at a joke.

"Do you really think I'd leave you alone here?" Anger that she could suggest such a thing flashed in Steve's eyes. He softened his tone. "I would never do that, Laura."

She managed a grateful smile. "Then I guess we'll wait for the porters together."

"That's too risky, with nightfall only a few hours away. They may have taken a route we don't know about. No, we have to make it to the village before sunset, and I'm not going to waste precious time waiting for porters who may never show up."

"What's the alternative?"

"I'll carry you the rest of the way."

"For five miles?"

He winked at her. "A piece of cake."

"But I'm too heavy!" she protested.

He gave her a slow once-over. "Not in my estimation, you're not. I doubt you're any heavier than my pack. I'll leave it here and come back for it tomorrow." He turned his back to her. "Hop aboard, sweetheart."

"You mean piggyback?"

"I suppose I could sling you over my shoulder caveman style if you prefer."

She didn't, so she wrapped her arms around his shoulders and her legs around his waist.

Steve shifted her weight around on his back until it felt balanced and comfortable. As he walked, he enjoyed the soft warmth of her against him, the rhythmic jiggle of her body rubbing against his.

"A lumpy bag of potatoes you're not, Laura," he told her after carrying her a half mile or so. "And you're a hell of a lot sexier piece of baggage than my backpack."

Despite everything, Laura smiled. "You have a way with left-handed compliments, Steven. Am I holding on too tight?" She had to cling to him to maintain balance, and this made her feel awkward and helpless.

"No, you feel just right," he told her.

"I doubt you'll be saying that after a few miles."

"Don't worry about me. I'm as strong as an ox. So just relax and enjoy the ride."

Resting her cheek on the broad ledge of his shoulder, Laura breathed in his musky masculine scent. It was so hard not to love him, so hard not to put her complete trust in him. She had never wanted to depend on him like this, and if she had any choice in the matter she wouldn't. The situation was as painful to her as her twisted ankle. She knew more than ever now the danger of falling in love with this man. Love was the last thing he wanted from her. And here she was clinging to him, soaking up his scent and his strength, adoring him more and more with each step they traveled. Falling in love was like losing control completely, and she could understand why Steve wanted no part of it. Well, neither did she!

The irony of the situation did not escape her. Wrong time, wrong place, wrong man. Once they reached the village, she would make herself stop loving him. Yes, that's what she would do. Believing it was possible to discipline her wayward heart, Laura let it stray for just a little bit longer in Steve's direction.

Chapter Eight

"Oh, look what's up ahead, Steven. A *chorten*."

They had passed through the forest and entered a glade. Laura was referring to a Buddhist shrine in the distance, a tall conical structure of whitewashed stones glowing in the sun. Long lines of blue-and-white prayer flags stretched from its spire and seemed to be waving their welcome as they flapped in the breeze.

"Time for a break," he announced when they reached the simple pristine shrine.

Laura slid off him, and he wiped the sweat off his brow with the red bandanna she had tied around his arm and he now kept in his shirt pocket as a talisman of sorts.

"I'm obviously not as light as you're pretending I am," she said.

"No, it's the sun that's getting to me, not your weight," he said gallantly. "After all the wet weather we've had, I'm not used to it."

"Are you used to women riding on your back?"

"I admit the situation's never come up before." He smiled slyly. "But when it comes to accommodating a pretty woman in any position she desires, I'm adaptable."

Laura ignored the innuendo, although she couldn't prevent her imagination from conjuring up the titillating images it provoked. She blocked them out and turned her attention to the shrine.

"This must be the village *chorten,* which means the village can't be too far away. I can probably make it there on my own two feet." She took a few experimental steps and winced.

"Poor Laura," Steve said. "You must hate being so dependent on me. I don't like needing other people's help, either. I think we're alike that way."

She appreciated his empathy. It made her situation a little less awkward. At the same time she wished he wasn't being so nice to her. She'd found it so much simpler to dislike him, but now that was impossible.

"Do you know what's printed on those prayer flags?" she asked, taking refuge in keeping their conversation impersonal.

"*Om Mani Padme Hum,*" Steve replied.

"That's right." She was surprised that he knew. "Jewel in the lotus," she translated. "A prayer that flies up to the heavens on the wind. I remember that from my childhood."

"Is your father a student of Buddhism?"

Laura stiffened. She'd all but forgotten that the purpose of this trip for Steve was to interview her father. "No, he's not," she answered brusquely.

"That's right, Adam Prescott is a man devoted to science," Steve said. "I suppose he wouldn't be much interested in anything unless it could be proven."

Laura said nothing.

"We're getting into yeti country," Steve went on. "Or at least the area where the legend originated. I'll be interested to hear what the villagers have to say about that elusive creature. Wonder if there have been any recent sightings.''

Laura remained silent as a stone. She wished her heart could harden like a stone, too. But it wasn't easy to be hard on a man who had carried her so far and would carry her farther still.

She looked away from him and watched the prayer flags flutter, and then, as if in answer to her own prayer, she saw a woman leading a little white Tibetan pony come out of the woods beyond. The woman wore the traditional Sherpa costume—a coarse handwoven blouse under a long black tunic and a striped woolen apron. Laura called out a Sherpa greeting to her, and the woman moved toward them, smiling shyly.

Steve laughed in amazement. "Is that pony a mirage or did you conjure it up, Laura?"

"The gods must have sent it," Laura replied, half believing exactly that. "Let's just hope its owner is willing to let me ride it to the village."

It turned out that the woman was more than happy to allow Laura the use of her pony once she understood the situation, which Laura managed to convey to her in the few Sherpa words she knew and a limping demonstration.

Steve lifted Laura onto the pony, a docile creature, and the woman took up the reins. She led them to her village, which was less than a mile away. As Steve walked alongside the pony, he felt disappointed that he couldn't have carried Laura *all* the way there.

The isolated village reminded Steve of the little town in Vermont where he'd grown up, also nestled in the mountains and protected by them. But instead of white clapboard, the Sherpa houses were built of mortared stone and heavy timbers, with projecting wooden balconies. They looked sturdy and well cared for, with neat yak pens and potato fields in back. Because of the monsoon rains, the alpine meadows surrounding the village were lush and verdant, and the whitewashed homes glittered against the emerald backdrop. Above the meadows the snowy caps of the mountains were turning pink in the setting sun.

Steve felt a surprising wave of nostalgia as he recalled his own hometown, so different from this one yet so alike, too. He promised himself that he would visit his stepgrandmother as soon as he got back to the States. It would be nice seeing her again and tasting her apple pie.

Kaba Par must have spotted Steve and Laura coming down the dirt path leading to the village, because he came running toward them before they got there.

Laura was impressed at how fast Kaba could run. He wasn't the least bit out of breath when he reached them. He seemed to thrive in this high altitude, getting energy from the rarefied mountain air. The higher they climbed, the more energetic he became. Now he beamed at Laura, delighted to see her on a pony.

"So you found better transportation than your own two feet," he said. "Good for you. Never walk when you can ride."

He looked so pleased that Laura hated to break the bad news to him.

Steve did it for her. "Laura won't be using her own two feet for a while, Kaba. She twisted her ankle on the way here. It's a pretty bad sprain."

"These things happen when Fate sees fit," Kaba said, philosophically resigned and composed as always.

"But it's the worst thing that could have happened!" Laura said. "I won't be able to hike for days, perhaps weeks. You must go on to my father's site without me, Kaba. Bring him the supplies and see if he's all right. I'm so afraid that he'll be cut off from all communication if the next weeks bring heavy snow up where he is."

Kaba nodded. "I will go if you want me to, but we will discuss it further over tea. The lama of a nearby monastery has offered us his hospitality and looks forward to meeting you. It is rare for Westerners to pass this way."

Obviously it was, because as they continued through the village, people hung over the balconies of their homes and out the windows to watch them pass. They didn't smile or call out greetings, but neither was there hostility in their silent stares, only avid curiosity.

On the way to the monastery Kaba and Steve hung back to talk privately as Laura rode ahead.

"I take it you didn't spot that police checkpoint I was so concerned about," Steve said.

"No, sahib. There was once a checkpoint here but it no longer exists. According to those I have asked, you will not come across one for many more miles."

"Seems like my luck is holding out." Steve watched Laura up ahead, her body swaying slightly as she rode. "I wish I could say the same for the memsahib."

Kaba allowed himself a show of regret. "A shame, such a shame. Perhaps if I had been there to guide her, this would not have happened."

"I watched over her during that rough section across the cliff face, just as I promised you I would, Kaba. And she came through just fine. The accident happened on an easy stretch through the woods. She tripped on a tree branch. Neither you nor I could have prevented that from happening."

"Yes, there is little anyone can do to prevent another's mischance. But her injury could be a blessing in disguise."

"Quite a disguise," Steve said sardonically. "I doubt Laura will see it as much of a blessing when we leave her behind tomorrow."

Kaba gave Steve a sidelong glance but said nothing.

"She's right to insist that the expedition continue without her," Steve went on. "And I admire her for being so rational and practical about it. Do you think she could stay at the monastery? She'd be safe alone there, wouldn't she?"

"Oh, yes, safe indeed. But women are not allowed to stay there."

"Surely the head lama could make an exception in this case."

"He has not power to make exceptions. It would go against hundreds of years of tradition. When he heard there was a woman in our expedition, however, he did offer her the use of a pilgrim's hut overnight. I feel certain that he will extend the invitation for as long as Laura needs a haven."

"Is this hut isolated?" Steve asked.

"It is a good distance away from both the village and the monastery. But an easy walk all the same."

"You forget Laura isn't going to find walking too easy for a good while, Kaba."

"No, sahib, I have not forgotten that." Another quick look at Steve's face. "Neither of us should forget that."

"One of the porters can stay behind and look after her," Steve suggested. "I'll take up the slack and carry his weight."

"You would be willing to leave the young lady behind with a porter? What if he gets it into his head to take advantage of the situation? It does not seem likely, but there is that possibility."

It was a possibility that made Steve's blood pressure shoot up. "Scrap that idea, Kaba. I've got a better one. We can hire a woman from the village to stay with Laura."

"I don't think so, sahib. The village women have neither the time nor the inclination to leave their homes and go live with an outsider. They have families to look after and much work to do."

Steve felt the frustration build within him. "Then dammit, *you* stay with her, Kaba."

"Very well," the guide replied mildly. "If you will lead the expedition on to Jewel Mountain, I will stay behind with Laura."

"If I knew the way, I would have gone by myself and arrived there already," Steve grumbled.

Kaba smiled.

"So you're saying it's up to me to stick around and play nursemaid to Laura?"

"I have said nothing of the kind, sahib."

"Listen, if I hang around waiting for Laura's ankle to mend, I might miss the opportunity to interview Dr. Prescott. And that's why I've come this far in the first place!"

"No need to shout. I know your reasons for coming very well."

Steve lowered his voice. "I only have *one* reason. To get a story."

"Ah, yes. That was the one you told me."

"I understand why you included me in this expedition, Kaba. You figured I'd watch over Laura. But I'm telling you that she'll be okay on her own. She makes the best of any situation and comes out on top. Hell, she would have crawled to the village if I hadn't been around to carry her."

"Fortunately she didn't have to, which points out the advantage of having you around, Mr. Slater."

"I'm under no obligation to stay with her," Steve insisted. He looked at Kaba with narrowed eyes. "What if I decide to follow you to Jewel Mountain instead?"

Kaba shrugged. "I cannot prevent you. And if you ask to share food along the way, I will not deny it to you. Nor will I report you if we pass a checkpoint. I will do nothing to interfere with another's chosen path."

"So you're leaving it all up to me? I can stay with Laura or go with you."

"You can do as you please, of course."

The trouble was, Steve didn't know what would please him now. He usually went his own way and never let anything stop him along it. That had suited him just fine in the past. But as much as he wanted to go on with the expedition, he felt a strong pull in Laura's direction. He picked up his pace and caught up with the pony. The Sherpani sang a mournful tune as she led it. Laura looked pretty mournful herself, Steve noted.

Laura looked at Steve, trying to read his expression. What had he and Kaba been discussing for so long? Her, no doubt. But what had the outcome been?

"I have some good news," he told her.

"I could use some." Her heart rose. Was he going to tell her that he would stay behind with her?

"Kaba knows about a hut where you can stay until you're able to hike again."

You, he'd said. Not we. Her rising heart took a nose-dive. But she managed a weak smile. "Great. That will be a lot better than my leaky tent."

"I would have left mine behind for you."

"How generous," she murmured. "But now you won't have to. The hut will suit me fine, I'm sure." She'd been foolish to hope that he would offer to stay with her, she realized. That was too much to expect from someone like Steve. Still, the sharp disappointment she felt made her eyes sting. She turned from him and looked straight ahead.

"At least it's only a sprain, not a break," he said. "You'll be as good as new in no time."

"No time," she repeated in a hollow voice. He had no time for her. He was too busy chasing after his damn story.

"Rest," he said. "That's the only cure for a sprain. But be sure to move around a little bit each day. Do you have any aspirin? I could give you my supply if you don't."

"Thanks, I have my own. Don't worry about me." As if he would! "Kaba will make sure to leave me enough rations to last until he returns from Jewel Mountain." She purposely left out mentioning Steve's return.

"Oh, I'm not worried about that," he said. "Kaba will make sure you have everything you need before we leave."

"And by the time he returns, I should be able to walk again," Laura continued, trying her best to sound optimistic. "If the passes are still clear of snow, I'm sure I can talk Kaba into making another trip up the mountain with me so I can visit my father."

"That sounds like a good plan."

Laura forced a laugh. "I'm glad you approve of it."

"And I'm glad you're taking this setback so well, Laura. If I were wearing a hat, I'd take it off to you."

"Thanks," she said dryly.

"It won't be so bad spending some time here. The Sherpa are kindhearted and friendly to strangers."

"I've already discovered that to be true," Laura said. She waved her hand in the direction of the Sherpani leading the pony. "That kind lady mentioned that she has a son who could help me out if I needed him. So I'll take her up on the offer."

Steve frowned. "How old is her son?"

"I'm not sure. But when she talked about him, she raised her hand so high, about the height of a child of ten or so."

"Oh, just a little boy." Steve sounded relieved. But then he looked worried. "You can't depend on a kid to help you, Laura."

"Why not? He can fetch water and firewood. What more do I need?"

"A little companionship, for one thing. You're going to be terribly lonely all by yourself in that hut."

The tears began stinging Laura's eyes again, and she squinted, pretending the low sun they were heading into was bothering them. "I've been lonely before," she said. "And I learned how to appreciate my own company. I'm not afraid of being alone."

"I doubt you're afraid of anything," Steve grumbled.

He stuffed his hands in his pants pockets and walked on beside her in silence. She could have at least asked him to stay with her, he thought. Not begged. Simply asked. But no, not Laura Prescott. She had everything all figured out and under control. She obviously preferred her own company to his.

There had been a moment when he'd felt that she really cared about him. He recalled the love and tenderness in her eyes when she'd looked at him as they lay together on the grassy crest earlier that day. And he had ruined that precious moment by pulling away from her emotionally. Now he regretted it. If he stayed with her, though, perhaps he would see that look in her eyes once more.

No, that was crazy. He didn't want Laura to care too much about him. Everything was settled. She would be fine by herself, and he would go on to his goal. He should feel relieved that she expected nothing from him now. He should be stepping with a lighter foot instead of skulking along beside her like some dejected dog.

"Little boys aren't very reliable," he said after a while. "What if he forgets to come one day, Laura? You'll be without water and fuel, that's what. It gets cold at night in the mountains. And sure, the Sherpa are friendly. But what if unfriendly bandits pass by the hut and rob you? Or worse!" His voice caught. He cleared his throat. "And there could be all sorts of wild animals lurking about the hut. Don't forget, we're in the middle of wilderness now."

"You certainly know how to cheer a person up," Laura told him.

"I just want you to be aware of the dangers."

"Well, now I am. Thank you for pointing them out to me before you departed."

"Do you want me to go on to Jewel Mountain, Laura?"

"Of course not. I don't want you bothering my father. You know that."

"Yes, I do, and that's not what I meant." Steve placed his hand on her thigh, feeling it move under his palm with every step the horse took. "Let me put it another way. Do you want me to stay here with you?" There. It was out. He had asked her directly.

She released an exasperated breath. "What an idiotic question! What do you think I want?"

It was settled, then, Steve thought, even though she hadn't even asked him to stay and had more or less called him an idiot to boot. But he couldn't leave her now. He didn't know why, only that he couldn't.

"I'll go tell Kaba I'm staying," he said.

When Steve dropped back, Laura covered her face with her hand and shed hot tears of relief. Then she quickly wiped them away without anyone being the wiser and said a little silent prayer of thanks.

Kaba accepted Steve's decision to stay with his usual aplomb. "This eases my heart," he said simply.

"Mine, too," Steve admitted.

"There is one small suggestion I would like to make, however."

"Oh?" Steve had a sneaking suspicion that he wasn't going to like it.

"If the monks assume that you and Laura are married, we should leave them at peace with that assumption. They would feel more comfortable, I believe, if they regarded the two of you as man and wife. As would the villagers. It is not the custom here for unwed couples to live under the same roof."

Steve thought this over for a moment. "Sure, let them assume what they want," he said. Making people feel more comfortable didn't go against any of his principles.

"Good," Kaba said. "I am glad that I didn't tell the head lama anything about the two of you except that you were American visitors. It is always best to say as little as possible at all times."

Steve strode back to Laura to tell her the news. "As of now, we're married," he informed her.

His casual declaration startled her. "If that's a joke, I don't get it."

"No joke, Laura. Just a temporary convenience. Kaba thinks we'll be accepted more easily around here as a married couple."

"Yes, that makes sense."

"It's no big deal, I suppose, to pretend that we're husband and wife."

"No big deal," she repeated, matching his indifferent tone.

* * *

Leaning against the doorway of the hut to keep her weight off her sprained ankle the next day, Laura watched Steve chopping wood. The sun beat down on his bare back, and his muscles flexed each time he whacked the log with his ax. His strokes were hard and swift. Chips flew around him, some catching in his thick dark hair.

The log had been a gift from the lama, delivered by oxen that morning. The monk driving the oxen had made a point of telling them that only dead or fallen trees were harvested from the forest. For the most part the Sherpa used juniper branches for kindling, and yak and zum dung for fuel. Steve had promised that he would respect this tradition.

It was a huge log, but Steve appeared up to the task of hewing it. Laura found his intensity mesmerizing. Although she had only intended to watch him for a moment, she couldn't turn her eyes away. The broad triangle of his back and his rhythmic movements captivated her.

But when he stopped to wipe his brow and glanced around, she pulled back from the doorway so that he wouldn't catch her observing him. This made her feel foolish, as if she'd been doing something wrong. She reminded herself that she hadn't been spying on him. She'd simply been watching him for lack of anything better to do. She stepped outside and called to him.

"The sun is so strong. Take a break in the shade, Steven."

He dug the ax blade into the wood and walked toward her, loose-jointed from the hard exercise. His khaki shorts rode low on his hips and his bare legs were long and muscular. She'd induced him to wear his hiking boots while chopping. Otherwise he would have performed the task barefoot, which she thought foolhardy.

"You must be thirsty," she said. His golden chest gleamed with sweat. Her own throat was dry.

"Yeah, I could go for a cold beer right now." He dipped a wooden ladle into the bucket of rainwater by the door and drank that instead. "Why don't you take a spin down to the supermarket and get a six-pack for me, honey?"

It was their latest game—Married Couple in Suburbia—and Laura took it up. "Sure thing. And I'll rent a movie at the Video Store, too."

"Great," Steve said. "We'll have a pizza delivered and watch it this evening. There's nothing good on TV."

Laura rather enjoyed this game. She found it an amusing contrast to their actual primitive living conditions. The stone hut had no running water or plumbing and only one small window above the hearth, which also served as a chimney.

It was a snug little hut, however. The roof was constructed of sheepskins and yak pelts, held together with woven rope and supported by roughly hewn wooden beams. Inside it was spotlessly clean and dry, and with the firewood Steve was chopping, it would also be warm.

But as comfortable as the hut was, Laura and Steve didn't feel comfortable in it. Now that they were completely alone, and would be until Kaba returned from Jewel Mountain, they felt ill at ease with each other. They'd managed to spend the night and most of the morning without getting too personal, thanks in part to their silly game. But Laura decided to drop the game and express her true feelings to Steve, or at least some of them.

"It felt good to have you lying in your sleeping bag beside me last night, Steven."

"Even though I snore like a bear?"

"You only snored the first night we slept together."

He refilled the ladle and dashed some water across his chest. The droplets clinging to the hair on it glittered. "I've never slept with a woman without making love to her before. You're a first for me, Laura."

"Should I feel flattered?"

"That depends on what you want. Maybe we should get that straight right now."

Maybe they should have stuck to their lighthearted game, Laura thought. "I don't know what I want," she answered honestly. "But I doubt it's the same thing you do, Steven. I would never make love with a man just because he's attractive and the situation happens to be... convenient."

"What about Kathmandu, Laura?"

"Why do you keep harping back to that night? If you were a gentleman, you wouldn't."

Steve tossed some water in his face and snorted. "I've never claimed to be a gentleman. But I've always followed my own code of honor."

"Does that code include romancing a woman just to get a story?" She hadn't meant to bring up that sore point with him again, but the words were out before she could call them back.

He said nothing for a moment but carefully ladled more water. From his severe expression Laura thought he might throw it in *her* face this time. But he sipped it instead, never taking his eyes off her. "What do you think my motive is now, Laura?" he finally asked. "Why am I staying here with you instead of going with Kaba to your father's camp?"

She didn't answer him because she wasn't sure.

"It seems nothing I can do will change your bad opinion of me," Steve said. "And I don't even know why I care what you think of me."

Neither did Laura. The one time she'd shown him tender regard, he'd pulled away. And he'd made no sexual advances now that they were alone. She sensed he wouldn't unless she made the first move in that direction, and if she didn't, he would accept that, too. So if he wasn't staying with her for love or sex, then why? Simple human kindness? No, Steve Slater didn't impress Laura as being overly altruistic.

Maybe he figured that her father would be more inclined to give him an interview if he showed up at the site with her in tow, the grateful daughter. At least his chances of getting a story would be a lot better than if he showed up there alone. Laura cautioned herself that this was all conjecture on her part. For all she knew, Steve really didn't have an ulterior motive for remaining with her. But he'd once told her that getting a story was all that mattered to him.

Whatever his reasons for staying behind, Laura still appreciated that he had. If they were going to get along during the days ahead, she would have to forget all about the way he'd deceived her in Kathmandu. Or at least not mention it to him anymore.

"Be careful you don't get sunburned," she told him in a conciliatory tone. "You should put on a shirt."

"But the sun feels so good on my back after all that rain. I hope this fine weather stays with us."

Laura was relieved that they were on a safe subject again. They couldn't get into too much trouble discussing the weather. Or the scenery. "It's so lovely here, isn't it?"

Steve nodded and they looked around them as the breeze fluttered through their hair. The hut was well situated on a grassy knoll close to a shallow brook that ran clear and cold. A river flowed about fifty yards behind the hut. Langur monkeys frolicked on its bank and on the roof of a dilapidated shed that must have housed livestock at one time.

Beyond the river were alpine meadows where zum and sheep grazed. A thickly wooded area lay to the left, and to the right Jewel Mountain supplied a picture postcard backdrop. It looked both close enough to touch and very far away. Steve gazed at it when he spoke.

"I'm not sorry I didn't go on with the others. This is exactly where I want to be right now."

Laura wanted to believe him. She resolved to stop analyzing his motives for staying behind. The most important thing was that he had, and she would be a fool to drive him away with her doubts.

She'd also be a fool to let down her guard with him ever again. The times she had, heedless passion had rushed in like a dam breaking, sweeping away all her good sense and self-control. She knew the danger of loving him too much. She had seen it in his wary eyes. So she kept that love deep in her heart, lying dormant but waiting to spring to life again with the warmth of his touch, the heat of his kiss. She couldn't let that happen. Their time together would come to an end, he would go away and she would be left with a flourishing love without anything to nourish it.

So when Steve went back to his wood chopping, Laura went into the hut, denying herself the pleasure of watching him anymore. Nevertheless, she could still hear the whack of his ax from inside, and her memory replayed the way his muscles had rippled in the sun.

"I thought you'd forgotten all about me, Steven."

Steve chuckled to himself. No doubt a woman as lovely as Laura wasn't used to men forgetting about her. Not that he had. He'd carried her to the brook so that she could soak her ankle in the icy water. And now he'd come back to get her after preparing a surprise for her in the hut.

"I had a few things to do," he said gruffly to hide his eagerness. He couldn't wait to see her reaction to his surprise. He bent down and examined her ankle. "That cold water did some good. It doesn't look as swollen."

"But my toes are numb." She wriggled them.

She had a slender, high-arched foot, and Steve had the impulse to kiss it. He'd never had the slightest desire to kiss a woman's foot before. What the hell was happening to him?

Laura was driving him crazy, that's what. All morning, in the hot sun, he'd wanted her, he'd ached for her. He'd been grateful for the opportunity to release his pent-up sexual energy chopping wood. And he'd put all that hard work to good use. It would give her great pleasure, he knew. He picked her up and jostled her to balance her weight in his arms.

"Hey, take it easy," she admonished. "I thought we decided that I wasn't a lumpy bag of potatoes."

He laughed. "You're tough, though, Laura. You're like me. You don't bruise easily."

That was sheer bravado on his part, Steve realized. She could bruise him with a mere word or suspicious look. When or how she'd gotten such power over him he didn't know, but somewhere along the trail she had managed to. Otherwise, why had he remained behind with her?

He carried her back to the hut and paused at the door. "Close your eyes," he demanded.

"Put me down first," came her counterdemand. But when he did, she still didn't follow his command. "Why should I close my eyes?"

"Because I asked you to, Laura."

"That's not a good enough reason."

He gave up. She would always be difficult. He would have to accept that, although he never had with any other woman. "Okay, walk right in with your eyes wide open," he said. "But don't waste any time taking off your clothes once you do."

Her gray eyes opened really wide over that suggestion. "Why should I do that?"

He smiled like the Cheshire cat. "You'll see."

He waited by the doorway as she hobbled into the room. When she let out an astonished cry, he went in after her.

"Oh, Steven, tell me I'm not dreaming."

"It's for real all right."

"But how did you manage it?"

"Never mind how. I did it, that's all. For you, Laura." And it had been worth all the trouble and effort, he thought as he observed the look of pure joy on her face as she gazed at the big wooden tub of hot water. "Now hurry up and get in before it cools down."

She didn't give him a hard time about that suggestion, almost tearing off her shirt buttons in her haste. But then she stopped in midmotion and looked at him. "Would you mind giving me a little privacy?" she asked shyly.

Steve backed away. "I'll wait outside."

Left alone, Laura shucked off her clothes, then attempted to get into the tub. But she couldn't manage it with a sprained ankle. Even without one, she would have had trouble. The tub rim was higher than waist level. She floated her hand in the water and sighed. Delicious! Every aching muscle in her body, every cell, every atom longed to join her hand in the warmth of that water. Modesty took a back seat.

"Steven!" she called. "Please come back."

He did in an instant. His eyes flickered over her nudity. A muscle on his cheekbone twitched, but his face remained an impassive mask. "Yes, Laura? What is it?"

"I'm afraid I need your help."

"That's nothing to be afraid of," he said.

No, perhaps it wasn't, Laura thought. At that moment she believed him to be the kindest, most thoughtful man in the world. "Will you please lift me into the tub?" she asked him.

His hands felt cool and rough against her bare skin when he picked her up. He lowered her into the warm water slowly, gently, and she moaned with pleasure.

"This is heaven on earth," she told him. "And where on earth did this tub come from?"

"I found it in the shed when I went hunting for an ax," he said. "And I remembered you said that you longed for a bath."

"But you had to lug buckets of water up from the river." She splashed around, her body as buoyant as her heart. "And you even heated it up for me!"

"Well, there didn't seem to be a hot-water faucet handy." Embarrassed that she realized what great lengths he'd gone to to please her, he turned away and stoked the fire under a big copper container.

Laura noticed his embarrassment, and it touched her almost as much as all his effort had. Tears of gratitude welled in her eyes. She didn't try to hide or contain them this time. "Thank you, Steven. You've made me very happy."

Her choked-up voice didn't sound very happy to Steve, and he turned back to her. He watched in amazement as the tears streamed down her face and into the bathwater. He had never seen Laura cry before. "Hey, cut that out," he said hoarsely. "You're going to get the water all wet."

She laughed as she wept. "This is the nicest thing a man has ever done for me," she told him.

And it was the nicest thing he'd ever done for a woman, Steve thought. He had worked like a man possessed to carry it off. But now he shrugged. "It gave me something to do. Sorry there's no bubble bath or loofah sponge, though."

That he had actually remembered those details touched Laura even more. "You're the sweetest man, Steven. You really are."

Sweet? No one had ever called him sweet before. And he'd never wanted anyone to, either. He supposed it was all right if Laura did this one time. Not that he wanted her to make a habit of it. Or maybe he did.

He brought her a bar of soap. "Want me to be your loofah sponge, Laura?"

His question hung in the air like the steam rising from the tub. Laura had stopped crying to regard him intently. He held his breath, waiting for her answer.

"Yes," she said.

He began rubbing the soap against the smooth expanse of her back, slowly, methodically, as if it were the most important task he'd ever performed.

Laura closed her eyes and luxuriated in the warmth of the water and the gentleness of Steve's touch. Her caution, her reservations, her firm resolutions concerning him dissolved. She could feel her heart expanding, the love for him blooming again. She waited with languid acceptance for his hands to roam to more intimate parts of her body. But he continued to scrub her back with a maddening thoroughness.

She swiveled around to face him, her firm high breasts bobbing in the water, a smile of invitation tilting up her lips. She knew where this could lead. She didn't care.

He dropped the soap in the water and took her in. His eyes glowed as hot as the fire in the hearth. But still he did nothing, eyes blazing as he looked at her.

"There's room enough for two in this tub, Steven."

"That doesn't mean you have to invite me to share it."

"Don't you want to?"

"I don't remember when I've ever wanted anything more." His voice was filled with longing.

He disrobed so quickly that Laura had no time to consider the repercussions of her invitation, but she didn't want to think. She simply wanted *him*.

When he got into the tub, his big body caused the water to slosh over the rim. Laura laughed, moving to make room for him.

The tub was deep and wide enough for them to stand in it without touching, but he pulled her against him, flesh to flesh in the warm, soothing liquid. His hands swam all over her body, skimming the curves.

"How beautiful you are, Laura. When you lie only touching distance away from me at night, it drives me wild."

She returned his touch tentatively, gliding her palms over the rough texture of his chest hair, the hard planes of his shoulders and arms. Then her hands floated away from him.

"We've been through too much together to be shy now," he told her.

She nodded in agreement. But it wasn't shyness that made her hold back. She wanted to prolong their pleasure together. She found the bar of soap that he'd let slip from his hand and smiled teasingly.

"My turn to be your loofah, Steven." Although she could clearly see his readiness to make love to her, she planned to drive him wild for a little bit longer.

She rubbed his chest with the soap, and then her caresses became a little bolder. He half groaned, half laughed. "Don't stop," he pleaded.

Laura had no intention of stopping what she had started by inviting him to join her. But after waiting so long, she wanted this moment to last. They had all the time in the world, after all.

Steve seemed to understand and let her set the pace. They passed the soap back and forth, sliding it around each other's body, then rubbed against each other, making the water ripple with their sensuous movements.

"My slippery little seal," Steve murmured.

They kissed often but lightly. A brush of the lips. A skim of tongues. They massaged each other slowly, voluptuously, an underwater exploration of mutual delight.

Steve relished every moment of it, although he had to keep reminding himself that patience was a virtue. He would hold back for as long as Laura wanted him to, even though her every touch caused currents of excitement to shoot through him, jolting him to the core. If they kept up this teasing underwater game for much longer, he mused, she would eventually manage to electrocute him.

"We could use more hot water," she suggested sweetly.

Was she kidding? He was burning up! Surely his body heat alone would bring the water in the tub to a boiling point soon. But in actuality so much time had passed that the water had grown tepid, and it was obvious that she expected him to do something about it. He gave a resigned sigh and sloshed out of the tub. He had gone through a great deal of trouble to please her, and a little more wouldn't kill him. Then again, maybe it would.

Laura watched him move across the small room to the hearth, dripping water on the clay floor. His wet golden skin shone in the firelight. When he turned around with the copper pot of hot water, her eyes traveled down the line of dark hair that went past his flat belly, and his masculine power made her body respond with a flash of anticipated pleasure. She couldn't wait for him to join her again.

He slowly poured the water into the tub. "I'm spoiling you," he said.

"You'll enjoy the benefits, too, Steven."

"I intend to, believe me."

When he climbed back in, he cupped her breasts, then bent his head to suckle.

Laura felt the pull of desire in her womb and half floating, half holding on to him for support, she wrapped her legs around him. He entered her so easily, so perfectly, she thought.

"See, we're made for each other," he told her.

And then he kissed her deeply as he moved inside her, filling her completely. His slightest movement made her muscles contract with pleasure. Supporting her bottom, he swirled her around the water, rocking her rhythmically. She gripped her legs tighter around his waist and moaned when sweet release poured through her. He took his own pleasure then, with faster movements, only freeing his lips from hers to whisper her name with supreme satisfaction.

They gazed into each other's dazed eyes for a long time. The water cooled. Their passion didn't. They got out and dried each other with the same towel as firelight danced over their bodies. Neither of them said a word. None were needed. It seemed to Laura that they understood each other completely now. At last. How could she have ever doubted this man? She adored him. She would never have doubts about him again, she promised herself. She didn't think of all the other promises she had made to herself regarding him and then forgotten to keep.

He pulled her onto the sleeping bag with him. He kissed and cuddled her; he tickled and fondled her; he made her feel cherished. She hugged him close.

"Oh, Steven," she said. "I..." She swallowed down the words.

She had been about to tell him she loved him. But the memory of his drawing away from her on the cliff made her hold back. Perhaps she didn't understand him completely, after all. That would take time, much more time. And they had days and days of it ahead of them, golden hours to explore each other and come to know each other in every way possible.

"You what?" he asked dreamily, then nibbled her ear-lobe.

"I want you again," she said instead of declaring what was in her heart because that, too, was true.

"Then take me," he urged.

And she did, responding to him with all the unspoken love within her.

Chapter Nine

Steve watched Laura sleep as dawn broke the next morning. He fought down the temptation to awake her with kisses. After their long night of love, she needed her rest. But as he studied her face, the soft slope of her cheek, the adorable shape of her mouth, desire for her made him restless. He couldn't get enough of her. He had thought that once he possessed her, her power over him would be diminished. But it had increased instead. He was more fascinated with her than ever.

He got out of his sleeping bag, careful not to disturb her. He wished they could sleep together, but neither bag was big enough to hold two. He imagined them in a real bed together, snuggled spoon-fashion, night after night. But as cozy as this image was, it made him uncomfortable. There was too much a sense of permanency about it.

He padded across the mud-plastered floor. It felt cool beneath his feet. The surface was slightly rough, textured by the fingermarks of the unknown plasterer who had smoothed the surface with his hands.

Steve liked the simplicity of the hut. His own life was simple. He'd always made sure to keep it that way. He could live anywhere and be comfortable with only a few possessions. He could pack up and be gone in five minutes flat, never looking back, never missing a thing he left behind. This gave him the sense of freedom he thrived on—or at least he had thrived on in the past. He had been everywhere in the world without becoming attached to any place in particular, or anyone in particular. Lately, though, a sense of being incomplete had been nipping at the heels of his freedom, tripping him up, slowing him down.

That's why he'd taken some time off for himself. Officially he was still on vacation. Yet he couldn't help himself from pursuing a story instead of relaxing. He always needed a goal, and his latest goal was to investigate Dr. Prescott's yeti research. Laura's injury may have sidetracked him, but only temporarily.

But for now he was more than content, he thought, lighting a small fire of juniper branches to drive the morning chill from the hut. He didn't mind the cold himself, but he wanted Laura to be comfortable when she got up.

He looked toward her. She hadn't stirred. He worried that he'd exhausted her with his ardent lovemaking. But she had been a willing, enthusiastic partner. She had been his equal in every way. He'd never enjoyed making love to a woman more. Enjoyed it? He'd reveled in it!

Still, he would have accepted a platonic relationship with Laura during this time in the hut if that's what she had wanted. His surprise of a hot bath had been a gesture of friendship and consideration, not a seduction ploy. Even so, he smiled with satisfaction over the results of his gesture as he walked over to the tub.

He dipped his hand in the cool water. It would take a long time to empty the tub and refill it with fresh hot water again. Still, he intended to do it every day for her because it gave her such pleasure, and time was one thing he had plenty of right now.

It wouldn't hurt to shave for her every day, either, he decided. As he'd studied Laura in the shaft of morning light coming through the small window, he'd noticed a slight redness on her cheeks and neck. His beard had irritated her delicate skin. He'd packed a razor, so he might as well use it.

When Laura opened her eyes, she saw Steve crouched by the hearth, feeding branches to the small fire in it. How good it was to see him first thing in the morning. She watched him as he stared at the fire, seemingly lost in thought. He was bare chested, wearing only his low-riding khaki shorts. She observed him for a long time before he became aware that she was awake.

"Good morning, sleepyhead," he said.

She stretched lazily in the confines of her bag. "What time is it?"

He brought up his arm to check his watch, then realized that he wasn't wearing it. "Half past dawn, more or less," he said. "But what does time matter here?"

It didn't matter at all, Laura thought. They had the whole long day in front of them. And many more after that. "What's that marvelous scent in the air?" she asked him.

"Burning juniper." He came to her and knelt by her bag. "How are you?"

Laura found that an oddly formal question but answered accordingly. "Fine, thank you. And you?"

"Me? Oh, I'm great. But you know, last night, maybe I was a little too...enthusiastic with you."

She laughed at his concerned expression. "You were wonderful."

Looking relieved, he stroked her face. "It's not so wonderful that I burned your cheek with my scratchy beard. Sorry about that. I'm heating water to shave. Did you pack a mirror?"

"Yes, but I lost it somewhere on the trail." She reached up and stroked his face, too, grazing the rough surface of hair with her fingertips. "I'll shave you, Steven."

He raised dubious eyebrows. "Have you ever shaved a man before?"

Until him, there was a lot she'd never done with a man before. "No, but I'm willing to give it a try," she said.

"I'm glad you're so game, but I'll be the one at risk."

"Oh, Steven, where's that great sense of adventure of yours?" she chided.

"It stops short of getting my throat slashed."

She pretended to pout. "Come on. Let me shave you. I won't hurt you."

He looked at her a long moment. "And I don't ever want to hurt *you*, Laura," he said.

He had turned serious on her. Rather than reassure her, his declaration upset her. "But will you?" she asked him in a small voice.

He shook his head slowly. "No," he promised. "Never intentionally. I care too much about you. I think you're the most wonderful woman I've ever made love with. But I don't..."

"You don't love me," she said, finishing the sentence he'd left incomplete.

"That's not what I was going to say." Yet he said nothing more.

Laura didn't press him. She was sure she understood. He was trying to tell her that whatever they shared was impermanent. But she already knew that and accepted it. She had no choice but to accept it. She loved a man who pulled back from love. It was her problem, not his, and she wasn't going to ruin their time together by dwelling on it.

"Well, are you going to let me shave you or not?" she asked.

"You promise you won't cut me?"

"No, never intentionally," she said, deliberately repeating his very words. "I care too much about you. I think you're the most wonderful man I've ever made love with."

"Do you really? Or are you just being cute now?"

"I meant every word."

"But those were my words, Laura."

"And did you mean them, too?"

"Every word." He unzipped her sleeping bag and pushed back the top layer to reveal her naked body. His leopard eyes took her in, and hunger sparked in them. "So soft," he said, running his hand along the expanse of her warm flesh.

She raised her arms and pulled him to her.

"I don't want to scratch you again," he said, drawing back.

"It doesn't matter." She pulled him harder. Nothing mattered but the pleasure he gave her. She wanted as much as she could have of him for as long as it lasted. She couldn't help herself. She couldn't hold back with him. She closed her eyes and pressed the back of his neck when his mouth found her waiting breast.

"Tilt your chin up," Laura demanded. She had the razor poised, ready to shave Steve's neck.

"Whatever you say, Laura." He did as he was told, and his Adam's apple bobbed when he gulped. "You've made me your slave."

So that's the way it was, Laura thought. They'd both become slaves to a passion that seemed limitless and uncontrollable now that they had given in to it.

By the position of the sun she guessed it was high noon now. They'd finally managed to leave the hut and go out into the bright sunshine. Steve was sitting on a rough stool and Laura stood between his long, spread legs, the copper bucket of hot water beside her. Although they were in an isolated area, with only grazing animals in the distance, she had covered herself with one of his denim shirts, which reached to her knees, and Steve had put on his khaki shorts just in case they got another surprise visitor from the monastery.

Laura carefully scraped the razor against the vulnerable skin of his throat, then stepped back to examine her work. She smiled with satisfaction. His face was revealed to her once more. Such a strong face, she thought. Too angular and irregular to be considered model-perfect, perhaps, but she preferred it that way. If she could have molded a face to please her in every way, it would have been his. And she had done a fine job of shaving it, she decided, except for that unfortunate nick beneath his left earlobe. She leaned toward him and kissed the spot.

Steve took this opportunity to cup the soft weight of her breast in his palm. Laughing, she pulled away and saw the hunger in his eyes once again.

"Let's go back inside," he said.

"You're incorrigible, Steven. Will you ever be satisfied?"

"But you satisfy me completely," he replied. "That's why I want you again and again." He rubbed his smooth face. "And now that I'm shorn, you can have your way with me."

"I already have!" she reminded him. "And you with me." She felt the hot sun beating down upon her and stretched under the luxury of it.

She stretched like a very satisfied woman, Steve thought. She looked so beautiful to him. Her lips were slightly swollen from his demanding kisses, and her gray eyes had a dreamy cast to them, as if she were still under the spell of his embrace. From their first kiss in Kathmandu he had predicted that she would be a delightful partner. But he had never foreseen how powerfully her sensuality would affect him. He'd been joking when he'd declared himself her slave, but now he feared the truth of it. With sunlight pouring over her, lighting up her hair and illuminating her skin, she looked like a goddess to him. He reached for her again, but she took a quick step back. She pointed her chin in the direction behind him.

"We're being watched," she informed him in a low voice.

Adrenaline shot through Steve's system. He leapt off the stool and turned around to face down the intruder encroaching on their territory. But when he realized it was only a small boy peeking around a birch tree, he relaxed.

"Hey, come over here, you," Steve demanded.

"You'll frighten him away," Laura said.

"Good."

"Oh, but he's so adorable." Laura smiled and beckoned to the child. He came forward a few paces. She urged him on with a few Sherpa words. He dared a few more steps. She called again. In this fashion he eventually made it to them.

"What is your name?" Laura asked him in his native language.

"Pemba, the son of Sonam," he replied in English.

"Sonam is the Sherpani who let me ride her pony," Laura told Steve.

"My mother sent me to be of help if needed," the boy said.

"How kind." Laura smiled at him. "And how well you speak English, Pemba."

"I learn at school," he declared proudly.

"Well, shouldn't you be at school now?" Steve asked him, frowning. He didn't need some kid hanging around their private paradise.

"No school, sahib. Teacher go far away for now." Pemba smiled broadly, apparently delighted by this. "I help you and your wife, yes?" He beamed at Laura.

"My what? Oh, right." Steve remembered that the villagers assumed he and Laura were married. "Well, we don't really need any help, thank you. We're managing just fine on our own."

Pemba didn't budge or even deign to look at Steve. He kept his lovely slanted eyes on Laura. "Good for my English to be here, memsahib. You learn me more, I work for you. One day I be a guide for tourists like my uncle. Make much money doing that."

"Ambitious little guy," Steve muttered. But he liked the boy for that and began to warm up to him.

"I'd be happy to teach you more English," Laura told Pemba. "But you don't have to work for us in return."

"Oh, yes," the boy insisted. "I want to. As you say in America, the deal does the deal."

"A deal's a deal," Steve said, correcting him and at the same time agreeing to the arrangement. "You're on, kid." He offered his hand to Pemba.

The boy hesitated taking it. "Onkid?" he asked in puzzlement. "What is that?"

"That means you can start work right away. You can show me how to gather fuel for the fire."

"Ah, zum dung. Okay. Onkid!" Pemba shook Steve's hand vigorously. "Thank you, sahib."

"Call me Steve."

"Mr. Steve," the boy said formally. "And Mrs. Steve," he said to Laura with a bow.

Steve and Laura looked at each other, smiled and shrugged.

In the days that followed, Mr. and Mrs. Steve and Pemba became good friends. Laura and Steve found him a delightful child, eager to learn, eager to help. He ran errands for them in the village, bringing back potatoes and barley, yak yogurt and cheese. He told them that the villagers were eager to make their acquaintance, and they promised to go there as soon as Laura's ankle was strong enough. Laura urged Steve to go without her, but he refused to leave her alone.

Pemba also showed Laura how to cook a few Sherpa dishes made with potatoes and dough, via instructions from his mother. As simple as the recipes were, Laura found them a challenge until she got the hang of cooking in the hearth. She was especially proud of her *rigi cour,* potato cakes baked on a flat stone over the fire. Steve declared her a master chef.

Laura couldn't help thinking of their time together as a honeymoon, although she constantly cautioned herself not to. They never spoke of a future together. They lived completely in the present moment, enjoying each sunny day to the fullest.

"Does the rest of the world still exist, I wonder?" Laura said dreamily to Steve as they sat by the riverbank watching the langur monkeys who gathered there. It was their chief entertainment.

"I almost wish it didn't," he replied, taking her hand and playing with her fingers. "Then we wouldn't have to go back to it."

She chose to ignore his reminder that they would eventually have to leave the peace and happiness of their isolated Eden. "Oh, look at Charlie and Mildred," she said, pointing to two of the monkeys. They'd given names to the ones who had distinguished themselves from the rest of the troop.

"I see old Charlie is still chasing after her." He laughed when the female monkey bared her teeth and spit at the other. "And Mildred is still playing hard to get."

"Poor Charlie," Laura said.

"He should stop wasting his time and go on to someone else."

"Is that the way you operate, Steven?" Laura asked archly.

"I thought we were talking about monkeys."

"So we were."

They sat in silence as the langurs chattered around them. Steve continued to play with Laura's fingers. "Maybe that's the way I used to operate before you came along," he said after a while.

What did that mean? Laura wondered. That he wouldn't go on to someone else now that he'd found her? She didn't dare ask him. It would break their unspoken but mutually understood agreement not to discuss their relationship or where it would lead.

"I was fascinated with monkeys as a child," she told him to get away from the subject they always avoided. "I could do a great imitation of one, sound effects and all."

"Do it for me now," Steve urged.

She shook her head. "I dropped that act after making the huge mistake of giving a performance when I first went to boarding school. The other girls found me ridiculous and called me Monkey Girl. It took me years to live down the nickname, but by senior year they finally accepted me."

"Why did you even care if they accepted you? I would have said the hell with them."

Laura laughed. "Yes, I'm sure you would have, Steven. But I did care. Terribly. Those girls were the only family I had when my father sent me away to school after my mother died. The rejection hurt."

"And his did, too, I'll bet," Steve said softly.

"He didn't reject me!" Laura protested. "He did what he thought was best for me, I suppose. He just didn't realize how hard it would be to adjust after being raised in the wilds for most of my life. I didn't know how to dress right, to talk right, to fit in at all."

"But you eventually learned how to blend in and be like all the others."

Laura thought she heard a note of criticism in Steve's voice. "Of course I did. I had no choice. Isn't that one of the keys to survival? Look at how those silver monkeys blend into their environment. Most wild creatures do that to avoid being spotted by predators."

"And you really are a wild creature at heart, aren't you, Laura?" He gently bit one of her fingers. "For all your declarations to the contrary, I spotted that in you right off. That's what drew me to you."

She had once believed that it was her famous last name that had drawn him to her. But she couldn't bear to believe that about him anymore. She loved him too much. "You're the one who makes me wild," she told him. "Before I met you, I'd become very tame."

"No, you only pretended you were, to yourself as well as to others," he said. "That was your camouflage to fit in. Was your fiancé part of the camouflage, too?"

"Jerome would have made the perfect husband," she replied. "Responsible, conservative and committed. I thought he suited me fine. We would have had a safe, normal, predictable life together."

Steve groaned. "How boring can you get? You were right to break up with him, Laura. You couldn't possibly be happy with a man like that."

"But he's the one who broke the engagement, not me."

"Only because you wanted him to, I'm sure. You must have forced his hand."

Had she? Jerome had accused her of running away, but at the time she hadn't seen it that way. She'd thought she was running to her father's aid, not running away from her scheduled marriage. She'd been in such a big hurry to get to Nepal, but would it have made much difference if she had waited a week, married Jerome and brought him here with her?

She hadn't wanted to share Nepal with Jerome, though. It would have been like sharing her other, secret self that she had locked up deep within her for so many years. Instead, she had chosen to share all her passion and high spirits with the man sitting beside her now. Why? The answer didn't matter to Laura. She had never been happier than she'd been these past few days with Steve. The joy of simply being alive and in love pulsed through her.

"Okay, Steven, you asked for it," she said, standing up. "My sprained ankle may hamper my style a bit, though."

And then she proceeded to do her monkey imitation for him. Although she hadn't performed it for thirteen years, she gave it her all, with the exuberance and enthusiasm she had felt as a child, sure that Steve would get a kick out of such an unconventional display.

And he did. He laughed and applauded and whistled for more. When she breathlessly sat down beside him again, he hugged her to him.

"You are the most gorgeous, desirable Monkey Girl in the world, Laura Prescott," he murmured in her hair.

And the warmth of his words and embrace filled her to the brim, replacing all the old hurts and fears and loneliness she had experienced as a girl.

Later that afternoon Pemba showed up at the hut door with what looked like an animated stuffed toy to Laura. A large one.

"What is it?" she asked the boy, her fingers itching to pet the bushy-tailed, short-faced, shaggy black creature.

"Don't you know, Mrs. Steve?" Pemba looked stunned by her ignorance. "Why, this is a yak calf."

"Oh, of course. There aren't any yaks where I come from, Pemba. That's why I didn't recognize a baby one."

"No yaks? Where do you get your milk and butter, then?"

"Ordinary cows, Pemba. Personally I buy my dairy products at a supermarket."

Steve came to the door. "Now you're going to have to explain to him what a supermarket is," he said, stepping outside. While Laura was attempting to do that, he circled the calf.

"It's for you and Mrs. Steve," Pemba told him.

He had lost interest in Laura's explanation, and she sensed that he neither understood nor believed her. Supermarkets were beyond his imagination, let alone experience.

"For us?" Steve asked. "What are we going to do with a yak?"

"But this is a special one, Mr. Steve. His mother die soon after his birth, so we take him into our home. Now he likes only to be with people. He is...what is the word...a put."

"A pet, you mean, Pemba." Laura extended her hand to the calf, and he covered it with wet slurpy tongue licks. "Oh, Steven, isn't he precious?"

A smile tugged at the edges of his mouth, but he put on a serious frown. "He's sure to be extra trouble to have around."

"No trouble," Pemba said. "He is weaned. All he requires is grass to graze on and kind words and pats. My mother thinks you find pleasure in having him with you during your stay here."

"Our very own baby yak," Laura said. "I think it's a wonderful idea. He can stay in the shed at night."

"He looks awfully big to be babied," Steve grumbled. But the calf kept nudging his leg, and he broke down and petted it. "Cute," he reluctantly admitted. "What's his name, Pemba?"

The boy shrugged. "A yak, Mr. Steve."

"Sherpa probably don't give animals personal names," Laura said.

Steve could tell that she was already trying to come up with one for the calf, however. He sighed with resignation. "Looks like we got us a *put*."

"That's what we'll call him. Put," Laura declared. "Okay?"

"Fine with me," Steve said. "Now all we have to do is teach him a few tricks." He pointed a finger at the animal. "Stay, Put," he said sternly. The yak didn't budge. "Amazingly brilliant animal!"

"I give full credit to the trainer." Laura kissed Steve's cheek.

Pemba observed them with a smile on his sweet face. "You are most happy here, are you not, Mr. and Mrs. Steve?"

Laura didn't reply. She wanted to hear Steve's answer.

"We couldn't be happier," he told the boy.

And Laura's heart blossomed.

"Then why go away?" Pemba asked. "Stay here and be my friends for good and always."

"Nothing is for good and always, kid," Steve said. "Everything changes with time."

Now Laura's heart wilted a little.

"The mountains never change," Pemba said.

"Sure they do," Steve replied. "So slowly that you don't notice it. But if more and more people come here, they'll change a lot faster. In some areas of your country, the mountains no longer have many trees left on them. Then the soil erodes, causing landslides and floods, and crops can't grow."

"*Bohut kharah!*" Pemba exclaimed. "Very bad!"

"Don't frighten the child," Laura murmured to Steve.

"Well, he should know these things. This land is his heritage." He ruffled the boy's hair. "You listen to me, pal. You don't want a lot of Westerners coming here to live, or pretty soon you'll have parking lots and pollution."

"And a supermarket?" Pemba asked, stretching out the new word he had learned. "If you stay here, will you build a supermarket to feed you? I would like to see one very much."

"Not here, you wouldn't," Steve told him. "Then you wouldn't need yaks and zums anymore."

"For fuel we would," Pemba said.

"It would take a heck of a lot of yak dung to keep a supermarket going, Pemba. Trust me, you're better off the way you are."

Pemba didn't seem convinced. "I would like all these things I hear my uncle speak of. He lives in Kathmandu and owns a picture box and a motorcycle. These are wondrous things. When I become guide like him, I will buy my mother a box that washes clothes. I will carry it all the way here on my back and surprise her."

Steve and Laura looked at each other over Pemba's head. They didn't know whether to laugh or cry.

"This program is getting boring, dear. Mind if I switch channels?" Steve asked. They were sitting on their sleeping bags in front of the small hearth fire and he had slipped into their Married Couple in Suburbia game.

Laura didn't play along this time. "You're not really getting bored, are you?"

Night after night they cuddled in front of the fire like this, and she found it an enjoyable pastime. The few candles they had didn't provide enough light for any other sort of occupation.

"Well, I wish we could get a good sports channel," he replied. "Maybe we should sign up for cable."

"I'm serious, Steven. Are you bored here with me?"

It struck Steve that she sounded like a real wife would. "With you? Never," he said, giving her a kiss on the cheek to appease her.

A perfunctory kiss, Laura thought. She was not appeased. "If you *are* bored, you could go into the village during the evening. There must be a place there where the men gather and talk."

"I have no intention of leaving you alone here at night, Laura."

She was sure she heard impatience in his voice. "I wouldn't mind."

"You say that, but you don't mean it. Besides, I don't want to leave you to go hang out at some local version of Joe's Bar and Grill. I much prefer your company."

"You say that but you don't mean it."

"I wish you wouldn't throw back my words like that, Laura. It's getting to be a habit with you."

She picked up the testiness of his tone. "And I wish you'd drop that dumb Married Couple game. You make marriage sound so mundane, so banal."

"Well, isn't it?"

She should have expected that reply from him. But that didn't make hearing it any easier. "No, it doesn't have to be," she told him with firm conviction. "My parents had a wonderful marriage. They were partners in every sense of the word. They never stopped delighting in each other's company, even though they were constantly together in the most isolated areas."

"In that case they had no choice but to get along."

"Why must you always be so cynical?"

He shrugged, moving his body away from hers in the process. "Because that's the way I am."

"I don't like it."

"The way I am?" His tone was defensive.

"No, just that part of you. The cynicism."

"You know what, Laura?"

She guessed he was going to tell her that he didn't give a damn about how she felt. She braced herself. "What, Steven?"

"I don't much like that part about me, either," he said instead. Now the edge was off his voice, replaced by a soft note of melancholy.

She reached out and touched his cheek. "Why are we quarreling?"

"Because that's what lovers do sometimes. It doesn't matter. It's not important." And this time he kissed her on the lips with more depth of feeling.

Laura accepted his kiss gladly, but she could not accept that what they had argued about was of no importance or didn't matter. But there was no sense in continuing a prickly discussion now that they had more or less made up.

"I wonder how Put is doing all by himself?" she said to get them back on an even keel.

"He's far too big to bring into the hut, if that's what you're about to suggest, Laura."

"Of course I wasn't. I know there's no room for him in here, and I would never suggest such a thing."

"Well, I see how you look with such fondness at that dumb animal. You've become putty in Put's hands."

"Hooves," she corrected, smiling. "I find his need for human affection so touching."

"I'll go check on him for you," Steve offered, jumping up.

"Oh, you don't have to do—" But he was already out the door before Laura could finish her sentence.

Left alone, she wondered if Steve had used the yak calf as an excuse to get away from her. As content as he claimed to be, she sensed an undercurrent of restlessness in him, rising closer and closer to the surface. Was he beginning to find spending so much time with her tedious? Was their relationship beginning to wear thin for him? She threw another juniper branch in the hearth and watched it flame and sizzle, then shrivel up.

It was pitch-black outside, and with no moonlight to guide him, Steve took cautious steps to the shed by the river. He breathed in the cool autumn air and felt a certain relief to be away from Laura. He had felt uncomfortable with their conversation about marriage. Not that he had interpreted her remarks as hints about their own possible future together. All the same, he knew that his deprecating replies had bothered her. Well, he couldn't help it. He had no affinity to that particular institution. He was just like his father, a chip off the rotten old block. At least he had been told exactly that by his stepfather enough times to believe it.

He pushed open the rickety shed door and heard the calf shuffle and snort.

"Please don't get up," Steve said in a parody of politeness. "I'll join you on the floor." When he sat down, the yak placed his head in Steve's lap and sighed contentedly. "Well, now you've done it, fellow," he said, stroking the shaggy dome. "You've won me over completely."

He liked being in the dark, quiet shed with the animal, breathing in its scent. It reminded him of boyhood days on the farm in Vermont, when he'd slept with the animals in the barn. His stepfather had made him sleep there as punishment for any infraction of his dogmatic rules. He would tell Steve he wasn't good enough to stay in his house. But Steve hadn't considered it punishment. He had preferred spending the night in the barn, away from his stepfather's loud menacing voice and his mother's whimpering responses to it.

Laura had been raised in a much different atmosphere and couldn't understand how miserable family life could be. According to Steve's long-suffering mother, she had married for *his* sake, to give her son a name and a home. Steve figured that she must have told him that to make him feel better about the situation, but it only made him feel worse. Because he'd been born, she had been forced to wed a brutal, cruel man. No children had resulted from this unhappy union. But this didn't make Steve's stepfather value him more. Instead, his resentment of Steve's existence grew.

"A marriage made in hell," Steve muttered.

The yak nudged a little closer, as if to comfort him. But Steve didn't need comfort. He never had. For as far back as he could remember, he'd been tough. How old had he been when he'd understood his stepfather's declaration that he was no good? Three? Four, maybe? I don't belong to you, old man, he remembered thinking. I don't belong to anybody.

Steve thought about all this now, in the privacy of the shed, although he hadn't given much thought to his childhood for years. But being with Laura touched all the soft spots within him, areas of his heart and memory that he had protected from even himself until now. That's why she made him so uncomfortable at times. And that was why he was stirred by her, too.

He noticed that he'd begun to shiver as he sat on the cold stone floor. The yak's soft breath wasn't enough to warm him. Only Laura's arms could. So what the hell was he sitting here keeping a *yak* company for?

"See you in the morning, pal," he said, standing up. "Sweet dreams."

When Steve left the shed, he looked up at the stars. They were so vivid in the moonless sky. Their twinkling brightness reminded him of Laura's eyes when she laughed. When he reached the hut, he called to her.

"Laura, could you come out here for a minute?"

He waited for her with his hands stuffed in the pockets of his canvas slacks, still feeling chilled. But when she appeared in the doorway, his heart warmed. Firelight glowed behind her.

"So you're back," she said. "You were gone a long time."

He couldn't make out her expression in the darkness, but her voice sounded sad. "Not that long," he said. "Put needed a little company."

"And you needed to be alone."

"Yes," he admitted. He realized that Laura was the only person who knew him at all. She was the only one he'd allowed himself to get close to for many years. Too many years. "And I needed time to get you a gift."

"A gift?" Now her voice was curious.

"Come outside and take a look." He helped her down the steep doorway step, concerned about her ankle. "Diamonds, Laura." He raised his arm toward the expanse of glittering stars set in a backdrop of black velvet.

"Oh, Steven, you shouldn't have." She laughed softly, head tilted up. "They really do look near enough to reach up and snatch out of the sky, don't they? It must be that we're so high up in the mountains that we're actually closer to them."

"Pick and choose the ones you want," he offered magnanimously.

"That Big Dipper brooch would be nice for dressy occasions," she said.

"And how about the Little Dipper for more informal ones?" he suggested helpfully.

She sighed. "It's so hard to decide. I think I would like just one perfect star and that will be enough."

"I know." Steve pointed to the North Star. "That's the one for you. It would make a nice ring, wouldn't it?"

"Perhaps a tad ostentatious."

"So what? If you've got it, flaunt it. And you certainly have got it, Laura." He grabbed her left hand in the darkness and pretended to slide a ring on it. "Here. It's yours. From me to you."

"I'll wear it forever," she promised. The imaginary star ring would most likely be the only one he would ever give her. Even so, his gesture pleased her.

He put his arm around her, and they gazed at the stars in silence for a moment. And then Steve cleared his throat.

"Let me tell you a little bit about myself," he said. "The way I grew up. I've never told anybody about it before."

That he was willing to share something personal with her pleased Laura even more. She pressed her body close to his to encourage him to go on. And he talked for a long time under the star canopy, expressing to her in a sometimes halting voice all the pain and alienation he had felt as a boy in his stepfather's house.

Laura soaked up his pain, taking it as her own. But she didn't interrupt him with superfluous words of sympathy, and when he was through talking, she had only one thing to say to him.

"You survived and grew up to become the fine man you are, Steven. That's all that matters in the end."

"I'm not so fine as all that," he said grimly. "You can't expect me to be as open and loving as you are, Laura. I never had a chance to develop a real sense of trust. Maybe that's why I come off sounding so cynical at times."

He was warning her. Once again he was warning her not to get too close to him. And once again her heart refused to heed his words. "What about your natural father?" she asked him. "Do you know anything about him?"

"Only that he was a newspaper reporter on vacation at a ski resort in Vermont where my mother worked. He apparently won her over one snowy night with a dinner out and a slow dance."

It wasn't lost to Laura that Steve had almost won her over with a dinner and a dance. "Did your mother contact him when she knew she was going to have his child?"

"Oh, yeah. She called the paper he claimed to work for in New York, but no one there had ever heard of him. So he either lied about that or gave her a false name. Either way, she was left on her own," Steve told her. After a moment of silence, he added, "Let's go inside before you get too cold."

The hut was warm and cozy, and when Steve took her into his arms and kissed her with deep passion, Laura's sense of foreboding dwindled away. But then she looked toward the hearth and recalled how the juniper branch she had placed in it had flared so gloriously, only to shrivel into nothing. Would that happen to their passion? Would Steve's desire for her eventually burn out, leaving her nothing but ashes and fragrant memories?

Laura refused to accept that as possible. She had never felt such deep love for a man before, and if she couldn't believe in him, she couldn't believe in herself, either. They fell onto the sleeping bag together, and as she raised her hand to caress Steve's face, Laura could almost see the star ring he had placed on her finger, a bright twinkling promise of forever.

Chapter Ten

"Goodbye, Steven." Laura waved from the hut doorway.

Little Pemba was pulling Steve in one direction, but Laura's forlorn expression was pulling him in another.

"I'm just going to the village, not the edge of the world," he reminded her. "I'll be back as soon as I can find some vegetables to buy."

"Good luck," she said. "And don't forget to buy soap if you can."

"Come, Mr. Steve." Pemba tugged at his hand.

But Steve didn't want to leave Laura alone. "Come with us," he said. "I'll carry you on my back."

That's the last thing Laura wanted. She would rather be without Steve than be so totally dependent on him again. "I'd rather stay here," she told him. "I've got plenty to do to keep me busy."

"Don't walk too much and overtax your ankle," Steve cautioned. "You don't want a setback now that it's almost healed."

"I won't," she assured him.

"I'll be back around sunset."

Since it was only morning, Laura was surprised that he planned to stay away that long. But she'd continued to sense his restlessness creeping into their relationship like an unwanted third party, and she hoped he would lose it with this trip to the village. She gave him a cheery smile.

"Don't worry about me. I have Put for company."

She waved until Steve and Pemba were out of sight, then went back inside and threw herself into household chores. She swept the floor with a broom fashioned out of twigs, which she found amazingly efficient, and washed the two wooden bowls that had contained their breakfast rice in an enamel basin of hot water. She gathered up some clothes that needed washing, and with Put following her, went down to the river. She used a smooth sheet of rock by the shore as her scrub board, then beat the clothes against it. She felt a great sense of accomplishment when she spread the clean clothes on the mossy bank to dry.

Her tasks done, Laura sat on the rock, dangled her feet in the water and enjoyed the beauty of the day. She had no appointments to keep, no social engagements or business obligations, no nagging problems to solve or customers to mollify. During these weeks away from the hustle and bustle of modern civilization, she had learned the simple art of sitting and doing nothing. Simple as it seemed on the surface, it was a difficult art to master. Absolute relaxation was not something most Westerners felt too comfortable practicing.

For example, Steve didn't like to relax. His intense, restless energy had been one of the things that had attracted Laura to him, but it was also one of the things about him that made her feel apprehensive. Although he'd become a part of her very existence, he could be gone in an eyeblink, off to his next adventure.

Laura was fully aware that this could happen. Indeed, she *expected* it to happen. But expectation was one thing, acceptance another, and her heart could not accept the loss of Steve some day. Laura knew by now that there was no reasoning with her heart. It would not react to logic, only emotion. And one day Steve would most likely break it.

But this day was so lovely—the breeze so crisp, the sky so clear, the sun so warm on her back—that Laura let all her misgivings drift away on a fluffy cloud floating by. The present was all that mattered, after all, and she was now living in paradise with a man she adored. He would return to the hut at sunset, and she would be there to welcome him with open arms.

Away from Laura for the first time in weeks, Steve was enjoying Sherpa hospitality at the only shop in the village. He'd stopped there to buy soap, but when the shopkeeper offered him a glass of tea, he could hardly refuse. Soon other village men gathered around him, curious to find out about him, and eventually a large jug of *chung* was brought out and passed around. Steve once again felt he couldn't refuse and allowed his glass to be filled more than a few times with the bubbly local beer made from fermented rice. He liked being with these rough mountain men who smelled of fire smoke, animal herds and the exertion of honest hard labor. Pemba's father, Akam, was among them, and acted as interpreter for Steve.

"Ask the men about yeti," Steve told him, more interested in gathering information than talking about himself.

And the Sherpa were only too happy to oblige. Each had a story to top the last man's.

"My father followed yeti tracks for three miles before they disappeared at the shore of a river," one said.

"*My* brave father followed the creature into the woods but lost sight of him there," the man seated next to him on the bench said. "He had arms that hung below his knees, matted hair all over his body, and he left a terrible stink in his wake."

"We know what your father looks and smells like, Bola," another man said. "But Mr. Steve wants to know about yeti."

Except for Bola, the other men thought this such a good joke that the jug of *chung* was passed around again.

A man wearing a fur-rimmed hat spoke up. "But yeti are no laughing matter, my friends. One killed my fine horse last year."

"That could have been a wolf or a black bear," another said. "You have no proof it was a yeti who attacked your horse."

"A yeti did break into a storehouse in a neighboring village and carried away all the meat that had been preserved for the winter," Akam said. He picked up a hot piece of dung from the shop hearth and lit his pipe with it. "Two men witnessed this."

"Hah! It would be wise to check these two men's larders for the lost meat," someone suggested.

"I heard from my grandfather that a yeti once killed a beautiful young girl."

"No, no," Bola said. "The story goes that the yeti kidnapped the girl and forced her to be his bride in his mountain cave. She escaped and went to Kathmandu, where she became a famous dancer."

"But that was another girl, not the yeti bride," one man protested.

"And it was a boy a yeti killed, not a girl at all," another said.

Everyone argued about this for a while. Steve became a little bored. "Please ask, Akam, if anyone in the room has had *personal* contact with a yeti." He was weary of hearsay and garbled gossip.

No one spoke up when this question was asked, however. And soon Steve became the center of conversation again. They wanted to know if most men in America were as tall, and if they also had such big feet. Steve had never considered his size-twelve feet especially big before, considering his height, but the Sherpa obviously did.

One of them suggested to Akam that he make his new friend a pair of boots. Much guffawing over this suggestion. But Akam took up the challenge and immediately knelt down to measure Steve's foot. Steve guessed that boot making was his profession, and pride in his craft spurred him on. Measuring a man for new boots was apparently another good reason to pass around the *chung,* and in deference to Akam, Steve couldn't let it pass by him without another refill.

By the time Steve left the smoky shop, the sun was setting and he didn't have much to show for his day away from Laura. He'd acquired a lumpy gray wad of soap, two bananas and a small bag of tea leaves during his marketing quest. He was offered as many potatoes as he could carry back to the hut, but that was the one food he and Laura had in good supply. Steve told himself that he would never eat potatoes again once he returned home. And then a little wistful voice deep inside him asked, *Home? Where is home?* The hut was the only one he could really lay claim to, and of course that was only temporary.

Everyone in the village was hurrying home now that the sun was losing its warmth. Girls led zums back from the alpine meadows, women carried brimming water pots on their heads from the spring, farmers left off hoeing and hungry, whimpering children were carried on the backs of older brothers and sisters.

So Steven hurried home, too, stopping only once along the way to ask an old woman swishing a goatskin full of yak cream if she had any butter or cheese she would sell him. She did—she drove a hard bargain—and the sale was accomplished to the satisfaction of both parties.

Dark was quickly descending, and Steve lengthened his stride and picked up his pace. He didn't relish the idea of walking through the woods in the dark, and he liked the idea of Laura alone in the hut at night even less. Why the hell had he stayed so long in the village? At first drinking *chung* with the men had been entertaining, but the pleasure had diminished as his desire to be back with Laura had increased. He felt the pull of her tugging at his heartstrings, and it occurred to him that home could always be where Laura was.

As Steve hurried back to her, he reviewed all he had heard from the village men about yeti. None of it was new to him, but he'd liked hearing the legends straight from the original source's mouth, so to speak. It was the Sherpa who had spread tales of yeti over the years.

According to them, yeti varied in height from four feet to sixteen feet. Descriptions varied, too, but the traits consistently mentioned were that a yeti's posture was like a stooped man's, his face was partially free of hair, he traveled alone and had a fondness for meat and alcohol.

Sort of like a number of hard-driving newsmen he'd known, Steve mused.

This hairy wild man was called *Metoh-Kangmi* by the Sherpa, the abominable snowman. He was said to have the physical strength to uproot trees and lift and hurl boulders a great distance. According to the Sherpa, yeti lived in caves high in the mountains, were nocturnal and carnivorous.

The yeti preyed on smaller mammals of the region, and when pickings were lean, attacked domestic animals and even humans in the isolated villages. He fastidiously discarded the intestines before consuming his prey.

He had a repertoire of calls, from low roars to high-pitched whistling, with yelps, mews and grunts in between. In summation, not the most charming member of the animal kingdom, Steve thought.

But was he *real?*

Steve laughed to himself. Who would want to make up such an unattractive creature? The yeti was an important element in the mythology of this mountain region, yet didn't seem to serve any religious purpose. The only use he had was playing the bogeyman role to keep disobedient children in line. But the Sherpa didn't like to frighten children, and so they were told they could easily get away from a yeti chasing them by running downhill. Why? Because the yeti's long hair would fall over his eyes and he would be unable to see them, of course!

Legends and fairy tales aside, Steve had met many a Western mountaineer who believed that yeti existed. They had seen footprints in the snow. They had heard shrill calls in the night. They had sensed an intelligent life-form observing them as they hiked a lonely trail in the moonlight.

Sort of like what Steve was sensing right now, he thought as a chill ran up his back and caused a prickly sensation at the base of his neck. He had entered the thick pine forest and could not overcome the eerie sensation that he was being watched. Not one to ignore his instincts, he spun around quickly and saw something, or some*one,* shuffle between the trees. Steve could hear a muted thrashing as the figure disappeared from view.

With nightfall fast approaching, he did not attempt to follow the creature. Besides, the twilight could have been playing tricks on his eyes. That was probably it. Shadowy dusk and imagination, combined with a belly full of *chung,* didn't make him the sharpest observer at the moment. Steve shook his head and smiled. He couldn't wait to tell Laura about his adventure on the way home. Yes, he was on the way *home* to his Laura, and no yeti was going to waylay him.

Lost! Laura couldn't believe that she was actually lost in the forest. Put had wandered off, and she had gone searching for him about an hour ago. She'd been so positive that she could find her way back to the hut again. But maybe it would have been smart to leave a trail of breadcrumbs or something. The twilight disoriented her. At the moment she had no idea where she was, where the hut was or where Put was. So the expedition had been a failure on all three counts.

Instead, she kept calling Put's name. Not that she expected the calf to respond to it. But perhaps he would respond to her voice. Why had the dumb animal roamed off like that? Laura had seen him at the edge of the woods as she'd picked wildflowers in the pasture, but had paid no attention. Put usually stayed put. Now he was gone, night was falling and wild animals were lurking in the shadows, ready to gobble little Put up.

As dusk descended, it began to dawn on Laura that wild animals might be inclined to gobble her up, too. She knew that the Asiatic black bear didn't take too kindly to anyone intruding into his territory, and this was black-bear territory. Laura had observed a bear nest in a berry bush just the other day, and recalling this made her shiver now. Or perhaps it was the cold night air that made her shiver. Without the sun to warm it, the mountain atmosphere could drop to below freezing in no time.

I could be in big trouble right now, Laura thought. Steve had no idea where she was. No one did. The sorry thing was that *she* had no idea where she was, either.

Keep calm, she told herself. You can figure this out. She looked up above the treetops, located the North Star, imagined its position in relation to the hut and proceeded in what she hoped was the right direction. Along the path she came across Put, headed in the same direction. He snuffled his greeting and nudged her hard with his soft wet nose.

Laura hugged him, relieved that she had found the baby yak at last. Now to find her way home with him. That Put had chosen the same route as she had gave Laura little reason to believe it was the correct one....

Okay, where was she? Steve sat on the stoop of the hut and tried to figure out the answer to that one. Where could Laura possibly have gone? It didn't make sense that she would decide to take a walk at twilight, especially in such an isolated area and with such a weak ankle. Besides, he had told her he would be back by now. Had she gone down the path to meet him on his way home? No, he would have passed her, of course. So where *was* she?

The horrible possibilities flashed in his brain like searing headlines: Drowned In The River; Kidnapped By Bandits; Attacked By Bear! *Captured By Yeti!* Steve leapt up from the stoop. *Laura Prescott Becomes Yeti Bride!* Calm down, that's crazy, he told himself. Dammit, why had he drunk all the *chung?* He wasn't thinking clearly at all.

She was lost, he decided after taking a deep, sobering breath. For some reason she had gone off and gotten herself lost. And he would have to find her. He would begin the search logically, sensibly, with calm rationale. Yes, that was the ticket. Rational behavior. But he wanted to wail at the quarter moon instead. Laura was missing!

Steve took another deep breath. He'd always prided himself on keeping a cool head during the most trying circumstances. And he would do so now. He would get a flashlight, search by the river first, and then the pine forest. If he couldn't find her, he would go to the village for help. He would get all the villagers to comb the forest and the surrounding area with him. He would insist they search all night, not wait until morning. He could not bear the thought of Laura spending the night lost and cold and frightened.

He buried his face in his palms for a moment, and when he took his hands away, his expression had solidified into one of sheer determination. He was only a man, but he would move heaven and earth to get Laura back, to have her in his arms once again.

He went into the hut and got a flashlight. Resolve burning through his veins, he didn't even think to get a jacket. He was sweating. He had never been so distraught in his life. And at the same time he was outwardly calm, like a walking, calculating android out to accomplish the mission assigned to him. Out to find Laura Prescott.

When he stepped outside, he saw her in the distance, all white in the pale moonlight, against a backdrop of dark, dense pines. He thought he was hallucinating. And then he realized that it wasn't a mirage conjured up by wishful thinking. It was the flesh-and-blood woman herself, walking toward him quite casually, slender hips swaying, the yak in her wake. Steve had been so convinced that she was lost that he had trouble accepting her found again, without any superhuman effort on his part. He stood there, motionless, as she came closer and closer.

And then, without thinking about it or willing it, he was running to her. He was running faster than he ever had in his life; he was *flying* to her. When he reached her he swept her into his arms and twirled her around and around. She laughed, and the sweetness of that sound poured through him, filling him with pleasure and relief. He put her down with dizzy delight and kissed her cheek, her nose, her chin, her eyebrow, her temple and finally her open, smiling lips.

"You must have missed me, Steven," she finally managed to gasp.

"Missed you? I thought you were lost to me!" he practically shouted back.

"I did get lost," she admitted. "I was hoping you hadn't come back to the hut yet. I didn't want you to know because I felt so stupid about it. You weren't too worried about me, I hope."

"A little worried." After this understatement he gulped some air. He could breathe again without that tight pressure in his chest and throat. His terrible burning concern turned to angry impatience. "You have good reason to feel stupid, Laura. What the hell were you doing in the woods at nightfall?"

She took a step back from him, as if his sudden irritation threw her off balance. "I was looking for Put. And it wasn't nightfall when I started my search. I've been walking around in circles for over an hour."

"That sure didn't do your ankle much good."

"It feels fine, thank you. As good as new."

"Lucky you didn't twist it again. You've got about much sense as a yak," he grumbled.

Tired, chilled, hungry, she took offense. "For a minute there I thought you were glad to see me." She brushed past him and strode to the hut.

He held back, not sure how to proceed with her. When he finally decided to tell her the truth, he had to run to catch up to her. He grabbed her arm before she stepped inside. What he had to tell her seemed so big to him that it needed the room of the outdoors.

"Dammit, of course I'm glad to see you, Laura. I died a thousand deaths during those horrible minutes when I believed you were lost, and I guess I'm still a little worked up over it."

She was touched by his confession. "That's all right, Steven. I'm back safe and sound." She couldn't understand why he continued to look so troubled. "There's no reason to be concerned anymore."

"But there is," he said. "Something happened while you were gone. Something that's left me stunned. And I don't know what to do about it."

"I don't understand." Laura looked around her. The hut and its setting looked the same to her. "What could have happened?" she asked him.

"I realized that I'm in love with you, Laura. That my life is nothing without you in it. That I could never love a woman more than I love you."

"Oh." His declaration stunned her, too. She hadn't expected it. Ever.

His smile was pained. "Is that all you have to say? Just 'oh'?"

"I'm sorry. But I'm at a loss for words at the moment."

"I've waited too long," he said grimly. "I've waited too long to tell you how much I love you and now you don't care."

That was the last thing she wanted him to think! She stood on tiptoe and wrapped her arms around his neck. "It's never too late to tell a person that, Steven. And of course I care. How could I not care when I love you, too?" It felt so wonderful, so liberating to be able to speak of her deep feelings to him now.

And he didn't pull back when he saw the love emanating from her eyes this time. He soaked it in, letting it saturate every fiber of his being. The glow of her love radiated through him, and he shined it back upon her.

"Then everything is wonderful," he said. "We feel the same way about each other, and nothing or anyone is keeping us apart. We're on top of the world, Laura!"

She nodded. But a cautious little part of her feared that neither love nor life was that simple. At the moment, however, everything was perfect, and she allowed her joy to brim over. She kissed him with tenderness, and he returned her kiss with reverence. They had reached a new plateau in their relationship and didn't quite know how to go on with it.

The solemnity of the moment was broken when Put butted his head against them impatiently. He was always impatient when he wasn't the center of human attention. Laura and Steve laughed, and with arms wrapped around each other's waist, they walked Put to the shed by the river and tucked him in.

When they returned to the hut, they were restrained at first. They kept smiling at each other. And bumping into each other as they settled in for the night. Steve lit the fire. Laura made tea. They shared the two bananas and some goat cheese, then roasted potatoes in the hearth.

"I'm sorry I couldn't get more provisions," Steve said.

"You did fine. I didn't expect you to bring back caviar and champagne."

"I wish we did have champagne," Steve said, taking up her hand as they sat by the fire watching the potatoes roast and playing with her fingers, which had become a habit with him. "We could toast our love."

"We don't need champagne to do that."

They clicked their chipped enamel teacups instead.

Steve told her all about his day with the villagers, taking on the mannerisms of each man as he described him to Laura.

"I wish you had been there," he said after repeating all the jokes and stories to her.

"But I feel as if I had been."

"Not me. I missed you all day. Next time I make a trip to the village, I want you to come with me, Laura. It's no fun experiencing new things without you along to share them."

She couldn't imagine his saying anything nicer to her. "Yes, I'll come next time. My ankle really is strong enough now. I don't feel any bad effects from my long walk today."

"Good. We'll make a day of it. We'll be sure to start back earlier than I did today, though. Those woods aren't the best place to be when it gets dark. You're not going to believe this . . ." Steve paused to add drama. "But I think I saw a yeti in the forest coming home."

Laura laughed. "You're right. I'm not going to believe it. Your head was filled with the stories the Sherpa told you, and you imagined it."

"No, I definitely felt a presence, an intelligent life-form of some kind. And I definitely saw something move between the trees."

"Oh, Steve, that could have been anything. Why, it could have been Put, for all you know."

"I said an *intelligent* life-form, Laura."

"Then it could have been me! We were all thrashing around the woods at the same time, after all."

"No, it wasn't you, my love. I would sense you anywhere, even in the dark."

His words warmed her. He had called her his love. At the same time, talking about the yeti made her edgy. Steve had said that nothing or anyone could keep them apart, but Laura had the premonition that if anything could come between them, it would be this mythical creature.

She snuggled against him and kissed his neck. She blew in his ear and ran her hands through his hair. "Are you trying to drive me to distraction?" he asked her, laughing.

She was trying to distract him, anyway. And it worked. He quickly forgot about yeti and began returning her kisses and nuzzling her back. Their sense of restraint melted away as they slowly undressed and discovered each other anew. With all the power of their mutually declared love, they came together with potent intensity. At the same time the potatoes exploded in the hearth, and they laughed over such apt sound effects. They laughed and loved each other all night long.

"Are you sure we'll be wanted there, Pemba?"

The little boy had just invited Laura and Steve to a village party.

"But of course!" he said. "The more the happier. My mother and father tell me to invite you and Mr. Steve as their special guests."

"We feel honored to be included," Laura told the boy.

The party was held at the village leader's house, and when Steve and Laura arrived, they learned that it was a naming ceremony for the daughter's newborn baby. Pemba and his parents brought them around the crowded room to meet other villagers, and they were made to feel most welcome.

The room was large, with a timber ceiling. The family brass and copper pots were displayed on high shelves and glowed in the firelight. Party snacks of popcorn, fried potatoes and spiced fried dough cakes were passed around on bamboo trays, along with mugs of *chung* and yak-butter tea. Laura found herself wondering if a party with a Himalayan theme would go over well back in New York. She hadn't thought about her catering business for weeks.

She and Steve soon became separated. The women gathered at one end of the room and the men at the other end, not unlike a lot of New York parties Laura had attended. Occasionally she smiled at Steve across the room.

How lovely Laura was, Steve thought. Her skin was tanned and her hair lighter from all the time they spent in the sun. Her eyes looked sun bleached, too, a silvery gray that fascinated him.

Her every gesture fascinated him—the way she leaned forward and listened intently to the elderly Sherpani at her elbow, the way she tossed back her hair and smiled, or glanced his way and gave him a different, more intimate smile. It seemed odd to see her surrounded by people. He'd gotten used to having her all to himself and felt a little uncomfortable about sharing her with others now. He couldn't take his eyes off of her.

Pemba's father, Akam, sharply poked Steve in the chest with his elbow. He came out of his Laura reverie and noticed that all the men were looking at him with knowing smiles.

"We guess you and Mrs. Steve are not too long wedded," Akam said to him.

Chuckles, guffaws, elbow poking all around.

"What makes you think that?" Steve asked.

Louder mirth.

"It is most obvious," Akam assured him. "We wish you much happiness." Mugs of *chung* were raised. "And many fine strong children. And many years of loving companionship with your bride."

It was not a toast Steve had ever expected to be made to him. All the same, he clicked mugs with the men enthusiastically and thanked them with complete sincerity.

"I would like to present you with a gift for being so kind to my son Pemba," Akam told Steve. Ignoring Steve's protests that a gift wasn't necessary, he went to the corner of the room and brought back a pair of black woolen boots soled with thick yak leather. "Most big boots I ever made!" he proudly declared.

Steve accepted them with a formal bow and then realized he was expected to try them on. As he did, all the people in the room stopped chatting to watch the procedure. Everyone cheered when they saw that the boots fit, and Akam was congratulated for this feat of shodding Steve's feet.

Two young men began playing Himalayan flutes. The women crossed the room and pulled their mates to the middle of the floor. Laura laughed at the way the men had to be wheedled and badgered into dancing by the women. She'd seen the same thing happen at so many of the weddings she'd catered.

The men formed one line, and the women another. Laura's arm was linked on each side by two of the women, and Steve was commandeered into the men's line the same way. The villagers sang along with the music, a slow, melancholy chant. And as they sang, they swayed back and forth.

Laura was just beginning to relax under the spell of the slow, hypnotic chanting when the rhythm picked up, along with the dance steps. The footwork became more and more complicated, with much kicking and stamping thrown in. The rafters shook, the polished brass on the shelves rattled, the people shouted and hooted.

Laura and Steve were swept along in the frenzy of this merrymaking. They caught an occasional glimpse of each other and laughed at the way they were desperately trying to keep up with the enthusiastic Sherpa. Somehow they both managed to. But when the dancing ended, they took the opportunity to thank their host, say good-night and escape into the night.

"Alone at last!" Steve said, hugging her to him as they walked down the dirt path.

"But it was fun, wasn't it? I saw you having a good time."

"Yeah, I did enjoy myself," Steve admitted. "But the best part was watching you have a good time. The men made fun of me because I was always staring at you. They figured out we were newlyweds." He laughed sheepishly.

Laura laughed, too, as embarrassed as he was. She knew that the very idea of marriage galled Steve. "The boots Akam made for you are wonderful," she said to change the subject.

"Amazingly warm and comfortable," he replied, as eager to get on a new subject as she was. "I intend to wear them for the rest of the trip."

It was difficult for Steve to imagine going on, however. It seemed he had already reached his destination. Or as Kaba would say, his *destiny*. Living in the hut with Laura seemed about as perfect as life could get for him.

Or did it seem so perfect only because he knew it was temporary? Steve really didn't know. For a man who thought he knew himself so well, he was fast discovering he had a lot more to learn. Laura had opened up new territories in his heart, and he needed time to explore them before he'd be able to understand them.

"Do you ever think about what you'll do when you return to the States?" he asked her.

His question surprised Laura. After all, he knew she ran a catering business, although they'd never discussed it in depth. They'd never discussed his work much, either.

"I intend to continue doing what I've always done," she told him. "In fact, I was thinking at the party how much I'd like to get the recipe for those dumplings stuffed with goat meat. *Mo-mo*, I think they're called."

"I doubt your fancy clients would go for goat meat at their board luncheons and cocktail parties, Laura."

"Or zum curd, either," she agreed.

"Then again, maybe such simple food would appeal to their jaded palates."

"Until they got bored with it," Laura said. "Did you notice how the Sherpa are never bored with life, Steven? They're so in tune with themselves and their surroundings. So complete."

"We've been that way, too, during our stay here," Steve reminded her softly, as if speaking to himself.

Laura squeezed his arm. "I know," she whispered back.

They walked home through the pine forest, and although it was dark, they came across not a single yeti. Laura teased Steve about thinking he'd spotted one the week before. He still insisted that he'd felt the presence of something strange and wonderful that night, but conceded that it could very well have been Laura.

"I'm not so strange," she said.

"But you are very wonderful," he insisted.

Chapter Eleven

A few days later, when Steve was down by the river trying his luck at fishing, Kaba Par showed up at the hut. Laura was overjoyed to see him. She would have kissed and hugged him, but held back, knowing it would embarrass him. The journey to and from Jewel Mountain had been a fairly easy one, he informed her.

"And my father?" she asked anxiously.

"Dr. Prescott looks much the same to me," Kaba said. "But with a beard now, and gray in his hair."

Yes, Laura had already imagined the beard. And the wild hair of a madman. "Is he living in a cave, Kaba?"

"No, no. He occasionally spends the night in one, he told me, but while I was there he stayed in his cabin. A very comfortable one, Laura. You are not to worry on that score."

"Did he seem rational to you?"

"Yes, most clearheaded, although he tended to dwell on the past. He talked a great deal about your beloved mother."

"That's not like him at all," Laura said. "He never discusses her with me. Oh, Kaba, are you sure he's sound of mind?"

"You must judge that for yourself." Kaba handed her a sealed envelope. "Your father sends this message to you. Read it and then decide what you must do."

Steve came up from the river then, and for some reason she could not explain to herself, Laura quickly stuffed the envelope under the waistband of her jeans to hide it from view as he approached. If Steve noticed this subterfuge, he showed nothing in his eyes or expression.

Kaba and Steve greeted each other warmly, and Laura volunteered to make tea. She left them chatting about the weather and trail conditions and went inside the hut. She could hear Steve's low, soft voice as she tore open her father's letter.

She read.

Dear Laura,
  To think that you are only a short distance away—what a surprise. I never expected you to come to Nepal.

Laura looked up. The tone of the letter was hardly jubilant that she had. She lowered her eyes and read on.

Of course I would like to see you, dear daughter. But I don't think it advisable for you to continue on to Jewel Mountain. Kaba Par informed me about your twisted ankle, and I remember that even as a child it gave you trouble. There is snow up here. And ice. Not good conditions for weak ankles.

No, Laura thought, looking up again. She wasn't going to let him dissuade her from continuing on to his camp. She wanted to believe that concern for her welfare motivated him to discourage her, but then she continued reading.

> *I considered coming down the mountain with Kaba to visit you at the hut where he tells me you're recuperating, but I can't spare the time from my work. I'm at a very crucial point in it, and frankly, Laura, your visit is ill timed. Really, dear, you should have checked with me first before taking on this outlandish trip. You were always a bit impulsive and headstrong as a child, but I thought the years had changed that in you. Apparently not.*

Laura had to blink back a few tears before she was able to read on. She didn't know what she'd expected from her father, but certainly not these sharp little reprimands. She forced herself to finish reading the letter.

> *What happened to your wedding plans, by the way? Write and tell me. And please return home now, Laura. I know you must be terribly disappointed to have come all this way only to end up not seeing me, but we'll get together soon, I promise you. For now I prefer to be left alone. Your loving father.*

Loving father! His abrupt, formal close made her so enraged she almost tossed his letter in the fire. But then she noticed a little arrow drawn on the bottom of the page and turned it over.

> *P.S. Do I sound heartless, my dear? I am only thinking of your own welfare, believe me. Of course I'd like to see you, and if you really feel up to continuing the journey, you are most welcome to visit me.*

*But I do not want that journalist Kaba told me about
to accompany you. Get rid of him, Laura, before you
come here. Wishing you good traveling weather in
whatever direction you choose, Dad.*

Steve came into the hut, and Laura crumpled the letter
in her fist.

"Not a nice way to treat a letter from your dad," he said
nonchalantly.

"Why assume it's from my father?"

"Well, who else on Jewel Mountain would send you a
letter via Kaba? Don't tell me you've got a yeti pen pal."

Laura forced a laugh. "That's so silly."

"Don't worry," Steve said. "I'm not going to ask you
what he wrote. I can guess. How's the tea coming?"

"Oh! I forgot to put on the water."

"No problem. I will." Instead he stared long and hard at
her. "I'm going the rest of the way with you, love. No
matter what your father has to say about it, I'm not letting
you go without me."

"I don't want to go without you anymore." Laura placed
her hand on Steve's arm. "But I want you to promise me
something before I bring you to his camp."

He stiffened under her touch. "Oh, Laura, please don't
ask me to do that."

"I have to," she said. "Promise me that you won't write
a story about my father if you discover that he's...not quite
right."

Steve looked confused. "Not quite right about what?"
And then he understood. "Oh, you mean if he's off his
rocker."

"I prefer not to phrase it that way. But yes, I'm concerned that his yeti research is unrealistic."

"Is that what you've been worried about all this time,
Laura? That I would write a story ridiculing the respected
Dr. Prescott? I'd never do that."

She gave a sigh of relief. "Promise?"

"Yes, of course I do," he said impatiently. "If it turns out your father is completely misguided, I'll drop the story. I've got better things to do than write about loony scientists."

Laura believed him. It felt so good to be able to believe what Steve said. It didn't feel so good to hear her father referred to as a loony scientist, though.

"Oh, Steven, what if he really is crazy?" She shuddered.

He hugged her to him. "Did his letter sound it?"

"No, just distant. But that's normal for him."

"You know, most scientists on the brink of a great discovery have been perceived as crazy at first, Laura. If that's any comfort to you."

It was. But his arms were even more of a comfort. "Dad wants me to get rid of you," she said.

"Well, you can honestly tell him you tried doing exactly that for the longest time."

"I'm glad I failed." But then Laura remembered something and pulled away from Steve's consoling embrace to look up at him. "The checkpoint, Steven! There's sure to be one before we reach Dad's camp."

He gave her his best catlike smile. "I'll think of something. I always do." He hugged her close again.

Kaba Par came in as they were embracing. He laughed. "I see you have become dear friends during this time of isolation," he remarked. He walked around them and heated water for tea himself.

The three of them sat at the rough table and made plans for the next day. Kaba was willing to take Laura and Steve back up to Jewel Mountain, but he was sorry to report that two of the porters had quit. And Cookie had decided to go back to Kathmandu because he missed his family so much. Laura was surprised to learn that he had a wife and seven children. She would never have guessed that Cookie was a devoted family man.

They decided that they could manage without these expedition members. The two porters had already carried the extra supplies to Dr. Prescott, and their services were no longer needed. They also had enough canned foods, smoked meat and cheese to survive without a cook for the remainder of the trip.

"Actually it's all for the better that Cookie won't be coming with us," Steve said.

"But I thought you liked him," Laura said.

"I do. Cookie's a good man."

"Then why do you seem so pleased that he's leaving the party?"

"Because he's so tall for a Sherpa," Steve answered. And he would say no more than that.

At the crack of dawn the next morning, Steve and Laura waited outside the hut for Kaba and the porters, who had spent the night at the monastery.

They had said goodbye to Pemba and his parents the day before, when they'd taken Put back to them. Pemba had cried a little, and so had Laura.

Now, as she stood staring at the hut with Steve, she felt like crying again. A special time had come to an end, and she feared that she might never be so happy again. But she didn't share this fear with Steve. She didn't want him to think she was dependent on him for her future happiness. They turned their backs to the hut simultaneously and walked down to the road where they could see Pemba and the two porters in the distance. The last leg of their long trek had begun.

The wind was cold, the sun was warm and the path they traveled for the next five days rose continuously. At seventeen thousand feet, after they had passed the tree line, there was snow to deal with, but not too deep as of yet.

Laura found the high altitude and chilled air both exhilarating and exhausting. The glistening snow-capped ranges were beautiful to behold, but it was difficult to walk and breathe at the same time. Muscles complaining, lungs straining, she didn't hesitate to take the strong arm Steve offered when they had to climb over boulders or up steep, ice-slippery slopes. Because he was her friend and lover now, the man she adored and trusted, she could accept his help gratefully and graciously.

They were only a day away from her father's site when the trail led to a checkpoint that could not be avoided because of its high vantage point. Since Kaba knew its exact location, they were prepared. Steve had come up with a plan that depended on Laura to work. Wearing his new Sherpa boots and the red bandanna around his head, he hoped that with his dark tan he could pass for Cookie. It was up to Laura to convince the guards.

She went into the small police station with Kaba Par and presented her traveling papers to the constable behind the metal desk, who was dressed in official khaki. He called in two assistants from the back room, and they all examined the papers carefully, although one, Laura noted, held them upside down during his perusal.

"Are you come to visit father, Laura Prescott?" the constable asked in halting English that he seemed quite proud of.

"Yes, he's expecting me."

"I know this man," he said, pointing to Kaba Par. "He passed same way less than month ago." He glanced out the small window his desk faced. "But with four porter, not two."

"Two left the party," Laura said hurriedly. "But the other two and the cook stayed on. I handed you all their papers."

The constable shuffled through the travel permits, then gazed out the window and studied Steve, who hunched under a heavy weight to look shorter.

Trying to distract him, Laura began babbling about the scenery, the weather, the condition of the trail. The two assistants smiled and listened to her with the utmost politeness, although Laura sensed they spoke not a word of English. The constable continued staring out the window.

"That cook," he finally said.

"Yes?" Laura held her breath.

"Very nice boots he has."

And that was it. He returned the papers to Laura, wished her and Kaba a pleasant journey, sent regards to the famous Dr. Prescott and escorted them to the door.

"Thanks for getting me through," Steve said to Laura as they left the checkpoint behind them.

"It was easy. Your Sherpa boots seemed to convince the constable you were legitimate more than anything I said."

"But one little word from you, and I would have been detained."

That was exactly the scene Laura had found great pleasure in imagining during the first part of their journey. She had even done her part in Kathmandu to guarantee it happening. And now she felt grateful that she still had Steve by her side. She didn't know what to expect from her father and didn't want to face him alone.

That night, as she lay beside Steve in his tent and the wind howled outside, Laura slept fitfully. In the haze of semiconsciousness, her father's injunction blared in her head. *I do not want that journalist to accompany you. Get rid of him, Laura. Get rid of him. Get rid of him.*

"I can't do that!" she cried out.

Steve awoke. "What is it, Laura? A bad dream?"

"Something like that," she said.

"You're anxious about seeing your father tomorrow, aren't you?"

"Yes, I suppose I am. And it's so spooky tonight. Is that the wind howling? Or wolves?"

Steve reached across the sleeping bag for her hand. "Only the wind, love."

And she believed him because she wanted to. She fell asleep cuddling his hand against her cheek.

* * *

Late in the afternoon the next day, they saw the rough stone cabin with its flat red clay roof in the distance on a bluff. Smoke was coming out of the chimney, white against the cloudless azure sky. Laura was tempted to ask Kaba to go on ahead and tell her father they had arrived. But she knew she should be the one to go ahead to have some private moments alone with her father. Steve seemed to be thinking the same thing.

"I'm going to rest here for a while," he said, removing his pack and lifting himself onto a sunny rock ledge. "You go on, Laura. Better prepare your father for my visit."

"Who's going to prepare him for *mine?*" she asked dryly. She forced a smile to show that she was joking.

"I wait with Mr. Slater for the porters to catch up," Kaba said.

Laura slipped off her rucksack, threw back her shoulders and walked to the cabin alone.

A nanny goat pacing in front of the door bleated at her when she arrived. There was no sign of her father. She cautiously pushed open the door and stepped into a large, dimly lit room.

As soon as her eyes adjusted, Laura saw him hunched in a chair by the fire, his back to her. His hair was shoulder length, streaked with gray. She feared what he would look like when he turned around to her. Her throat clenched, and she had difficulty pronouncing the one-syllable word. "Dad?"

He sprang from the chair with an agility she hadn't expected from his hunched posture and faced her with a smile and open arms. "Laura! I was hoping you would come, dear."

She almost cried out in joy and relief. He was all right! She could tell that instantaneously from his sharp blue eyes and receptive expression. She ran into his arms and felt the familiar warmth of his hug. Then he held her at arm's length to get a good look at her.

And she stared back at him, taking him in with a fond smile. "You look so different with a beard, Dad. And what's with the shaggy hair?"

"This is how I always look when I'm working. I only spruce myself up when I visit you."

"You've gotten a bit grayer," Laura said.

Her father laughed. "And you, my dear, have gotten even more beautiful. The older you get, the more you remind me of . . . your mother."

"Thank you. That's the loveliest compliment you could give me. Kaba mentioned that you spoke a great deal of her while he was here."

"Yes. It was good for me, remembering those precious years when we were a happy family."

"You never reminisce about those years with me, Dad."

"Of course I don't." He turned gruff on her. "You've got your whole life ahead of you, Laura. Why dwell on the past?" As if shooing away the very idea, he waved his hands toward a chair by the fireplace. "Sit down, sit down," he said. "Make yourself at home."

She took the seat he'd motioned to and looked around. There were rough-planked bookshelves against the walls, packed tight with scientific journals and books, a number of which her father had written. Every inch of additional wall space was taken up by data charts and diagrams of various animal species. The small kitchen area was neat as a pin, there was a ladder leading up to a sleeping loft and sheepskins covered the clay floor. Kerosene lamps gave light, the large fireplace gave warmth and all in all it was a snug, cozy place, Laura concluded.

"I didn't expect your living quarters to be so substantial," she said.

"Sherpa helped me build this cabin last spring." Her father hung a copper kettle over the fire. "Should have sent you pictures of it, I suppose."

"I wish you had, Dad. Then I wouldn't have been so worried about you spending the winter here."

"Is that why you came all this way? To check out my living conditions?"

"Partly."

She got up and walked around the room. There was a framed photograph of her and her mother on his neatly arranged desk. She picked it up and smiled, remembering the scene so vividly. Africa—fifteen years ago. She had climbed halfway up a tree to take a picture of a chimpanzee. Her mother stood at the base of the tree, taking a picture of her. And her father had snapped this picture of them both taking pictures. It had been published in *Life* magazine with the caption: Wildlife, Childlife, And Zoologist Prescott's Wife.

"Partly?" her father repeated.

Laura put down the photograph and turned to him. "Frankly I was as concerned about your mental condition as much as your physical one, Dad. Your interest in yeti seemed so strange to me."

Dr. Prescott smiled. "Thought I was off my rocker, did you?"

Exactly Steve's words. Laura didn't look forward to telling her father that he had accompanied her. "Well, what was I to think, Dad? You always claimed yeti didn't exist."

"That's right, my dear." His smile broadened. "Nothing exists until proven. That's always been my approach."

"Does that mean...are you trying to tell me...have you actually proven beyond doubt that such creatures are real?"

Her father nodded, beaming, eyes sparkling. "Still think I'm nuts, Laura?"

She looked at him closely. She hadn't seen him so happy and fit in years. This discovery had given him a new lease on life. And the clarity of his gaze told her it was for real.

"Oh, Dad!" She knelt beside him and took his hand. "What a tremendous scientific breakthrough!"

"Not one I'm ready to make known yet, however. The yeti have come to trust me, and I want more time to get to know them in private. In fact, I may never reveal my research."

"What? But wouldn't it be wrong to keep back such a discovery?"

"Ah, but wouldn't it be equally wrong to destroy the yeti's world by making it known?"

"Perhaps it would," Laura said. The water in the kettle began to boil, and she busied herself making tea for them, delaying the moment when she would have to tell her father about Steve.

"If you want milk, I'll get some from the nanny," her father offered.

Laura smiled. "Aren't you the gracious host."

"Nothing but the best for my little girl."

"Please don't go through the trouble. We have to talk, Dad."

"No trouble at all," he said, ignoring her last remark. He took a bucket from the shelf, went outside and called to the goat. Laura followed him.

"Dad, there's something I should tell you."

"Hmm?" He wasn't really listening, too intent on cornering the goat, who didn't seem inclined to be milked at that moment. "Wait a second, honey. Let me just get a hold of nanny. Maybe if you could corner her on the other side, it would help."

"Oh, forget it, Dad! I don't want milk in my tea in the first place!" Laura said with impatient frustration. It was always like this with them. If he hadn't found the goat as an excuse to distract him, he would have found another way to avoid having a serious conversation with her.

"That's right," he said. "You don't like milk. You never have." He left off chasing the goat. "Now, what is this you want to talk about so urgently, dear?" But before she could reply, he asked another question. "Where's Kaba Par, anyway?"

"Down below, waiting for the porters."

"Thanks for sending along all those supplies, by the way," her father said. "Not that I needed them, mind you. I've got enough provisions to hold up for two long winters, let alone one. But it was thoughtful of you, anyway. How's your ankle?"

"Fine. I made it up here, didn't I?" she replied, sounding just as gruff as her father.

"So what happened to that scheduled wedding of yours? I thought the next time I saw you, you'd be married to what's-his-name."

"You know very well that his name was Jerome, Dad."

"Was? Sounds like he's history."

"We broke up a week before the wedding."

"Good. Didn't much care for the man—too much of a stuffed shirt in my opinion—but I didn't want to interfere with your life by telling you what I thought of him."

"You certainly have done an excellent job of never interfering with my life, Dad." Her tone was flat.

Her father gave her a closer look. "Are you upset about this breakup, Laura?"

She sighed. "No. He wasn't the right man for me. I realize that now."

"It's difficult to find the perfect mate," her father said, gazing at the glorious mountain vista beyond his cabin. "Only a fortunate few manage it. Your mother and I were two of them, and a day didn't go by when we didn't thank our lucky stars for each other. The perfect mate comes along once in a lifetime, Laura. Sometimes never."

She nodded and swallowed hard, moved by his words. Then she took a deep breath and made her confession. "Dad, that journalist you told me not to bring here.... Well, I brought him."

"How could you have gone against my wishes like that?" her father asked, his tone becoming cold. "Where's your common sense, let alone your sense of loyalty?"

"I've never been disloyal to you," Laura told him. "Steven would have found you without my help, he was so determined to interview you. He heard about your yeti research from Sherpa, not from me. If you don't want to talk to him you don't have to. But I trust him, Dad, and I think you should too because he's—"

"Trust him!" Dr. Prescott exploded. "Trust him with the most important discovery I've made in my lifetime? Never! You were wrong to bring him, Laura. Very wrong." With that he marched back into the cabin and slammed the door in his daughter's face.

She had traveled thousands of miles, Laura thought bitterly, to get a door slammed in her face. How like her father to cut off communications so abruptly. He had cut her off since she was thirteen. And she was tired, sick and tired, of retying the familial bond that had kept them connected through the years. So she didn't knock on the door and entreat him to reopen communications. She walked away instead, back rigid.

"It didn't go well," Steve guessed from Laura's expression when she returned to the ledge where she'd left him less than half an hour before.

"It never does with him. I should never have come. The good news is that he's perfectly sane. But the bad news is that he wants to be left alone."

"Maybe he'll be more receptive tomorrow. We can camp here for the night."

"I doubt he'll be more receptive to you, Steven," she told him bluntly. "He's adamant about not discussing his work with a journalist."

"Did he discuss it with you?"

She met his searching eyes. "Not in depth. And whatever he said to me was in confidence. Don't expect me to repeat it to you."

Steve nodded. "I won't ask again. And I shouldn't have asked the first time. I apologize."

Laura touched his arm. "Apology accepted." She turned to Kaba, who had silently observed them in conversation from his perch on a neighboring ledge. "I'm sure Dad will welcome *you,* Kaba. He considers you a friend."

"Then I will go to him," Kaba said. He stretched in the last afternoon rays of sun and slid down from the rocks. "The porters can help you make camp here. Do not look so sad, Laura. Your father cares for you deeply."

"He sure has a funny way of showing it."

"He has trained himself not to show it, perhaps. But do not give up on him. Come back to the cabin tomorrow."

She sighed. "I will, of course. As impossible as he is, he's the only father I have."

Steve decided that a bonfire would cheer Laura up and went with the porters to the mouth of a river about half a mile away to gather wood.

That evening the glow of the fire did lift her spirits, and she snuggled against him appreciatively.

"Why are you so kind to me?" she asked him sleepily as the fire warmed her body and his presence warmed her heart.

"Because it makes me feel good," he told her. "When I give you pleasure, it gives me pleasure. It's as simple as that."

He was always making things sound so simple, Laura thought. But she knew they were always more complicated than they seemed. Her relationship with her father was complicated. And her relationship with Steven was, too. She didn't know where she stood with either man. She was prepared, in the end, to stand alone. But now it felt so good to snuggle against Steven, to press her cheek against the hard muscle of his upper arm and close her eyes.

Steve let her sleep against him as he stared at the dwindling fire. The porters had gone off to spend the night in a cave they had found by the riverbank, Kaba was with Dr. Prescott and Steve felt as if he and Laura were alone in the universe. He enjoyed the sensation.

As he was thinking this, he heard a scrambling in the distance and became immediately alert, ready to spring into action. Laura awoke as his body tensed against hers.

"What is it, Steven?"

"Sounds like someone or something running along the stone path toward us," he whispered. He pulled her to her feet. "Get behind me, out of the light of the fire."

A moment later two small slender men came leaping into the circle of light.

Steve chuckled. "It's only the porters, Laura."

But they looked scared out of their wits, and both of them talked at the same time, in a babble of Sherpa phrases and Nepali. The one word that Steve understood and heard over and over again was *yeti*.

"They keep referring to a cave," Laura said.

"The one where they planned to spend the night, no doubt. They must have seen what they thought was a yeti in it," Steve said. "I know where it is. We collected firewood in that area. I'm going to check it out."

"But it's dark, Steven," Laura protested. "You could get lost."

"There's a full moon. And if the porters made it back to camp in a terrified state, I'm sure I can manage to do the same in a calm one."

"But what if there really is a yeti in that cave? How calm will you be about that?"

"Not very," Steve admitted. He dug into his backpack and pulled out a flashlight.

"But I'll be lucky to get a glimpse of the creature, Laura."

"I'm coming with you," she said.

Steve shook his head adamantly. "It could be dangerous. You're not coming, and that's final."

"The only way you can stop me is by tying me up."

He looked as if he were actually considering it for a moment, then turned away from her and started hiking down the stony path with long strides. Laura had to jog to keep up with him. After a while he slowed down.

"Okay, you can come with me," he told her as if he had any say in the matter.

When they reached the cave, Steve ordered Laura to stay behind while he went inside, and this time she didn't argue.

"Please, please, be careful," she begged him.

Since he had no intention of tussling with a wild caveman, or ape, or whatever the yeti was, Steve promised with the utmost sincerity that he would be.

Following the beam of his flashlight, he proceeded into the cave with caution. He heard a crunching beneath his feet and gazed down in disgust. Rodent bones. Deeper into the cave he discovered a nest of large juniper branches, obviously yanked out of the ground by their roots. That would take enormous strength, Steve thought. He didn't think he'd enjoy shaking hands with a yeti.

He beamed his light around the cave and was disappointed to see nothing but damp rock face. What did he expect? A yeti flair for interior decorating? Still, he was disappointed. What did a few rat bones and a juniper bed prove?

"Well?" Laura whispered when he came out of the cave. "Did you discover anything?"

"No need to whisper," Steve told her. "Whatever was in there is gone now." But he kept his voice low, too, for some reason. It just seemed the wisest thing to do.

And then they heard it—a mewing sound, like the crying of a sea gull, followed by a whistling of three long individual notes. Laura trembled. The hairs on the back of Steve's neck stood up and took notice.

"It came from that direction," he said, pointing to the left.

And then they saw it—a lone figure standing atop a boulder about fifty yards away, silhouetted in the moonlight.

"Good Lord, that's my father!" Laura whispered hoarsely.

"What the devil is he doing baying at the moon like that?"

"Oh, Steven, I don't know. He acted so normal when I visited him."

They watched as Dr. Prescott once again went through a series of mews and whistles, this time throwing in a few excited yelps for good measure. Laura moaned and covered her face with her hands. If she hadn't been so upset, Steve would have found the performance amusing. He'd never been put off by harmless eccentricity. He gave Laura a comforting hug.

Then they heard and saw *it*—the creature, the yeti—mewing and whistling in return as he came out of the shadows to climb the boulder. He climbed with grace and speed, and when he made it to the top, he stood upright beside Dr. Prescott.

They bowed to each other and touched foreheads in traditional Himalayan greeting. The yeti's head was long and pointed. His hairless face looked white as ivory in the moonlight. He was about the same height as Dr. Prescott and appeared to be half man, half beast.

He made a few quick gestures. Prescott gestured back. The yeti shook his head. Prescott shrugged. The yeti grunted a few times, and Prescott laughed heartily. The yeti responded with sharp yelps that could have been laughter, too, and slapped Prescott's back so hard that he lost his balance. But the yeti caught his arm to steady him, then released it and patted his back more gently.

He bowed again. Prescott bowed back. They touched heads again. And then, with a catlike whine, the yeti went over the side of the boulder and disappeared from view. Dr. Prescott waved goodbye, then climbed down the other side much more slowly and carefully.

Laura and Steve, both speechless, continued to stare at the top of the moonlit boulder, now an empty stage. They tightly clutched each other's hand. Neither realized how tightly. They were numb and stunned.

And then Steve felt a firm grip on his shoulder. His blood turned cold. Laura felt a lighter touch on hers. She screamed.

Chapter Twelve

"Don't be frightened, dear. It's only me."

"Dad!"

Steve shrugged off the man's hand and turned around to face him. His heart was thumping at a wild rate, but he maintained his cool. "Dr. Prescott, I presume."

Adam Prescott chuckled appreciatively. "Hardly an original line, but an appropriate one, nonetheless. And you must be that damn journalist."

"Steve Slater." He put out his hand, curious to see if Prescott would shake it.

He didn't. "So you saw my friend."

Steve nodded. "Not many men can claim a yeti as a friend, Dr. Prescott. Could you call him back? I'd like to interview him."

"No doubt he's watching from the shadows, but he won't come near you. I'm the only human he trusts, and it took me a long time to win that trust."

"I'd settle for an interview with you, then," Steve said.

"And I have no choice but to grant you one, now that you've witnessed our clandestine meeting. Come back to the cabin with my daughter and me, Slater. We have to talk."

No one said a word as they hiked the stony trail, Prescott leading the way. Laura walked behind her father, but in front of Steve. She felt caught in the middle. Her devotion to her father pulled her heart one way; her love for Steve pulled it the other way. She hoped and prayed the two men could resolve their differences before her poor heart split in two.

When they entered the cabin, they found Kaba seated in the lotus position in front of the fire, either meditating or napping. It was hard to tell with Kaba. He opened his eyes immediately and smiled at them calmly, not looking the least surprised at seeing the three of them together in the middle of the night.

"Met up with them at the boulder. They saw the yeti," Dr. Prescott explained succinctly.

"Such a privilege," Kaba said.

"Kaba speaks highly of you, Slater," Dr. Prescott told Steve. "So I guess you're worth talking to."

Steve gave Kaba a nod of thanks.

"Kaba also told me how determined you were to keep Slater away from my site until he won your trust, Laura. So I was wrong to accuse you of disloyalty."

Laura accepted her father's gruff apology with a smile.

Kaba rose, lifting himself up from the floor as if pulled up magically by a string. "I will go outside and await the sunrise, a spectacle I never tire of."

"No need to leave," Dr. Prescott told him. "You already know everything I'm going to tell Slater now."

"Then no need to stay, either," Kaba said and went out the door, closing it softly behind him.

Dr. Prescott opened a cupboard and took a dusty bottle from it. "Cognac," he said. "Guaranteed to be at least twenty years old because I've had it in my possession that long. Saved for special occasions.'' He shook the bottle. "And there's still a little left. You both look as if you could use a swallow of it. I sure did after my first sight of a yeti.'' He poured a little brandy in two tin cups and handed them to Laura and Steve.

Laura took a sip and made a face, but she needed the warmth of it. She was still in a mild state of shock.

Steve tossed his back in one gulp. "Much appreciated, Dr. Prescott," he said. "And I'd appreciate information from you even more. How did you first make contact with a yeti?''

"Purely by accident, as is often the case with great discoveries," he said, gesturing for Laura and Steve to sit before the fire. He remained standing and paced around the room as he talked. "I came here to study the snow leopard. Never had the slightest interest in yeti. Wouldn't have dreamed of wasting my time or grant money investigating a creature that scientists before me had concluded was mythological. But then one day..." He paused and looked at his daughter. "Now, don't get upset when I relate this, Laura.''

"I won't," she promised, but turned pale anyway.

"One day, in an unexpected spring snowstorm, I lost my way. I was only a few miles from my cabin, but it could have been thousands. I walked in circles for Lord knows how long and couldn't find my way back. I became snowblind and could have died from exposure.''

"Oh, no, Dad!''

"Well, I didn't die. Here I am. So let me finish my story, Laura," he said in his gruff, impatient way. "I was rescued by a hairy creature who carried me to his cave. He covered me with his body, which didn't smell too pleasant, but the warmth of it saved my life. After the storm he led me back here and disappeared. But I had to prove to my self that he wasn't an illusion, and devoted all my energy to finding him again."

"You mean he *let* you find him again," Steve said.

"Exactly!" Dr. Prescott turned his piercing blue eyes on Steve. "He allowed me to make contact again. No yeti can be discovered unless he wants to be. For some reason I will never understand, this one wanted my friendship. Perhaps it's a breakthrough in yeti evolution, this desire to form a relationship with a human being."

"But why you, Dr. Prescott?" Steve asked.

He laughed harshly. "Why me, indeed! Don't you think I ask myself that question at least a hundred times a day? It could be for the simple reason that I am here, in his environment, and he's had the chance to observe me closely and see I mean him no harm. But whatever the reason, I'm the one he chose to prove his existence."

"Proof," Steve said. "That's the key, isn't it?"

"That's right, Slater. So it doesn't really matter that you witnessed me communicating with a yeti in the moonlight. If you report what you saw, no one will take it seriously."

"But they will, Dr. Prescott," Steve replied in a voice as controlled and as challenging as his. "I'm an established journalist with a good track record for reporting the truth. And you're a reputable scientist. I could write the story without any further information from you and it would receive worldwide attention. So instead of daring me, give me more facts."

The two men glared at each other. It was a clash of intelligence and masculine pride. And Laura felt the energy of it shooting through her.

"Or have you failed to get the proof?" Steve pressed. "After being handed this opportunity on a silver platter, have you found yourself unequal to it, Dr. Prescott? Maybe I should write a story to alert other zoologists to come here and take advantage of a yeti who seems to want his existence documented."

"No!" Prescott cried. "This is *my* yeti! And I have all the data, all the proof that he exists. I have a detailed log of his daily habits. I have photographs and voice recordings. I have skin and hair samples. I have plaster impressions of not only his foot but his hand. I know where the skeletons of his ancestors are buried and I know where his mate and his offspring dwell. I have enough intrinsic, cognate and corollary evidence to prove, without a shadow of a doubt, that the yeti exists, Slater. But I'll be damned if I'll show it to you!"

Steve smiled and sat back in his chair. "Thank you, Dr. Prescott. That's all I wanted to know. You don't even have to show me the evidence because I believe you. And because of your reputation, so will the rest of the world if I quote you."

"But you can't," Dr. Prescott said. "If my discovery got out now, it would cause havoc in the scientific community. I'm not ready to have my privacy destroyed like that."

"Don't worry, Dad," Laura spoke up. "Steven promised me he wouldn't write about you."

"No, I didn't, Laura."

"What?" She looked at the man she loved, her gray eyes wide and stunned, as if he'd just shot a bullet between them. "But you did!"

"All I ever promised you, Laura, is that I wouldn't write a story making your father look like a fool. The one I intend to write will make him go down in history as a famous scientist."

"I don't want to be famous," Dr. Prescott protested. He reconsidered his statement. "At least not yet. No, Slater, you can't write about this until I'm ready to make the facts known. I have so much more research to do."

"My story won't stop you from doing it."

"But it will! Think of the repercussions, man. Never mind the scientists who will come here in droves. What about the tourists who will inundate the area in search of the cheap thrill of hunting down the abominable snowman? This isolated place will become a carnival."

"That's not my concern," Steve said. "Every story I report has repercussions. If it didn't it wouldn't be worth reporting."

Laura looked at Steve as if he were a stranger. "Steven, don't you understand? This isn't just another *story*. There's so much more at stake here."

"If I don't report this, someone else will," he replied coolly. "It's no secret in this area that your father has made contact with a yeti. The Sherpa know, and sooner or later, others will. At least what I write won't be sensational. I'll do my best to report the facts."

"I need time," Dr. Prescott said. "Give me that, Slater. Kaba told me that you were a good man who cared for my daughter. On that basis I trusted you."

"That's not fair," Steve said. "You're using emotional blackmail now, Dr. Prescott. You're right, I do care for your daughter. Very much. But I can't let that influence me now."

"Well, it should. You can't claim to care for Laura and then disregard her feelings concerning this matter."

"I have to keep emotions separated from my objectivity as a journalist."

"Then you're a cold man, Slater. I only hope my daughter realizes that your work takes priority over her."

"Has your love for Laura ever interfered with *your* work?"

Dr. Prescott stepped back as if Steve had physically struck him. "That's none of your business."

"It is now. You made it my business by bringing it up. The way I see it, Prescott, you pushed Laura out of your life when she was a child in order to pursue your career. So you have no right to lecture me about priorities."

"Get the hell out of here," Dr. Prescott told him.

Steve didn't budge. He turned to Laura. "Are you coming with me?"

She didn't answer him. She had remained silent during their exchange, although she felt badly used by both of them for making her the basis of their contention. She knew that whichever man came out the winner, she would be the loser.

"Laura?" Steve asked again. "Are you coming?" When she didn't respond a second time, he went out the door.

Her heart felt like a Ping-Pong ball, hit back and forth between the two men and out of her control. She followed it in Steve's direction and ran after him.

"Wait!" she cried.

He turned to her immediately. "So you finally made up your mind. You understand what I have to do, don't you?"

"No," she said, not moving an inch more in his direction. "Please, Steven, promise me you won't write about the yeti. Let it go."

"I can't. It's too big. Too important."

Her face became a rigid mask of dignity. "In that case, you're letting me go."

"Don't give me an ultimatum, Laura," he warned. His own expression took on the same rigidity.

"It's not an ultimatum," she said. "It's your free choice. You can have me. Or your damn story."

"I want both."

"Well, you can't have both." She turned away. She went inside and left the door open for him. But he didn't come back.

At first Steve didn't notice that he was being followed. He heard slight noises behind him but discounted them as the sounds of birds or small creatures thrashing in the brush. Then he heard a little sigh that could only be human and turned around. Kaba, a few yards behind, smiled at him.

"So it's you," Steve said. "I should have guessed. You're always around when I need you, Kaba."

"And do you need me now, sahib?"

"Drop the sahib, will you, Kaba? I know you consider yourself superior to me in every way."

"Not in every way," Kaba said. But he dropped the sahib. "Indeed, I do think you need a friend now, Steve. I did not intend to, but I overheard your last conversation with Miss Prescott. It was not a pleasant one."

"Most partings with women aren't," Steve declared. "You love them and then you leave them."

"Is that the way it is with you?"

"Yeah, it always has been. The leaving part, anyway. Love used to be a stranger to me. I never put much trust in it."

"And now?"

"It only confuses the issue, Kaba. I'll be going back as soon as the sun rises."

"Back to where?" Kaba asked.

Steve shrugged. "From where I started. All the way down the long trail. Will you be coming with me?"

"No," Kaba said. "My duty lies with Miss Prescott. But one of the porters will show you the way."

"I can find it myself," Steve said. "Going back is much easier."

"Always," Kaba agreed. "It's the going into unknown territory that's so difficult."

Steve was silent for a moment. "I went into unknown territory by falling in love with Laura. And it sure wasn't easy. She's not an easy woman, Kaba."

"You must be greatly relieved to be away from her, then."

"You bet. For a while there I thought I'd be stuck with her for the rest of my life."

"But you aren't?"

"Nope. Clean break. I brought her to Jewel Mountain and now I'm leaving her there. Her choice, not mine. Never look back, Kaba. That's the secret to my success."

"I will keep your secret," Kaba told him, then coughed into his hand.

Or did he laugh? Steve wondered.

"Quite a night," Laura said to her father. She didn't know what else to say, what to do with herself. So she sat down on the sheepskin before the fire and stared at it, not seeing anything at all.

Her father continued to pace the room, as if Steve's exit hadn't been important enough to interrupt his aimless shuffle. He cleared his throat a few times. He pulled at his beard and ran his hand through his shaggy hair. He stopped by his desk to examine the photograph of his wife and young daughter.

"I'm sorry, Laura," he eventually said.

She looked up at him blankly. "For what?" Her eyes were cloudy pools of misery.

"Everything! I don't suppose I handled that situation with Slater very well. Shouldn't have brought you into it. I used you to try to protect my own interest."

"But it had no weight with him, did it?" Laura asked herself that more than her father. She looked back at the fire.

"I think he objected more on principle than true feelings. You can't corner a man like that. He'll strike back. And he struck back where it hurt me most, Laura. Do you agree with him? Do you think I pushed you out of my life in order to pursue my career?"

"All I know is that I wanted to stay with you more than anything after Mother died. But you sent me away."

"I wanted you to remain with me, too!" Her father sank down on the chair next to her and lightly ran his hand through her hair. "I would have been greatly comforted by your presence during those awful bleak years of grief. But to let you stay with me would have been the most selfish thing I could have done. I would have had your companionship and devotion. But what would you have had, dear?"

"My father's companionship and affection," she replied softly.

"But that's not enough for a young person! Even if your mother had lived, we would have sent you away to school at that age. Our life in the wilderness was too isolating. We wanted you to have a good education and a chance to choose your own life-style, not the one we imposed on you. The last promise I made your mother, when we both finally accepted that she wouldn't get well again, was that I would let you go after she died. That I would *make* you go."

Laura looked up at her father again. "You never told me that, Dad."

"No, I wanted you to believe that it was all my idea. I thought that would be the easiest way. I didn't want your pity, Laura. I really couldn't bear that. I wanted you to leave me behind and get on with your life." He wearily rubbed the back of his neck. "In the beginning all you would do when I visited you at school was beg me to take you home again, Laura. That hurt me so much because you couldn't understand that we didn't *have* a home anymore. Not without your mother. She gave our life a warm center of stability."

He stood up and began pacing again. "It's a lonely life I have now, but one I've become accustomed to. My work keeps me distant from people, but I find it fulfilling. Besides, it's the only work I know."

"I can't imagine you doing anything else," Laura said.

"I admit I found it less painful to let you go by losing myself in my research, Laura. I thought it was the best way for both of us to survive such a great loss. But I was wrong, wasn't I?''

He stopped in the middle of the room, arms out, palms open as if in supplication as he waited for her answer.

And Laura could not find it in her heart to tell him that he had been wrong. What did it matter, anyway? The past could not be changed.

She got up and slowly walked to him. "I invite you back into my life, Dad."

His eyes misted with tears. "And I accept the invitation. Thank you, daughter. I've missed you."

"And I've missed you, Dad!"

They hugged awkwardly, not used to demonstrative emotions with each other. They laughed, a little embarrassed, and Dr. Prescott turned his face to stealthily wipe the tears from his eyes.

"So!" he said, looking back to her. "Could you stay here with me for a while so we can get reacquainted?"

"Yes, I'd like that very much," she said. "But I can't stay too long. I have a business to run back in New York."

"And I promise I'll make time to visit you there at least twice a year from now on."

"That would be wonderful." Although she smiled, her eyes still held deep sadness in them.

"You should have gone with him when he left here tonight," her father told her.

She shook her head.

"Yes," he insisted. "I see that so clearly now. He was right. Your relationship with him has nothing to do with his decision to write about my yeti discovery."

Laura sighed. "It's more complicated than that. By making Steven choose between me and his story, I found a way to make it easier for him to part with me. Because he would have eventually, somewhere down the trail."

"Then I misunderstood. Kaba led me to believe that the two of you were in love."

"Love means different things to different people, Dad. For me it means a lifetime commitment. For Steven..." She shrugged and laughed with bitter resignation. "Well, it doesn't mean the same thing for him. As much as I hurt now, I know that he would have hurt me even more if I delayed the inevitable. It's just as well we parted on top of the mountain than on the bottom of it."

"You forced his hand, Laura," her father reminded her in a gentle tone.

"It didn't take much, did it? I gave him the out he was looking for." She moved to the door. "I might as well close this now. He isn't coming back."

And she did, with a firm thud that vibrated through her being. She would never be the same again, she knew. She would never love a man as much as she loved Steven. But he was gone now.

It was comforting to realize how little a man really needed to survive in life, Steve thought as he marched down the mountain alone in the dark. All he needed was a strong back, a good mind, an independent nature and a few ambitions.

That thought was so cheery that he began whistling. But the tune bothered him. It was romantically cloying and reminded him of holding a strange, lovely woman in his arms one rainy night in Kathmandu. He could think of no other tune, though, so he stopped whistling. The music continued to play in his head, each off-key note plucking on his heartstrings.

To drive it out he began mentally composing the story he intended to write as soon as he got back to civilization. Unknown Humanoid Discovered—The Missing Link. Yeah, that sounded pretty good. But he could do better than that once he got in front of a typewriter. Right now he really didn't feel like working on it.

For some reason the image of little Pemba popped into his head—Pemba leading the yak calf to the hut. Pemba would surely have his fill of Western visitors once news about Prescott's discovery made the headlines.

Steve recalled lecturing the Sherpa boy on ecology. How sanctimonious he must have sounded, he thought now. How two-faced! Sure he wanted the area to remain pristine, but at the same time he wanted to be the one to break a story that would attract visitors to overpower the environment. Yeah, *you*, Slater. The guy who complained so contemptuously about Mount Everest being defiled by tourists. Now the same thing could happen to Jewel Mountain, and you could take all the credit.

And what about that yeti? As soon as the story broke, the creature's peace would be destroyed forever. His habitat would be overrun, his burial grounds dug up, his body or one of his relatives dissected—all in the name of scientific knowledge. Well, that's progress, Steve thought sardonically. You can't stop progress.

But he stopped in his tracks. He wasn't going to do it, dammit. Let someone else write the story eventually. It wasn't going to be him. He took off his backpack and sat down on the side of the trail, amazed by his own decision. He couldn't recall making such a selfless one in years. And it felt good. Real good.

Although his decision remained firm, his euphoria faded after a moment. He didn't feel good anymore. He felt... lonely, empty and confused. What was he walking away from now? If he didn't write the story, then he had no excuse to leave Laura. But if he went back up that mountain for her, that would mean only one thing. That he intended to stay with her. Always. Was he ready for that? Was he capable of a permanent relationship?

Yes! his heart answered. Laura had already proven to him that he was capable of love. She was *his* missing link—

the part that made him feel whole, and he wanted to spend the rest of his life with her.

The sky was brightening in the east. A new day was dawning, and a new life was possibly waiting for him up on the mountain. Would she accept him if he returned to her now? She had left the door open, hadn't she?

Steve stood up and began walking faster, faster up the trail he had just come down. He couldn't bear the idea of having the sun rise without Laura in his arms. He passed the site where they'd made camp the afternoon before. Kaba and the porters were there, building another fire with the dead wood they had gathered. The porters greeted Steve with a show of surprise, since they had said goodbye to him only a short while before. Kaba merely smiled as Steve hurried past.

He saw her in the pale dawn light, standing outside the cabin on the bluff. She was gazing to the east, waiting for the sun to show itself. He called her name, and it echoed off the mountaintops.

"Laura! Laura! Laura!"

She turned and saw him waving to her. "Steven!" she cried, and his name blended with hers in the bouncing echo.

She ran down the path, he ran up it, and they met halfway, with such force that they almost knocked each other down as they embraced. And at that moment the sun appeared over the top of the mountain peak and beamed rays of gold-and-red light upon them.

"I can't leave you. I could never leave you," he said.

"I love you!" she told him. "I was wrong to make you choose between me and your story."

"It doesn't matter. I won't write it. I just can't do it."

They were both gasping, out of breath, their hearts beating furiously.

"Marry me," he said, inhaling deeply. "You're my wife already. So let's formalize it."

"That means forever, Steven."

"That's the only way I want you, Laura. Forever."

And as they kissed, to seal their promise, the long, high-pitched whistle of the yeti pierced the silence from high above the clouds.

*   *   *   *   *

Note to Reader: Many names of regions and mountains in this book are fictitious to avoid revealing the true location of the yeti.

This is the season of giving, and Silhouette proudly offers you its sixth annual Christmas collection.

SILHOUETTE

Christmas Stories

1991

Experience the joys of a holiday romance and treasure these heart-warming stories by four award-winning Silhouette authors:

Phyllis Halldorson—"A Memorable Noel"
Peggy Webb—"I Heard the Rabbits Singing"
Naomi Horton—"Dreaming of Angels"
Heather Graham Pozzessere—"The Christmas Bride"

Discover this yuletide celebration—sit back and enjoy Silhouette's Christmas gift of love.

COMING NEXT MONTH

#709 LURING A LADY—Nora Roberts
Barging into his landlord's office, angry carpenter Mikhail Stanislaski got what he wanted. But, for the hot-blooded artist, luring cool, reserved landlady Sydney Hayward to his SoHo lair was another story....

#710 OVER EASY—Victoria Pade
Lee Horvat went undercover to trap Blythe Coopersmith by gaining her trust. She gave it too freely, though, and both were caught...struggling against love.

#711 PRODIGAL FATHER—Gina Ferris
It wasn't wealthy, stoic Cole Saxon's wish to reunite with his prodigal father; it was A-1 wish-granter Kelsey Campbell's idea. And from the start, Kelsey proved dangerously adept at directing Cole's desires....

#712 PRELUDE TO A WEDDING—Patricia McLinn
Paul Monroe was a top-notch appraiser. Sensing million-dollar laughter behind Bette Wharton's workaholic ways, he betrayed his spontaneous nature and planned...for a march down the aisle.

#713 JOSHUA AND THE COWGIRL—Sherryl Woods
Cowgirl Traci Garrett didn't want anything to do with big shots like businessman Joshua Ames. But that was before this persistent persuader decided to rope—and tie—this stubborn filly.

#714 EMBERS—Mary Kirk
Disaster summoned Anne Marquel home to face the ghosts of the past. With tender Connor McLeod's help, could she overcome tragedy and fan the embers of hope for tomorrow?

AVAILABLE THIS MONTH:

#703 SOMEONE TO TALK TO
Marie Ferrarella

#704 ABOVE THE CLOUDS
Bevlyn Marshall

#705 THE ICE PRINCESS
Lorraine Carroll

#706 HOME COURT ADVANTAGE
Andrea Edwards

#707 REBEL TO THE RESCUE
Kayla Daniels

#708 BABY, IT'S YOU
Celeste Hamilton

SILHOUETTE®
OFFICIAL SWEEPSTAKES
RULES

NO PURCHASE NECESSARY

1. To enter, complete an Official Entry Form or 3"× 5" index card by hand-printing, in plain block letters, your complete name, address, phone number and age, and mailing it to: Silhouette Fashion A Whole New You Sweepstakes, P.O. Box 9056, Buffalo, NY 14269-9056.

   No responsibility is assumed for lost, late or misdirected mail. Entries must be sent separately with first class postage affixed, and be received no later than December 31, 1991 for eligibility.

2. Winners will be selected by D.L. Blair, Inc., an independent judging organization whose decisions are final, in random drawings to be held on January 30, 1992 in Blair, NE at 10:00 a.m. from among all eligible entries received.

3. The prizes to be awarded and their approximate retail values are as follows: Grand Prize — A brand-new Ford Explorer 4×4 plus a trip for two (2) to Hawaii, including round-trip air transportation, six (6) nights hotel accommodation, a $1,400 meal/spending money stipend and $2,000 cash toward a new fashion wardrobe (approximate value: $28,000) or $15,000 cash; two (2) Second Prizes — A trip to Hawaii, including round-trip air transportation, six (6) nights hotel accommodation, a $1,400 meal/spending money stipend and $2,000 cash toward a new fashion wardrobe (approximate value: $11,000) or $5,000 cash; three (3) Third Prizes — $2,000 cash toward a new fashion wardrobe. All prizes are valued in U.S. currency. Travel award air transportation is from the commercial airport nearest winner's home. Travel is subject to space and accommodation availability, and must be completed by June 30, 1993. Sweepstakes offer is open to residents of the U.S. and Canada who are 21 years of age or older as of December 31, 1991, except residents of Puerto Rico, employees and immediate family members of Torstar Corp., its affiliates, subsidiaries, and all agencies, entities and persons connected with the use, marketing, or conduct of this sweepstakes. All federal, state, provincial, municipal and local laws apply. Offer void wherever prohibited by law. Taxes and/or duties, applicable registration and licensing fees, are the sole responsibility of the winners. Any litigation within the province of Quebec respecting the conduct and awarding of a prize may be submitted to the Régie des loteries et courses du Québec. All prizes will be awarded; winners will be notified by mail. No substitution of prizes is permitted.

4. Potential winners must sign and return any required Affidavit of Eligibility/Release of Liability within 30 days of notification. In the event of noncompliance within this time period, the prize may be awarded to an alternate winner. Any prize or prize notification returned as undeliverable may result in the awarding of that prize to an alternate winner. By acceptance of their prize, winners consent to use of their names, photographs or their likenesses for purposes of advertising, trade and promotion on behalf of Torstar Corp. without further compensation. Canadian winners must correctly answer a time-limited arithmetical question in order to be awarded a prize.

5. For a list of winners (available after 3/31/92), send a separate stamped, self-addressed envelope to: Silhouette Fashion A Whole New You Sweepstakes, P.O. Box 4665, Blair, NE 68009.

PREMIUM OFFER TERMS

To receive your gift, complete the Offer Certificate according to directions. Be certain to enclose the required number of "Fashion A Whole New You" proofs of product purchase (which are found on the last page of every specially marked "Fashion A Whole New You" Silhouette or Harlequin romance novel). Requests must be received no later than December 31, 1991. Limit: four (4) gifts per name, family, group, organization or address. Items depicted are for illustrative purposes only and may not be exactly as shown. Please allow 6 to 8 weeks for receipt of order. Offer good while quantities of gifts last. In the event an ordered gift is no longer available, you will receive a free, previously unpublished Silhouette or Harlequin book for every proof of purchase you have submitted with your request, plus a refund of the postage and handling charge you have included. Offer good in the U.S. and Canada only.

SLFW-SWPR

SILHOUETTE® OFFICIAL SWEEPSTAKES ENTRY FORM

4-FWSES-4

Complete and return this Entry Form immediately – the more entries you submit, the better your chances of winning!

- Entries must be received by **December 31, 1991**.
- A Random draw will take place on **January 30, 1992**.
- No purchase necessary.

Yes, I want to win a FASHION A WHOLE NEW YOU Sensuous and Adventurous prize from Silhouette:

Name _____ Telephone _____ Age ____

Address _____

City _____ State _____ Zip _____

Return Entries to: **Silhouette FASHION A WHOLE NEW YOU,**
P.O. Box 9056, Buffalo, NY 14269-9056   © 1991 Harlequin Enterprises Limited

PREMIUM OFFER

To receive your free gift, send us the required number of proofs-of-purchase from any specially marked FASHION A WHOLE NEW YOU Silhouette or Harlequin Book with the Offer Certificate properly completed, plus a check or money order (do not send cash) to cover postage and handling payable to Silhouette FASHION A WHOLE NEW YOU Offer. We will send you the specified gift.

- -

OFFER CERTIFICATE

Item	A. SENSUAL DESIGNER VANITY BOX COLLECTION (set of 4) (Suggested Retail Price $60.00)	B. ADVENTUROUS TRAVEL COSMETIC CASE SET (set of 3) (Suggested Retail Price $25.00)
# of proofs-of-purchase	18	12
Postage and Handling	$3.50	$2.95
Check one	☐	☐

Name _____

Address _____

City _____ State _____ Zip _____

Mail this certificate, designated number of proofs-of-purchase and check or money order for postage and handling to: **Silhouette FASHION A WHOLE NEW YOU Gift Offer,** P.O. Box 9057, Buffalo, NY 14269-9057. Requests must be received by December 31, 1991.

- -

ONE PROOF-OF-PURCHASE

4-FWSEP-4

To collect your fabulous free gift you must include the necessary number of proofs-of-purchase with a properly completed Offer Certificate.

© 1991 Harlequin Enterprises Limited

- -

See previous page for details.